MW00699227

Praise for *The Sec*.

"*The Secret Keys of Conjure* is an admirable, wise, and above all useful introduction to the vast territory of African-American and European-American folk magic. Respectful always to those who developed the intertwined but differing cultural traditions of hoodoo and kitchen-witchery, Chas Bogan defines the terms, explains the spiritual principles, and provides the recipes and rituals that every practitioner needs to know in order to practice old-school rootwork and natural magic in the modern world. This is a book I will recommend to my own students."

—catherine yronwode, rootworker, author of *Hoodoo Herb and Root Magic: A Materia Magica of African-American Conjure*, and co-proprietor of Lucky Mojo Curio Company

THE SECRET KEYS OF CONJURE

© Devin Hunter

About the Author

Chas Bogan (San Francisco, CA) is a professional Conjure doctor who practices at his store, the Mystic Dream. He is an initiate and practitioner of various metaphysical traditions, teaching classes on Conjure and Feri at the online school of which he is a founder, Mystic Dream Academy, as well as at conventions and festivals. He also produces talking boards (Carnivalia) and spiritual supplies steeped in Hoodoo (Modern Conjure). Find him online at ChasBogan.com.

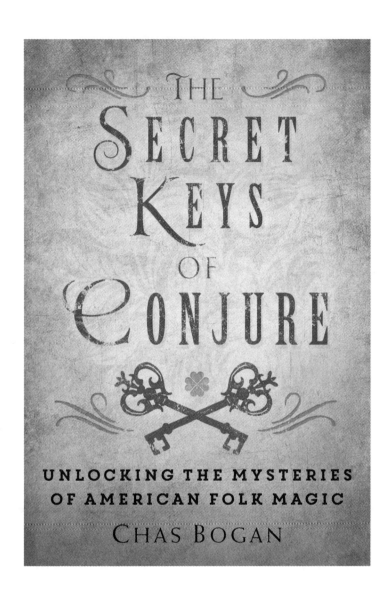

THE SECRET KEYS OF CONJURE

UNLOCKING THE MYSTERIES OF AMERICAN FOLK MAGIC

CHAS BOGAN

Llewellyn Publications
Woodbury, Minnesota

FIRST EDITION
Second Printing, 2019

Cover design by Ellen Lawson
Interior illustrations by the Llewellyn Art Department
Zodiac man image by Mary Ann Zapalac

Llewellyn Publications is a registered trademark of Llewellyn Worldwide Ltd.

Library of Congress Cataloging-in-Publication Data
Names: Bogan, Chas, author.
Title: The secret keys of conjure : unlocking the mysteries of American folk
    magic / by Chas Bogan.
Description: First Edition. | Woodbury : Llewellyn Worldwide, Ltd., 2018. |
    Includes bibliographical references and index.
Identifiers: LCCN 2017047404 (print) | LCCN 2017053048 (ebook) | ISBN
    9780738754444 (ebook) | ISBN 9780738752891 (alk. paper)
Subjects: LCSH: Hoodoo (Cult) | Magic—Southern States. | Folklore—Southern
    States.
Classification: LCC BL2490 (ebook) | LCC BL2490 .B64 2018 (print) | DDC
    133.4/30973—dc23
LC record available at https://lccn.loc.gov/2017047404

Llewellyn Worldwide Ltd. does not participate in, endorse, or have any authority or responsibility concerning private business transactions between our authors and the public.

All mail addressed to the author is forwarded but the publisher cannot, unless specifically instructed by the author, give out an address or phone number.

Any Internet references contained in this work are current at publication time, but the publisher cannot guarantee that a specific location will continue to be maintained. Please refer to the publisher's website for links to authors' websites and other sources.

Llewellyn Publications
A Division of Llewellyn Worldwide Ltd.
2143 Wooddale Drive
Woodbury, MN 55125-2989
www.llewellyn.com

Printed in the United States of America

Dedication

To my loving partners, Storm Faerywolf and Devin Hunter, for the many conversations that helped me organize my thoughts for this book, and for picking up the slack around our home and business while I was writing it.

To my many teachers, especially cat yronwode, without whom my knowledge and experience of these subjects would be so much more limited.

To my good friend Grey Townsend, for so many inspiring conversations in and outside of the hot tub. To Shelby of Coastside Conjure, for all her support, especially as it pertained to working with saints.

To those who attended my in-person classes for *A Course in Modern Conjure*, Jo Jenson, Rowan Rivers, Christine Rossi, and others, and helped me flesh out my thoughts and lessons in a way that has evolved into this book.

To the various communities that have supported my work:

- The Brotherhood of the Satyrs
- The various student communities at Mystic Dream Academy, most notably Black Rose Witchcraft and BlueRose Faery tradition
- The Mystic Dream Psychic Guild

To all those folks who have frequented my shop, the Mystic Dream, and shared with me their magic. I have learned volumes simply by listening to others tell how Conjure is practiced by them.

Contents

Tricks   *xi*

Recipes   *xiii*

Foreword by Jacki Smith   *xvii*

Introduction   *1*

  I: *The Keys to Divination:* Unlocking Psychic Awareness   9

 II: *The Keys to Ritual:* Unlocking Blessings   25

III: *The Keys to Curios:* Unlocking Good Luck   47

IV: *The Keys to Language:* Unlocking Healing   69

  V: *The Keys to Cleansing:* Unlocking Spiritual Purification   89

VI: *The Keys to Knots and Stitches:* Unlocking Protection   107

VII: *The Keys to Personal Concerns:* Unlocking Influence   123

VIII: *The Keys to Scent:* Unlocking Sexual Enticement   143

IX: *The Keys to Sweetening:* Unlocking Love   163

  X: *The Keys to Setting Lights:* Unlocking Wealth   185

XI: *The Keys to Powders:* Unlocking Justified Hexes   205

XII: *The Keys to the Graveyard:* Unlocking Spirit Conjuration   223

XIII: *The Master Key*   245

Resources   *259*

Bibliography   *261*

Index   *265*

Index of Popular Formulas   *273*

Tricks

I

To Determine a Child's Fate   13

Bible and Key   15

White Plate Reading   16

To Discover Your Fortune in a Dream   19

To Dream True   19

To Remember Your Dreams   19

To Keep Bad Dreams from Coming True   20

To Keep from Dreaming   20

To Avoid Bad Dreams   20

Other Methods for Purposeful Dreaming   21

IV

To Safeguard Against Burns   72

To Take Out a Burn   72

To Stop Bleeding   75

To Join Two Lovers   80

V

Uncrossing Rite   93

The Water Rite   100

A Foot Washing   101

VI

Law Keep Away Patch   110

Thimble Spell   113

A Trick of the Light   116

Witch's Ladder for Protection   121

VII

Harmless Witch Bottle   131

Dominant Hand Mojo   133

Conjure Ball to Influence Someone   136

Jack Ball Trick to Influence Someone   139

Beef Tongue to Stop Gossip   142

VIII

Magic Mirror Spell   154

IX

To Soften a Hardened Lover   171

Honey Jar to Sweeten Someone   177

For Shared Residency   180

To Make Them Propose   180

To Make Them Accept Your Proposal   181

To Keep Your Mate at Home   181

XII

To Find a Spirit Guide   226

To Sound Eloquent   232

La Madama's Aid in Cleansing Cards   236

Saint Expedite for a Quick Resolution   241

XIII

Keys to the Crossroads   251

Recipes

II

Anointing Incense   27

Crown of Success Incense   28

Three Wise Men Cocktail   34

Blessing Herb Blend   42

Temple Incense   44

Warm Blush Blessing Incense   45

Home Blessing Incense   46

Peace Incense   46

III

Green Fast Luck Herb Blend   49

Red Fast Luck Herb Blend   49

Yellow Fast Luck Herb Blend   50

IV

Dragon's Blood Ink   78

V

Chinese Wash   91

Four Thieves Vinegar   92

Peace Water   97

Quench Water   97

Purifying Laundry Wash   99

Seven-Day Herbal Bath for Peace of Mind   99

VI

Asperging Solution   115

VII

Boss Fix Herb Blend   126

Controlling Tea   126

Jack Ball   137

VIII

Glamor Oil   146

Look Me Over Oil   147

Cleo May Oil   147

Desire Me Oil   148

Goona Goona Oil   149

Carnation Oil   150

Satyr Oil   150

Van Van Oil   159

Hoyt's German Cologne   161

IX

Dixie Love Oil   167

Chuparosa Oil   167

Bridal Bouquet Oil   167

Return to Me Oil   168

Hold Me Incense   169

Gingerbread Effigy   173

Rock Candy Wand   174

Simple Syrup   175

Briar Trap Cocktail   175

XI

Run Devil Run Herb Blend   210

Love Breaker Conjure Ball   212

Confusion Powder   213

Damnation Powder   214

Hot Foot Powder   220

Break Up Powder   220

Goofer Dust   222

XIII

Confidence Oil   246

Eloquence Bottle   246

Memory Drop Oil   247

Wisdom of Solomon Oil   247

Abramelin Oil   248

Master Key Oil   248

Foreword

by Jacki Smith

THE SECRET KEYS IMPLY that once attained, you are privy to all that is unlocked. That is the lie that we tell ourselves when we are looking for a quick fix and instant expert status. This is the lie that we believe when we value the savant over the long-suffering adept. The truth is that once you attain a secret key, you then begin the journey. Once you unlock what that key restrains, you are now responsible for what is inside Pandora's box.

Folk magic comes from need, usually great need, that has created a reserve of nervous or desperate energy. When a seeker finds faith in spiritual solution, the burst of energy that comes from releasing those worries into a trick or a spell is the quickening of the magic. This is what makes Conjure and folk magic so powerful. we are using the primal energy of survival, the primal energy of creation. The energy can also make us heady and trick our ego into thinking we are experts and powerful magical doctors.

Is this one of the reasons Conjure spells are called tricks? We trick ourselves to move out of our own energetic way and we trick the momentum of our lives to the lives of others to change course. We can also trick ourselves into thinking there is no need to hone our craft, that we can turn to a book or a website and find the quick reference we need for our next crisis. In Conjure, your anima, or magical spirit, needs to be fed, worked with, and exercised for it to continue to power your magic. You must work your magic or your magic will not work for you. You must practice and know what magic feels like and acts like in your life to know its effect upon you or your client.

When you study with a Conjure doctor, they push you, they trick you into growing, they challenge your ego and humble you in front of your own spirit to experience the divine in action. Teachers are not necessarily kind, as they know more growth and knowledge are gained from adversity than from balance. This rare relationship is experienced one-on-one and is custom to the teacher and seeker. In the Kongo, you would sit in the funk (essence) of your elder to absorb the lessons they were teaching. In our twenty-first-century world, we no longer have the luxury of an elder to learn from. We have more seekers than elders, and we no longer have the abundance of time to apprentice at the feet of our aunties.

Conjure is no longer in the shadows, it is no longer limited to the Hollywood definition of black magic. There are more practitioners of magic than any of us realize. There are soccer moms who make mojo bags, there are teachers who calm their classrooms, and there are entrepreneurs who cleanse their offices. With this acceptability we can find more books and resources for our work. We can talk more openly about magic and not be placed in the category of crazy. With acceptability, we unfortunately run the risk of whitewashing this tradition and losing the powerful cosmology of why this magic works.

We saw this in the popularity of witchcraft as an outcropping of Wicca. As Wicca became more acceptable, the dark origins of magic based on primal need were washed away: never to curse or cause harm, and never to do magic for oneself, for personal gain, or in vengeance. This became known as "white magic," and "black magic" was relegated to Conjure and African traditional religions. Through the help of the entertainment industry, black magic was portrayed as being practiced by black people and was seen as inherently negative. The bad guys in the magical TV shows all wore black or were black, and collectively we continued to agree to the stereotype. The more primal the magic, the riskier it was to tip into the evil side. New Age spirituality ushered in the call to treat everything with love and light. It called for the Pagan traditions to be gentled and interpreted with the teachings of Jesus and filled with Christ consciousness. It called for us all to evolve past our primal needs and trust in the universe to provide. It became one-sided and denied us all the legitimacy of our shadow side.

Conjure is not light in its inception. Conjure comes from marginalized, oppressed people whose struggle to survive and thrive created these magical traditions out of need. Over and over, generations of people tested and proved their magic and were able to rely on its foundation in the toughest of times. When your life or wellbeing is in the hands of another, your shadow side is the tool you turn to. Our shadow side protects us. It is the place where our spirit can rest and recharge. Just as a flower grows only at night, our spirit needs the cool calm of our shadow side to assess all that we experience and how we can grow from it. To deny our primal needs and our shadow side is to cut our personal power in half and hobble our self-actualization.

Conjure, like our primal energy, is always there. It calls to us, as it is a tradition that was never broken. There is no need to reinvent or reclaim the tradition; there is only the need to listen, awaken, and learn. Conjure is not a system of ethics or a religion. It favors neither the shadow nor the light side of a spell, but it does favor the need to find balance and joy in life. There is not a key to be given, but a key to pick up. We hold all the Secret Keys of Conjure within us, and Chas Bogan is helping us awaken to them and interpret them.

Book learning of these oral traditions is legitimate as long as you push yourself, test yourself, laugh at yourself, and create a relationship with the energy that is awakened within you. An author who is truly teaching you will make you uncomfortable. They will invalidate your misconceptions and won't pander to your need to be instantly amazing. They will force you along the journey of discovery with them and inspire you to reach for more. This is the experience you will find in *The Secret Keys of Conjure*. You are studying at the feet of a master, and you will be immersed in the funk of wisdom that Chas Bogan has imparted in these pages.

When I started my study of Conjure and Hoodoo, I was obsessed with how it shaped the American folk magic tradition in a unique way not found anywhere else in the world. I wanted to research and write about how Conjure, Spiritism, Jewish mysticism, and the Golden Dawn were the four pillars of our unique American experience. I wanted to write about it because I wanted to learn it! The more I researched, the more there was to know, and eventually life got in the way and kept my focus on my own magical product and practice.

When I first started reading *The Secret Keys of Conjure: Unlocking the Mysteries of American Folk Magic*, I literally started jumping for joy because THIS IS THE BOOK I WANTED! This is all the information rolling around in my brain unconnected and unfinished. Chas did it. He connected these traditions in a way that breathes life into the experience. He took the power of the oral tradition and brought it to the black and white page. This is the history of American magic, and I am humbled to be a part of it.

Chas brings balance, understanding, and origin to the things we have been doing for generations. He gives you the keys and challenges you to get uncomfortable and grow. He challenges you to embrace both your light and your shadow side to find balance in your magic. Chas brings a respect for and understanding of our Conjure ancestors, without whose bravery and consistency we would not have this unbroken magical tradition to immerse ourselves in.

Conjure is calling. It is ready to come out of the magical closet and show all its sides. Chas Bogan is the sage authority we were looking for to help us unlock the mysteries within ourselves.

—*Jacki Smith*
Founder of Coventry Creations (coventrycreations.com), creator of the Motor City Hoo Doo products, author, teacher, psychic, and enchantress

Introduction

I STAND AT THE crossroads. The fullness of the moon, the chill of the west wind, and the hoot of an owl in the distance all conspire to create an atmosphere for magic. From around my neck I remove the amulet I wear when doing work at the crossroads, made from two crossed skeleton keys tied together in the center. They represent the crossroads themselves and further symbolize the keys to spiritual mastery. Though these keys are physical, what they unlock is internal, and by touching them to my forehead I am able to open to my psychic and magical potential. It is only now, my awareness having been opened, that I hear approaching footsteps amidst the rustling of leaves, and I ready myself to make the pact that will aid me in the writing of this book.

How to petition and work with the spirit of the crossroads is the subject of the closing chapter. For now, following the deal made that night, I find myself deeply engaged in writing about a subject I have long studied and practiced. I have been blessed to have learned firsthand from a variety of skilled Conjure workers, whose traditions form the foundation of my personal practice. Throughout the years that I have owned an occult store in the San Francisco Bay Area, the Mystic Dream, I have had the advantage of both teaching and learning from those who frequent my establishment. My own line of spiritual supplies, which includes oils, powders, baths, and so forth, has been branded with the name *Modern Conjure*, while my in-person and online class is named *A Course in Modern Conjure*. Over the years this course has evolved, as my interactions with students have informed me of their concerns and misconceptions, and my material has been adapted in consideration of how it may best be presented to people of diverse backgrounds. I am pleased by the opportunity to write this book, as it once again allows me to present these deep wisdoms and rich practices in a manner more fully informed and fresher than my earlier work.

The map of North America is forever changing, its ancient trails intersecting with modern highways, bridging old traditions with new innovations and bringing local customs together with immigrant practices. At the crossroads, where such exchanges occur, powerful magic is made. To unlock this magic requires certain keys, various tricks and enchantments, and their attainment and operation is the goal we now embark upon.

The magical folkways of North America share many traits yet are sometimes segregated by such factors as region, race, and religion, all of which, as we shall see, influence how Conjure is practiced and perceived.

Regionally, people from across the country bring their own home-spun traditions to the table, and we find distinct influences such as New Orleans Hoodoo, Appalachian Granny Magic, Ozark folk magic, Low Country rootwork, and others, many of which do not possess a descriptive name but whose practitioners refer to it simply as *the work,* or *jobs,* or something similar. Throughout this book I will commonly use the words *practitioner* or *worker* to refer to those engaged in Conjure. Regional communities have their own concerns, be it the stability of a crop, the need for warmth in winter, or protection from common enemies. The materials employed in folk magic often vary according to what can be found in a given area, such as herbs and animals, as well as what materials are made available through local industry, such as horseshoes or railroad spikes. Additionally, there is a long tradition of commercial trade for such materials that has supplied exotic items to rural practitioners and delivered conventional magical products to workers who have left the fields of their upbringing.

Racial identity shapes magical beliefs and techniques. Concerns arising from racial inequality establish magical responses, often seeking to influence biases and protect against racially motivated threats. The needs of a race are not always clear to those outside of it. For example, one of the products I craft and sell is *Law Keep Away*. I have had more than one conversation with white customers who were under the impression that the product's sole purpose is to protect criminals from capture. These are customers who have never had the experience of being pulled over because of the color of their skin, and therefore have no immediate understanding of why someone might want to avoid the police. Misunderstandings often occur when people try to truck with traditions that were not developed with them in mind. Additionally, certain resentments exist, such as when the descendants of slave owners adopt the very practices meant to protect against their ancestors.

Folk magic in North America often features Christian imagery and scripture. Many magical beliefs and customs can be traced to Native American, African, and European traditions, which were integrated into Christian iconography and celebrations either to hide practices considered heretical or to integrate the old ways with the dominant religion. Theological interpretations that encourage magical actions, while not addressed in all Christian denominations, are fundamental to the practice of many faithful workers, who sometimes both curse and heal according to cultivated interpretations of scriptural injunctions. Although many Conjure practices draw inspiration from the Bible, certain practitioners reject Christianity, these often being devotees of African traditional religions, or Neopagans, who may consider Christian influences a matter of forced conversion and cultural dominance rather than an inherent element of Conjure practice.

Given the historical challenges the United States has encountered in the attempt at creating a society that values differences of region, race, and religion, it is to be expected that these topics are often contentious, arousing such questions as *Should regional traditions be transplanted elsewhere? When does cultural borrowing give way to colonial appropriation?* and *How should nonbelievers utilize traditional psalms?* North American culture continues to be shaped by such issues, as do our magical traditions. Those engaged with the larger Conjure community are sure to encounter individuals who will stress that one can practice Conjure only if they are from a certain region, or are part of a particular racial background, or a believer of a specific faith. The unpacking of these issues is beyond the scope of this book, and it is not the right of this or any single author to grant permission to or define suitable action on behalf of the whole. It is incumbent on the reader to become educated and engaged with the larger community in order to understand diverse perspectives and determine appropriate behavior.

The word *Conjure* itself has its roots in Latin, appearing in Old French and Middle English to describe one who commands. Its modern connotation as one who invokes spirits solidified sometime around the thirteenth century. Its use in North America to describe a style of magical practice is owed to African-Americans, for whom Conjure is synonymous with rootwork and Hoodoo, though often with a more benevolent connotation. Variations of this term, such as Southern Conjure and Appalachian Conjure, were popularized in the early part of the twenty-first century, referring to shared regional practices that had no definitive name. At the time of this writing, the term Conjure is becoming more prominent, used often as an umbrella term for American folk magic. As a result, many are eager to preserve the word's deep association with Black culture, as well as its predominantly Protestant and Southern roots. Indeed, those communities that have created, retained, and nurtured its traditions from the past to the present must be engaged if one is to have a full experience of Conjure.

Beyond the earlier divisions discussed, time serves as another. Changes wrought by time serve as a gauge of authenticity for some. For example, practices born on plantations by those living under the condition of slavery are sometimes regarded differently than urban innovations occurring after the Great Migration. By this measure, practices involving humble materials found on the farmstead are seen as superior to those later manufactured by spiritual merchants and sold to and employed by urban practitioners. This book is presented without prejudice in terms of time and innovations and seeks to explore the fullness of Conjure as it is practiced today. As this work serves to train the reader in the useful practice of folk magic, to ignore advanced methods would be equivalent to favoring penicillin as a truer and more authentic medicine than amoxicillin, despite the superior efficacy of the latter.

While Conjure has over time been influenced by other occult practices, the magic at its core is both simple and complete. Certain actions result in certain changes. Throughout this book we will examine the doctrines that support this notion. However, it is important to stress that this type of magic often resides in the actions and ingredients that are being worked with. While many practitioners work with focused intention, visualization, and various forms of psychic energy, such elements are not always seen as essential, nor are the curios we use mere symbols meant to unlock our inner power. Rather, they are seen as themselves possessing power, which is put into service though specific actions.

While some spells are open to change, not everything can be adapted to suit the new practitioner. I hope that after we have explored the concepts underpinning this type of magic, you will be able to discern what elements are open to adaptation and which are set. Modern practitioners come from diverse backgrounds, and as a result hold different values. Some value the syncretic nature of Conjure and its ability to integrate with other traditions of magic, while others consider themselves purists. Conjure in the early twenty-first century has been influenced beyond its strong African origins, having added practices originating in Kabala, ceremonial magic, Spiritualism, Theosophy, and others. Much as North America has benefitted from immigration, Conjure has adopted practices from as far away as China, Ireland, and the Middle East. Ever practical, Conjure seeks to utilize what works. While some champion innovation, others seek a sense of tradition and authenticity.

Throughout its development, Conjure has assimilated various practices, though with consideration to its underlying doctrines. These will be explored throughout the text, but what is important to note here is that although Conjure may embrace other esoteric practices, it is not a tradition in which anything goes. Some practices fit well with Conjure, but others do not. One can only change a thing so much before it loses its original value. An often used metaphor for this is a lasagna. Some ingredients in this dish can be changed to a certain degree, but at a certain point it ceases to be recognizable. You could use gluten-free lasagna noodles or substitute ground turkey for beef and likely still have a nice dish, but if you were to use pita bread in place of noodles or banana slices instead of meat, your dish could not be called lasagna by most standards.

Of course, there will always be those who claim that their grandmother did it best, and everything else is a pale reflection of the true recipe. Such prejudice aside, there is truth to the fact that there is more to an experience than the exact execution of traditional ingredients. It may not have been grandmother's recipe that was best, but rather the time spent with her in the kitchen, hearing her tell the old stories, smelling her rose-scented perfume, and knowing that the magical legacy of one generation was being passed directly to another. While everyone may be capable of creating a dish equal in flavor, not everyone will share the same cherished experience of making and eating a meal. The balminess of a summer night, the laughter of family, the devotion felt when the sun rises to illuminate creation—these may be what constitute true magical ingredients to some. It is important to respect the intimate relationship that others have to these traditions while working to deepen your own.

Along with conveying the history that has shaped Conjure, my purpose with this book is to describe and celebrate the actual practices seen today. Existence does not equal authenticity; however, I would rather portray the diverse landscape of contemporary Conjure than argue about what others have gotten wrong. Name just about any item known to be used in folk magic, such as War Water, lucky green rice, or nation sacks, and there is someone passionate about its authenticity or lack thereof. Seeing that all of these items are currently used and well known, they are most certainly important to the practice of many Conjure workers, which is the ultimate concern of this book.

Conjure has demonstrated much acceptance of other cultures and their magical customs. It seems that when a person is looking for strong magic, there is a tendency to elevate those practices that are outside the individual's culture. Some of the earliest Hoodoo merchants were found in what were referred to as *Hindu stores*, such as the one in Harlem run by "Alleged Yogi and Professor Phillips" from the 1940s. As a current owner of a magical supply store, it has been my observation that people tend to find magic in the mystique of exotic practices. It is also the unfortunate case that folks tend to detach from those traditions most familiar to them. It sometimes takes a tourist's lens for us to see how remarkably magical our own culture is. Were you to hand a tourist the opposite end of a wishbone and explain to them the mechanics of silently making a wish and pulling for the longer half, it would sound wonderfully peregrine; however, those of us who grew up with this practice often overlook its value. Often the superstitions and tricks we learn as children are seen through our adult eyes as childish, forcing us to look elsewhere, to places where we are told that yogis levitate, or shamans heal, or sensei kill with a touch. The more outlandish and unbelievable the claims, the more likely we are to believe that there is just a bit of magic behind the exaggeration.

North America has recently seen a deepening interest in its folk magic, among Neopagans especially, who since the conception of Wicca in the 1950s have become the dominant practitioners of magic within American culture. For many this interest marks a return to the ways of their ancestors. Practices that fell out of favor because they were common, too "country," are being revisited, sometimes to the chagrin of those who never did abandon such ways. Many are finding freedom in folk magic. For some, this includes the freedom to express their religious heritage, since the history of Neopaganism is partly a reaction against Christianity, and its community is often openly hostile to any mention of Jesus or the Bible or the notions of sin and salvation. Freedom from ethical dogma constitutes another reason for the popularity of Conjure, as the prevalent ethics of modern Neopaganism frown on magic meant to control or curse others. These new converts to Conjure sometimes bring certain issues with them. Unlike European Paganism, which has required deep research to be uncovered, reclaimed, and recreated, Conjure never died out. This point is an important one to make, as many approach Conjure as though they have come to rediscover and save it, rather than as guests entering into a thriving, diverse, and passionate community.

Conjure thrives within the collective starscape of American folk magic, its influence seen in many other traditions, just as many of its practices are admixtures from others. Through the study and practice of Conjure, many of the core beliefs and practices that are fundamental to folk magic in North America can be understood. We will revisit and expand on some of these ideas throughout this book, but for now we must move on to the real work. Having begun here at the crossroads, we seek now a deeper journey toward the life-changing magic ahead of us.

❧ I ❧
The Keys to Divination: Unlocking Psychic Awareness

WHAT PORTENT IS REVEALED when a knock at the door follows the fall of a broom, or a black cat slinks across your path, or an egg yields a bloody yoke? Those of us who follow the ways of Conjure plot our course according to such omens. We recognize how fate is foretold by the world we inhabit; that small events foreshadow larger ones, and that our movements, as well as those of everything around us, tell a much larger story than most people are aware of. To be deeply connected to the world around us, to understand the dialogue being spoken by each falling leaf, cold draft, and cooing dove, is what we seek to master. Everything that exists has its own nature, its own awareness. The broom, for instance, has a more direct relationship with the ground than we do, and is known to fall over when unfamiliar foot-steps approach our threshold. This recognition that everything around us is alive and able to communicate with us is the key to unlocking psychic awareness.

Academically, this concept of the world being alive is known as *animism*, from the Latin *anima*, meaning "spirit," "breath," "the vital, animating force." This belief, which anthropologists see prominently in various native cultures, predates the development of religious orthodoxy. The ability to see common objects as alive is something easily witnessed in the activities of children, for whom fairies may soar in the form of dandelion seeds, and button-eyed teddy bears may serve as fierce protectors against monsters beneath the bed. Present Western thinking divides matter into forms that are considered either animate or inanimate, alive or inert, and holds that opposing views are symptomatic of an undeveloped mind or primitive culture. But those of us who perceive that everything has its own consciousness are advantaged, for there is the potential to connect with and learn from everything in our environment, to interact with our world rather than merely exist within it.

Resources on omens and their meanings abound, and some of the better ones on our topic are included in the resources section of this book. It is important to note that discernment is always necessary when interpreting an omen, for the meaning of any omen may vary. The wind speaks a language all its own, its gusts having an often recognized meaning that may be referenced in books; yet the wind may occasionally address you in a more personal manner that only you can interpret, blowing the hat from your head much as a friend might playfully slap some sense into you to signal a needed change of course. As with any conversation, an understanding of sentiment is needed, and so, in order to understand the wind, you must first befriend it. This needn't require a mysterious ritual; rather, you will find that the more you listen, paying attention to those things around you and approaching them as conscious beings, the louder they will speak and the more skilled you will become in interpreting them. The ability to interpret signs requires more than the mere knowledge of augury, for when hearing a creak in the rafters you must know if it is merely the house settling or if the house is speaking its mind. Knowing the temperament of the house is important. Is this a young and alarmist property, squeamish about every clogged drain? Or is this an old home prone to nag and mutter? You must understand the messenger if you are to understand the message.

The term *two-headed doctor* describes someone gifted with psychic perception, as though the person has one head that occupies the physical world and another that observes the realm of spirit. The exact gifts of such doctors vary. One may be able to tell you what spirits surround you, or profess knowledge of what future events will befall you, or have such a tactile awareness of your sins that their own skin quivers and blushes. They may sense these things in various ways, such as through clairaudience (audibly), claircognizance (knowing), clairsentience (feeling), clairvoyance (vision), or combinations thereof. Knowing the strength of your abilities is essential to exercising them; otherwise you may struggle to hear an ephemeral whisper when you could simply close your eyes and see the words written in your mind's eye.

But where do you begin if you have no experience at being two-headed? Are psychic abilities inherited, or can they be learned?

Popular Formulas for Psychic Abilities

In each chapter of this book we will explore popular products used in Conjure for various purposes. For some of these formulas we will explore recipes and methods for making your own. It has long been the tradition that such products are purchased from certain suppliers, whose establishments are sometimes known as candle shops or Hoodoo drugstores. In modern times these products have become available from online retailers. Many of these products come in the form of blended oils, and although we will not focus on how to make oils until chapter 8, the following are topical to the discussion of psychic-enhancing products. You are not expected to learn how to make all of these concoctions, though you may become eager to do so, as there is an added satisfaction and intimacy that comes from using a formula you have made yourself.

5 Circles Oil

I have not seen this particular formula on the commercial market in contemporary times, but it is mentioned in such popular references as Lewis De Claremont's *Legends of Incense, Herb, and Oil Magic* and Anna Riva's *Golden Secrets of Mystic Oils*. Both texts suggest the existence of a five-layered *aura*, believed to be a field of energy generated by an individual and visible under certain conditions. This formula is said to aid the psychic in traveling through the aura, opening them to greater psychic awareness.

Divination Oil

The product aids in fortune telling. My favorite is made by Otherworld Apothecary, which I like to dab on my third eye (the space just above and between the eyes).

Fortune Teller Oil

This product is for the professionals. The suggested use for Fortune Teller Oil, according to *Papa Jim's Magical Oil Spellbook,* involves pouring some in a glass of water and lighting a blue candle prior to giving a reading,

Aunt Sally's Lucky Dream Oil

The goal of formulas such as this one is to reveal beneficial information through your dreams, most often in the form of lottery numbers or auspicious symbols that may be translated into numbers. Lucky Mojo Curio Company produces a great product called Aunt Sally's Lucky Dream Oil, inspired by the same Aunt Sally whose dream book we will learn more about shortly.

Psychic Vision Oil

Various similar names for this oil exist, such as my own Second Sight conjure oil, which I produce for my brand, Modern Conjure. While the names of these formulas emphasize clairvoyance, they are generally used to boost whichever psychic ability one focuses on.

The appreciation of a good brand name may in time become something of a lost art, at least in certain online marketplaces where items are given lengthy names so the products will appear more often in searches, giving us names such as "Third Eye Psychic Hoodoo Clairvoyant Divination Conjure Wicca Dream Omen Oil."

Other formulas utilized for psychic abilities include those created for general occult power, such as Abramelin, Black Arts, Master Key, and others, which we will explore in our final chapter on magical mastery.

Signs of a Seer

While I believe that many of us possess the ability to awaken our psychic skills, there are those who are inherently suited to the task. Those who are especially blessed in this regard can be recognized through certain portents, such when a baby is born with a caul.

Having an intimate experience with death also marks a child as being blessed with "the sight," such as when one is born from a womb shared with a stillborn sibling or is born posthumously from the mother.

Certain families are known for their powers, so their descendants encounter various expectations from their communities. Even outside of such families, the seventh son of a seventh son would be expected to have the sight. The Seven Sisters of New Orleans[1] come to mind, famed for the spells they cast, although according to Junior Wells's 1957 song they could not help him cope with his own "Two-Headed Woman."

An auspicious time of birth also plays a role in determining who has the potential to be two-headed. It is said that a child born on Christmas Day will possess the power to see spirits, as will one born on Good Friday. Being born on the Feast Day of Saint Francis of Assisi may impart the ability to understand and communicate with animals. Knowing a child's potential allows their caregivers the opportunity to set them on the best course to develop their gifts.

Believers in reincarnation suggest that certain birthmarks are related to the ailments and injuries of past lives, and that those who exhibit them remain connected to their former lives and therefore walk between time periods, being better able to know the past and future.

....

TO DETERMINE A CHILD'S FATE

This method to determine a child's fate comes from Harry M. Hyatt's *Hoodoo, Conjuration, Witchcraft, Rootwork.* On a boy's first birthday, lay before him on the floor a deck of cards, a bottle, a Bible, and a piece of money. If the child selects the deck of cards, he will be a gambler; if the bottle, a drunkard; if the Bible, a preacher; and if the money, a hard worker.

---

1. The true number of women and their relationship is questioned by a number of sources.

I once was making small talk in line at the supermarket with a woman who pointed out the gray skunk patch at the back of my head. She said she was taught it was a sign that a person had been touched by the Devil. This tickled me. Perhaps in another time or place I would have been branded a warlock. One is reminded of the infamous witch trials, when a simple skin tag could be interpreted as being the Devil's mark, the nipple from which your demon familiar was said to suckle.

Childhood events play a strong part is determining the fate of a seer. In her book *God, Dr. Buzzard, and the Bolito Man*, Cornelia Walker Bailey discusses the expectations of her Saltwater Geechee community that she could see ghosts, based on the fact that she was pronounced dead as a child but later recovered. This is what Joseph Campbell calls a *shamanic crisis*, a critical event in a person's life that dramatically changes their consciousness and is sometimes accompanied by spiritual wisdom and psychic gifts.

If you find yourself discouraged because you lack a supernumerary nipple or your mother outlived your birth, fret not, for many spiritual gifts can be developed. We are not all cut out to be an accountant, or a dentist, or a pianist, and not everyone is called to be a Conjure worker. Sure, we all can say a prayer, light candles, and visit crossroads, but magic requires a calling. Interest can magnify scholarship, but should you want to be anything other than an armchair occultist, it will require both passion and action. To become proficient in the art of prophesy you may utilize products or spells to boost your abilities, but success ultimately comes from *doing*. Passion, along with practice, develops skill. Even someone born with a caul and reared with the wisdom of their granny-witch grandmother must engage their innate talents, or they will never realize their full potential. If you never listen for the words within the rustling leaves, then there is little chance you will ever hear them.

It is said that *knowledge equals power*, and the knowledge of how to read signs is especially valued. For those living day by day, knowing when to sow lima beans can be essential to their survival. The meanings of omens are an inheritance from our ancestors, a special gift given by God that especially benefits the needy, who may have little else in terms of education and resources. Traditionally this type of work has been championed by the disenfranchised, for whom such skills fortified their survival and might bring monetary profit as well. There is a long history of seers serving as professional readers for people of higher social influence. We see this depicted by American artist Harry Roseland around the turn of the twentieth century. Many of his paintings depict the same black female reading palms and tea leaves for white women sitting before her. While images of sewing are also prevalent in paintings such as this one, we can assume that this woman earned a portion of her income by reading signs for others. It is no wonder that the art of fortune telling is often outlawed by those who seek strict class divisions, as readers wield special influence over individuals of higher station.

Learning a form of divination is paramount in order to gain the knowledge you need, when you need it, rather than wait for the rooster to announce a death by crowing between dusk and dawn. Conjure doctoring is a sort of medicine, and in order to prescribe the correct cure one must first make a diagnosis. Except for times when Spirit directly inspires me, I do a reading prior to suggesting a remedy. Although there is no single form of divination common to all workers, there are some that are often associated with Conjure practice, most notably the following trick.

....

BIBLE AND KEY

For this activity you will need the following:

- A Bible: An average book size works well. Avoid an oversized family Bible, as it may become damaged—along with the feet of those engaging in this practice.
- One key, typically a large skeleton key
- Something to tighten around the Bible and hold it closed, such as ribbon, rubber bands, rope, or a belt

Place the key inside the Bible. Some will choose to place it on a page of scripture that they feel aligns with the question they wish to ask, while others will simply place it near the Bible's center. The book is bound, and two people dangle the Bible between them, with their fingers pressed against the protruding key (or else a ribbon is tied to the key, in which case their fingers press against the ribbon). At this point one or both of the people involved ask a question, then name off some possible answers. For example, say you were wondering who impregnated the preacher's daughter. You could name off various suspects, and when the rogue is named, the key will slip between the fingers holding it or otherwise slide out from the Bible.

Variations of this trick exist. A similar job may be done with a pair of scissors instead of a key, often with the two hands opening and closing the scissors until the blades escape from the book.

....

White Plate Reading

This method is used to ascertain if evil spirits are attached to someone. The individual in question stands or sits. The front of the plate faces the person being diagnosed, a short distance from their body. Movements are made with the plate to scan the body, as though the plate were a mirror meaning to capture images of the person's anatomy. I prefer to do this in the form of three crosses in the front followed by three in the back, moving down and across, and repeating that same motion. The concept is similar to that of photography, with the belief that an image of the invading spirit, should there be one, will appear as soot after the plate is passed over a candle flame. The plate is ritually washed afterward, cleansing the patient of the spirit that was captured on its surface. This is followed by protection work to prevent the spirit's return.

State of Mind

The ability to read a situation is crucial to understanding the real issue. My experience as a professional reader involves working with folks who feel that something is amiss but do not know what, or with folks making wrong assumptions about another person's motives and actions. Before reaching for the cursing candles, you may wish to throw some bones to discover that the husband is sneaking off at night to feed a motherless litter of puppies, not heading to a seedy motel room. Such a scenario is unlikely, as people more often prove to be awful, but due diligence is important. When determining what action to take in the form of a spell, it is essential that we have the correct diagnosis, lest more harm than good be done.

Temperament is key in many ways. Your mood affects your reading. Consider one popular portrayal of the fortune teller—that of the dire carnival gypsy who predicts mostly doom and gloom. Such a character is commonly burdened with a hard life and the curse of her own gift as a soothsayer. Your burdens may be fewer, but be careful not to bring them with you when you attempt a reading. Additionally, just as a negative mood will overshadow your readings, a Pollyanna attitude will sugarcoat every interpretation. Understand that readings are often colored by your emotions, expectations, and prejudices. This is where understanding the nature of being two-headed is beneficial, for a successful reading may depend on the ability to move from your physical head, clouded as it is with egotistical concerns, to your other head, whose perceptions are not similarly clouded—a *shift in consciousness*, as it is often referred to.

Psychics accomplish this change of awareness in different ways, some quite effortlessly and others needing triggers, sometimes dramatic ones. Consider the iconic fortune teller depicted in various films, eyes rolling back into their head and uttering strange sounds until their demeanor changes abruptly and they speak with grandiose authority. Most authentic workers are not so theatrical, though style is always welcomed. Doctor Buzzard gives us a good example, as we can imagine how his iconic purple glasses easily altered his perception and, what's more, made him look cool as jazz.[2] Readers work in individual ways, and there is no shared way in which we all switch our psychic power on and leave unwanted judgments aside. You must experiment to find a way that works best for you.

Workers have varying ideas of where the messages they receive emanate from. Some find psychic intuition inside themselves, others hear voices from deep within the roots of the earth, and some perceive divine knowledge as shining down from the sky like heavenly light. A

---

2. Doctor Buzzard was the name taken by Stepheney Robinson (1885–1947), though he may not have been the first or last rootworker from Beaufort County in South Carolina to use that moniker.

devout spiritual worker may point to God as the source of all extraordinary knowledge, while another may attribute it to their ancestors. Whatever you believe the source of your insight to be, it is important to show respect. If the broom blesses you with a message, show it due care, such as by washing its straws or oiling its stick. Honor the tools you use, be they cards or bones or yourself. There is a long tradition in Conjure of getting paid for your talents as a diviner, and if you choose to be paid, then respect yourself enough to insist on it. If you credit your ancestors for being the voice that whispers knowledge in your ear, then be sure to honor them, with flowers or whiskey or whatever works as an appropriate show of thanks. Tangible shows of gratitude are valued in folk magic. You must water the vine that feeds you.

Dreams

Sometimes the secret knowledge we seek doesn't come from observing outward signs or forecasting with tools but occurs when we close our eyes at night. In Conjure, dream divination is a rich tradition known as *dreaming true*.

Too often our days are filled with the drudgery of mindless tasks. The hour commute to work is barely noticeable. Our foot accelerates and brakes almost automatically while we remain aware of little more than the blur of passing taillights. It is not in our day-to-day life that we are most awake; rather, it is in our dreams that we become intimate with our internal environment, alert in that fashion peculiar to dreaming. When in our mundane life we encounter something out of the ordinary, such as seeing a coyote in the playground or hearing a song in the supermarket that had been playing in our head all day, our attention brightens and we become fully present. On such occasions we are pressed to find meaning. The unexpected owl feather that lands on the window of our car must mean something. Suddenly we come alive and engage with the world in a search for purpose. Every event that seems auspicious, whether ordained by angels or a mere coincidence, has the power to inspire us. While some may dismiss such thinking as hickish and superstitious, it may be what makes us fully cognizant. Expanding one's consciousness is not a benefit only for those who meditate, but is realized whenever we become imaginative. That is when we become greater, creating more potential for magic.

As I write this, Otis Redding has begun singing his classic "I've Got Dreams to Remember," and the synchronicity with our current topic evokes a connection to what had a moment ago been mere background noise. This provides the perfect atmosphere for magic, so let's continue with some tricks to help you dream.

To Discover Your Fortune in a Dream

Repeat the following verse nine times before bed, and your dreams will reveal the means to making you rich:

> *New moon, true moon,*
> *Star in the stream,*
> *Pray tell my fortune in my dream.*[3]

To Dream True

- Dream beneath a new quilt.
- Dream with a slice of wedding cake beneath your bed.
- Count seven stars on seven consecutive nights, and on the final night your dream will come true.

To Remember Your Dreams

- Drink a cup of tea or coffee before bed.

  The trick of drinking something caffeinated before bed helps you have more active dreams and awake from them easily, at least for folks who fall asleep quickly. (You may wish to engage in some physical or mental activity that will wear you out and make falling asleep easier.) Caffeine generally takes a good twenty minutes to surge through your system, by which time you will hopefully have fallen into a dream.

- Tell yourself thirteen times before you fall asleep that you will remember your dreams come morning.

---

3. Harry M. Hyatt, *Folk-Lore from Adams County, Illinois*, no. 5933.

- Keep a journal that you write in immediately upon waking.
- Sleeping with a mirror beneath your pillow will reflect your dreams back to you.

To Keep Bad Dreams from Coming True

- Before bed, read Psalm 23 (*The Lord is my shepherd ...*).
- Take a feather or a bit of stuffing from your pillow and burn it.
- Tell someone your dream—or don't.

   The act of telling someone your dream, or even just speaking it aloud, is said to cause it to come true. Alternatively, some say just the opposite is the case. Sometimes the prohibition is time-sensitive, such as not recounting your dream before sun-up or breakfast.

To Keep from Dreaming

- An open pair of scissors beneath your pillow will keep you from dreaming.

   We see an open pair of scissors working as a protection charm in various other situations as well. An open pair of scissors appears as a cross (+) or an X, both of which are protective symbols, given an extra edge because of the blades.
- Place both shoes at the foot of your bed and you will not dream.

   In addition to placing your shoes at the foot of your bed, some say to lay them upside down or under the bed. The notion here seems to be that your spirit will have trouble walking in the dream world if your physical shoes are encumbered.

To Avoid Bad Dreams

- Walk backwards to bed.
- Place a cup of water beside your bed.

   Water is often presented to spirits as a simple offering, and by placing water beside your bed it is believed that malevolent spirits will be attracted to the water and not you. Make sure you do not drink the water come morning, but dispose of it by throwing it against a tree.

OTHER METHODS FOR PURPOSEFUL DREAMING

- Sleeping in the clothes of one who was murdered will cause you to see the murderer in a dream.
- Sleeping on another's photograph will cause them to dream of you.
- To dream of a future mate, consume something exceedingly salty before bed and your future mate will offer you water in your dream.

The Colors of Our Dreams

Consider the classic American film *The Wizard of Oz*, which—spoiler—ends with the understanding that the events that transpired were all just Dorothy's dream. The real world of Kansas is starkly black and white, whereas the film is colorized once the door opens to Oz. Color plays a key role in our dreams, giving added meaning to objects. To dream of a horse means one thing, but to dream of a purple one is a horse of a different color. To figure out what such an animal might mean requires an understanding of color associations. Different cultures ascribe different meanings to colors. While white means purity and new beginnings in North America, in China it is a mournful color, the color of bone and death and funerals. Here is a list of the more general color meanings associated with Conjure:

Black: Cursing, hex breaking, protection

Blue: Contentment, dreaming, peace

Brown: Grounding, law, stasis

Gold: Solar, wealth in large amounts

Gray: Balance, neutrality, secrecy

Green: Money, healing, growth

Orange: Action, confidence, creativity

Pink: Flirtation, friendship, reconciliation

Purple: Influencing, mystery, spiritual development

Red: Anger, passion, sexuality

Silver: Lunar, wealth in small amounts

White: Cleansing, devotion, purity

Yellow: Clarity, joy, willpower

We will work with these correspondences throughout this book, especially when we explore how to work with candles in chapter 10.

Dream Interpretation

The importance of dreams may best be seen in the influence of dream books that came into fashion in the late 1800s, when publications such as *Aunt Sally's Policy Players' Dream Book* offered lists of common dream images and their interpretations, along with lucky numbers. These numbers could be used for gambling, such as with the game of Policy, popular in many African-American communities. Numbers were chosen in sets, the most popular being a set of three called a *gig*. There were well-known gigs, such as the *washerwoman's gig*, whose numbers are 4-11-44, and which, in some editions of the book, is held on the cover by the figure depicted as Aunt Sally (a fictional character, as far as anyone knows, depicted as a mammy with her dark skin and headscarf). Aunt Sally would later serve as the namesake for a line of Hoodoo products produced in the 1930s by King Novelty Company and later by Lucky Mojo Curio Company. Dream books could also be used in reverse for the act of decoding numbers, as with the song by Blind Blake titled "Playing Policy Blues," in which he declares his desire to pair a certain gig of numbers with her gig, an act that a good dream book would have been able to interpret as sexual innuendo.

Over the years I have purchased a nice collection of dream books with delightful names in the titles, such as Kansas City Kitty, Egyptian Witch, and Red Devil.

Let's take a look at contemporary dream interpretation. While dream books are part of a rich heritage, they are less favored now than in their heyday, as shifts in culture have come to stress personal authority. Not everyone is satisfied with the interpretation of a goose as given, for instance, in *Madam Fu-Fu's Lucky Number Dream Book;* rather, an individual's relationship to a goose as a symbol is likely to be stressed. I have chosen *goose* specifically, as one of my earliest memories is of feeding ducks at

Oakland's Lake Merritt and being bitten on the butt by a particularly sassy goose. If a goose appears in my dream, it is not a symbol of prosperity but of butt hurt. The goose is there to tell me to let go of whatever is irking me. It can be helpful to play a game of word association when attempting to find meaning in a symbol for which you have no recognizable relationship.

Physically speaking, dreams are symphonies of firing synapses to which our mind applies meaning. Yet a popular concept describes the brain as being a radio when we dream, receiving broadcasts from our spirit when in dreams we wander otherworldly realms. It may be that the nature of this otherworld is to be cryptic, or that our brain cannot quite make sense of the signal and is made to create a symbolic facsimile. Modern perceptions of dreams tend to define them as an extension of an individual's psyche. The landscape is understood to be generated by and to take place within one's brain.

Contrary to this belief that the landscape of dreams is personal to the dreamer is another stating that dreams take place in another world, one opposite our own, and therefore all aspects of a dream mean the reverse of what they would in our waking world. Thus to dream of a birth is to foreshadow a death, to dream of rain portends a sunny day, and to dream of a new beginning signals a swift conclusion.

Through environmental omens, fortune-telling tools, and prophetic dreaming, the Conjure doctor is able to diagnose situations through psychic knowledge. It is only with an understanding of situations that we are able to prescribe cures.

II

The Keys to Ritual: Unlocking Blessings

THE ROOT IS READY to be awoken, to find its purpose, not as a plant or shrub or tree but as an ally to a powerful conjurer. You place the root in a bowl and pour whiskey over it with three tips of the bottle, blessing it and urging it to awaken. Imagine you can feel it now, the tiny spirit within the root beginning to stir. As it awakens, you speak to it, telling it things about its better nature, how it is strong, how it is loyal, how it is skilled at magic. You can sense it growing now, sending out invisible shoots that compose its growing spirit body. Soon you will have a giant to serve as your ally in the spirit world. For now, the root soaks in the whiskey, gaining in strength, as you prepare for the spell it will aid you with.

In the previous chapter, I discussed how the environment around us speaks in signs. Now we must learn how to communicate in kind, through the eloquence of ritual. By talking back, we participate in the narrative of our world, commanding dangers to move from our path and inviting blessings to take their place.

To accomplish this, we must become fluent in the language of symbolism and ceremony. Remember the broom, and how in falling it announced an impending visitor. Say you wish to be rid of such a guest now. The simple act of standing a broom upside down, straws facing the ceiling, is said to make visitors take leave.

Shoo away any remaining negativity from your home by sweeping out your front door. Sweep into your home at dawn to invite in the blessings of a new day.

These actions communicate your desire. But to whom is this communication being made? The answer depends in part on the worldview of any given worker, which we will examine in the following paragraphs.

Many a worker will say the broom itself interprets your actions. While the exact metaphysical machinations of how it then grants your request may be unknown, many perceive each object as possessing an indwelling spirit able to travel beyond its physical form to service your request. Stories abound in folktales wherein objects are discovered to have magical powers. For Conjure workers, such magical objects are all around us, often unassuming in their power.

Other workers, often religiously devout, emphasize that such actions as upturning a broom are a way of speaking to God through creation. It is believed that the world was designed to respond to certain actions, sometimes miraculously. Understanding which actions garner the best results constitutes true spiritual wisdom.

Although I use the metaphor of ritual being a symbolic language, it is important not to approach the roots we will be working with as mere symbols. There is an all too common belief, influenced by New Thought ideology, that all magic comes from within the magician. However, this belief is not foundational to folk magic, which finds that magic is contained in the materials we use and released through specific actions. Rather than diminish the role of the broom to a mere symbol, we will address it as an individual with its own power.

The distinct dialect of Conjure relies on precise timing. It observes both the orbit of constellations as well as clock hands, and is punctuated by gestures aligned with specific directions. In this chapter we will be examining these procedures through our interaction with botanical allies.

Popular Formulas for Blessing

A blessing in its simplest form confers favor upon a person or object. Conjure practitioners perform various blessings in our work, often blessing ourselves and our tools at the onset of favorable workings. The difference between what one considers a blessing as opposed to a type of general well-wishing spell is intimately tied to compassion. There are blessings bestowed by God and those given by a mother to her offspring, even the casual blessing of someone who has sneezed; each is a show of compassion. Here are some of the formulas that serve to bestow blessings.

Anointing

The purpose of anointing something, which is most often done with oil, is to bless it with divine influence, making it holy. There are also numerous religiously inspired formulas that serve the purpose of anointing, such as Holy Trinity, Holy Type, Bible Bouquet, and others. The following incense recipe comes from Exodus 30:34–35.

....

ANOINTING INCENSE

- 1 part benzoin
- 1 part frankincense
- 1 part galbanum
- 1 part myrrh

Blessed Mary

We could list a number of religious figures eager to confer their blessings upon folks, but they often serve other purposes as well, whereas Blessed Mary is all about the blessing. This product is designed for people, especially children, who are in need of the Blessed Mother's love.

Blessing

Merchants often offer an oil labeled with this generic name, used for unspecified blessing needs. A blessing directs divine compassion toward an object or goal, and is best used for things that have some tangible form, something you can touch or a well-laid plan. If you have no car, there is little point in saying a blessing for your trip; you are better off doing some other form of work that will draw a vehicle your way. A firm principle behind magic and prayer stresses that requests be specific. While in a strict sense anything that benefits you may be called a blessing, being blessed with money or love or health requires working a type of magic unique to each of those conditions.

Crown of Success

This formula allows you to define success, drawing to you such things as money, love, or recognition. This is achieved through its ability to bless your head, to crown you.

....

CROWN OF SUCCESS INCENSE

- 1 part bay leaves
- 1 part five-finger grass (cinquefoil)
- 1 part frankincense resin
- 1 part myrrh resin
- 1 part patchouli

House Blessing

Home is sometimes a place of sadness and strife, which this formula seeks to remedy. Any positive emotion (joy, confidence, peace, etc.) can be a blessing. Another popular house-blessing formula is called Happy Home.

Blessings are frequently the work of clergy who rely on their access to the divine and the authority of their respective orders, which have traditionally been Protestant and Catholic. The decentralized framework of Protestantism allows for individuals to pursue their own religious authority and even create their own ministry, sometimes as a member of a larger denomination or as an independent church. Many spiritual workers, often with honorifics attached to their names such as Deacon, Sister, Preacher, or similar appellations, serve as self-appointed clergy of their own church—whether it be in a dedicated building, their office, or simply their internal vision. Wherever your personal sense of authority comes from, be it from your religion or pure humanity, learning how to bless is essential. While there are many ways to bless, let's stick with our theme and explore how herb blends are particularly suitable for blessing work.

Finding Our Direction

Whether we believe our universe was created by a deity or by happenstance, there exists an observable order to things. Time moves forward, gravity pulls things earthward, water flows downstream. Following the ways of creation aligns you with nature. It utilizes inherent energy. You are working with the world to create change when your actions follow the natural order. Spells that work with creation tend toward more positive works, what in occult phraseology is said to be of the *right-hand path*. As one of its definitions, the word *right* also means correct. The term *right-hand path* therefore reflects a prejudice: since most humans are right-handed, it places virtue in normality. (Left-handed people have even faced persecution for their difference, including being labeled as witches.) Accordingly, acts going against the natural order are said to be of the *left-hand path*. These directional terms are used to differentiate between work performed for benefit versus destruction.

Destructive work, such as curses, is called *witchcraft* in the nomenclature of more traditional Conjure communities. While there are several positive uses of the word *witch*, such as with water witching or granny witches, it is most often a negative term describing one who uses malevolent magic (this despite attempts by modern witches to rebrand the term with a positive connotation). Witchcraft is understood to be transgressive, working against the natural order. An example of this can be seen in the ritual of the black cat bone (an analogous rite requires a toad bone). This spell requires a sacrificed black cat, whose bones are tossed into a stream to detect the one containing mystical power, which reveals itself by floating upstream rather than down, transgressing the natural order. This is a familiar spell to make one powerful in the art of sorcery, though thankfully it is found more often in folklore than in practice.

Given the power that resides in deviancy, it is understandable that certain things deemed unlucky by some are understood to be magically powerful by others. Black cats, coffin nails, the number thirteen, and even the Devil himself are all regarded for their power. Sometimes to beat the odds one must become odd, and work against the natural order. This emphasis on order, or its transgression, governs ritual actions, such as timing and directionality.

Directionality plays a distinct role in our work, in regard to where we face and which gestures we use. As a general rule, we face or throw to the west to weaken and to the east to strengthen. When doing work to draw something toward us—say, money or love or luck—the gestures we use pull toward us. When sending things away, we push away from ourselves.

When harvesting a plant, the tradition is to face east, toward where the sun rises to bless each day, whereas when gathering herbs for cursing some may choose instead to face west, the direction of the setting sun and therefore of decrease and death.

This concern for directionality governs the spectrum of Conjure practices, such as the folding of prayer papers, the dressing of candles with oil, and the washing of one's body for spiritual bathing, and will be employed throughout this book.

Signature of a Plant

American folk magic inherits much of its herbal lore from the tribes native to these lands, especially the Cherokee, Chickasaw, Choctaw, and Seminole tribes, in addition to African and European influences. Before modern Western medicine evolved into what it is today, it was the root doctors, the hedge witches, the grannies and the cunning men who were sought within their communities for their healing talents. The compounds that would later develop into the complex medicines of pharmacology were present in roots and stalks and leaves, which often were brewed into teas, soaked in alcohol to make tinctures, mashed to a pulp for poultices, stirred into fat to make granny grease, or administered as smoke. The simplest of these remedies had purging effects, bringing sickness out through the various orifices of the body. Many of the basic spices we use for flavoring in our food have antimicrobial properties that safeguard us from certain pathogens. Herbs can have natural properties that are analgesic, antibacterial, antifungal, anti-inflammatory, antiseptic, antiviral, diuretic, stimulative, and sedative. Moreover, there is a spiritual understanding of such botanicals not just as chemicals but as spirits with individual interests and specialized talents.

A popular tenet regarding botanicals is the *doctrine of signatures*, which states that plants that resemble a certain part of the body can be used to treat that part of the body, fashioned so by a Creator intent on communicating purpose through design. For example, bloodroot (*Sanguinaria canadensis*) *bleeds* a sap that is dark red in color, like blood, and—in accordance with the doctrine—treats conditions of the blood (one example being its medicinal use in improving circulation). Beyond the realm of medicine, and closer to our subject of folk magic, plants are used in ceremony based on this same doctrine. Thus a lucky hand root (aka salep root) often resembles a fingered hand, and is therefore used to grab hold of favorable conditions such as luck, money, and love. Ever adoptive of the exotic, Conjure has integrated such diverse herbal curios as African guinea peppers, Chinese bat nuts, Peruvian palo santo sticks, asafoetida from India, and herbs from lands far afield. There are many good books that serve as references beyond what can be listed here, my top suggestions being *Hoodoo Herb and Root Magic* by catherine yronwode and *The Master Book of Herbalism* by Paul Beyerl.

It is important to know what part of the plant is useful for your purpose. This differs according to personal practice; however, roots are often preferred, thus the reason why this type of folk magic is referred to as *rootwork*. To say you *put roots on* someone suggests you have worked magic on them. This emphasis on roots may be related to their proximity to the ancestors, who having been buried and now occupy the earth, and from whom roots are fed. Unlike other parts of the plant that can often be extracted with little or no harm to the plant, root removal is fatal to plants without extended root systems. Sacrifice therefore becomes a theme, and it is understood that in the same way plants and animals are killed to feed us, so must we sacrifice plants for the purpose of feeding our magic. The level of involvement in killing a plant is more intense than in harvesting its parts, thus your relationship to it is stronger (although its spirit lives on in your work). It is not uncommon to utilize different parts of the plant for different types of work, such as the following:

Root: Commanding, cursing, power

Stalk and Bark: Stability

Leaf: Growth, health

Bud: Potential, road opening

Bloom: Sexuality, spirituality

Seed: Fertility

Fruit: Wealth, prosperity

The relationship between the worker and the materials they conjure with depends on the worker's beliefs. Among certain Christian practitioners, especially those influenced by the style of ceremonial magic put forth in popular grimoires, it is common to command the spirit of an herb to do your bidding, with the belief that God gave humans dominion over the earth, as expressed in Genesis 1:26. Here is a Pennsylvania Dutch prayer that expresses dominion over an herb:

> *In the name of Jesus Christ, I conjure you [insert name of the herb] that I may conquer by St. Peter, who holds the Keys, and by the moon and the stars, that you aid me to conquer all of my enemies, both seen and unseen, known and unknown; both spirit and human, male and female, and all the powers that are working against me.*[4]

Others seek to build a working relationship with the spirit within the plant. Approaching it as an ally follows the animistic philosophy that a living being resides within, such as the concept behind plant devas found in Theosophy. Beyond acknowledging individual spirits, there are practitioners influenced by New Age beliefs that postulate a collective spirit representing an entire genus, such as the concept of plant archetypes popular in Findhorn literature. Such relationships between plant

---

4. C. R. Bilardi, *The Red Church or The Art of Pennsylvania German Braucherei*, 264.

allies and root doctors tend to emphasize mutual respect, in which the plant spirit is petitioned to help with a need, and in turn that spirit is honored with praise, and possibly coins or libations.

There are various ways of developing a relationship with the spirit of a plant, such as the description that began this chapter. Some workers have an innate ability to close their eyes, cup an herb in their hands, and call out the spirit within to commune with it. Another might place an herb beneath their pillow and seek its spirit in dreams. When safe to do so, one may ingest an herb, or anoint oneself with its essential oil and breathe in its scent or the smoke that arises when it is burned. Interacting with the spirit directly is not an ability that everyone possesses, but it is still important to approach the work with the knowledge that there is a spirit working with you.

I like to imagine an ember within each root, waiting for my breath to feed it oxygen, glowing brighter, until I see its spirit emerge as a living flame. Some folks like to caress or tap a root gently, as you would to awaken a slumbering child. Others will coo to it, like to a pet, child, or lover. I was taught to give it a name resonant with its purpose, or, if it has a traditional name, such as High John the Conqueror, then that is used, and sometimes altered, like *Lover John* if its use is for love, or *Brave John* if for courage. Let us say that you are working with angelica root to draw romance; you might address her as *Angel Love*, telling her flattering things about herself, such as how alluring she is and how she can make hearts swoon.

Bathing the root is considered an essential step by many, though the nature and purpose of this varies. Some workers have described how they are enacting a baptism, and these tend to momentarily submerge the root in holy water. Colognes are commonly used as well, such as Hoyt's. This works well for individual roots, though for a bowl of dried herbs you may wish to simply sprinkle or mist them, so that your herbs do not become a soggy mess.

More common is the act of soaking the root, often in whiskey. Other liquors are known to be used as well, such as champagne for romance. I often use Goldschlager when working for money, as that liqueur contains cinnamon and flecks of gold leaf, both of which resonate with money work. If you want to get fancy, here is a wonderful whiskey cocktail sure to wake up your root.

....

THREE WISE MEN COCKTAIL

This recipe includes equal parts of three different whiskeys. Traditionally it is made with whiskeys named after their makers, namely Jim Beam, Jack Daniel's, and Johnnie Walker.

- 1 part Kentucky bourbon whiskey
- 1 part Tennessee whiskey
- 1 part Scotch whiskey

Herbs may not always make good allies. Bad allergic reactions can be an indicator that a plant spirit is not compatible with you, although I have known workers who considered their red eyes and wheezy breath a form of sacrifice. Something I suggest is finding the essential oil of a plant genus you wish to work with, when such is available, and noting your reaction to it. The first time I smelled rue I could not get enough of it, and it has proved to be one of my strongest allies. Other people I know hate the smell of rue oil and often express that they have a hard time working with it. These spirits have their own personalities, which is what gives them their specific abilities. With some wooing, most can become the allies needed to bless your work.

Once you have determined which plant to work with, it becomes important to know when your work should begin.

When the Time Is Right

Plants are considered to be more powerful when harvested at auspicious times. Herbs are often available to us in dried form, especially if they have a popular use in teas. A more intimate experience is to be had with those plants that you grow and harvest yourself. Pay attention to those native to your environment, that catch your eye on the trail or from planter boxes along city streets. Plants that seek to share their magic with you are said to grow along your path, seeking your attention.

Should you be lucky enough to have access to fresh plants, you will want to know the best time and manner in which to harvest them. The life cycle of a plant is often taken into consideration. Say you wish to work with basil for the purpose of fertility; you may choose to harvest it when it has gone to seed. A rose picked for a love spell is most potent when it has bloomed, when it is at its most fragrant. Some plants reveal their magic only in their chosen time, such as angel's trumpet, whose bell-shaped blooms perfume the air only after dusk.

Sometimes a need is immediate or an opportunity is so promising that it is wise to take swift action, whether or not conditions are aligned with traditional associations. More often, workings are planned for, and ingredients are gathered for a given time according to the nature of the job. For instance, the best time to perform a blessing ritual is considered to be dawn, at the cusp of a new day when potential is at its fullest. The opposite of that—say, work done for cursing—may best be done under the cloak of night (especially if you wish your work to remain secret) or else as the sun sets, should your goal be to see someone's power and influence lessen like the light of the setting sun. The emphasis here is on the increasing and decreasing influences of light and dark. A common understanding is that past midnight, the influence of darkness has reached its zenith and the increase of light is in effect, thus it is a good time for positive work. Past noon, the sun begins to set, and this is the time when light is decreasing and darkness is increasing. Factors such as daylight saving time, along with the observable decrease in daylight throughout the season, are taken into account differently by workers. It is up to you to decide if your work should be scheduled according to the clock or natural observation, determining whether 12:00 p.m. serves as the height of the sun's influence or if you ought to wait for the more exact moment when the sun stands fullest in the sky.

Another way in which mechanical time may influence a worker is through observation of an analog clock, by taking note of when the arms are simultaneously rising or falling. When they are rising toward heaven—say, between 6:30 and 7:00 and each subsequent hour until 11:30 rises to 12:00—it is an exalted time, ideal for bringing an increase of love, money, health, etc. Oppositely, when the hands both point more toward the earth—say, between 12:00 and 12:30 and each subsequent hour until 5:00 lowers to 5:30—jobs may be done for decrease, such as to lessen the influence of a rival. Both forces, increase and decrease, may be useful depending on your approach. For instance, if you were doing healing work against a tumor, you could utilize the hours of decrease to weaken it, whereas during the period of increase the focus would be on strengthening the patient's immune system. Time is a factor in dictating if it is more appropriate to banish the bad or call in the good.

Moon Phases

The moon has always governed magic. Its phases are easily seen by the naked eye, with no need for the charts or mathematics of astrology. For many workers, the moon marks the best time to perform a particular spell.

New Moon: This is a time of newness and renewal; time to plant seeds for new projects.

Waxing Moon: This is a time of increase; good for work seeking to draw favorable conditions.

Full Moon: The moon at its fullest and brightest; good for peace work and matters of inspiration.

Waning Moon: The moon is decreasing; time for sending things away and seeing them diminish in power.

Dark Moon: The moonlight has faded and the night is dark; ideal time for secretive and cursing magic.

When planning a spell, these phases are taken into account, often in relationship to what astrological sign the moon is in.

Astrology

The influence of astrology in early North American culture is evident in the planting instructions given in almanacs and the horoscopes printed in newspapers. Almanacs have aided North American families, particularly farmers, since the late 1700s, the most popular being the *Farmer's Almanac* (new editions are still available today under the name *Old Farmer's Almanac*), first published in 1792. The public's basic understanding of astrology was subsequently adopted by many folk magicians. Astrological lore helped dictate life on the farm, determining when to plant and harvest, when to breed livestock, when to raise a barn, even when to cut one's hair or perform surgeries on parts of the body. Most often this was in relation to which sign the moon was in, as the moon, more so than the sun, was regarded as governing our bodies, and those of livestock and plants.

Rootworkers often use planetary correspondences to determine what times are best for the execution of spells. The moon travels through all twelve houses of the zodiac about once every twenty-nine days, meaning it resides in any given sign for nearly two and a half days. Tables for the moon's course are available from various publications, for those wishing to do the calculations themselves. However, a good almanac will include what sign the moon is in on any given day, along with advice for what duties may best be performed or avoided at such times. Such lore can be seen in the following examples.

- Flowers planted in the sign of Gemini will bear luscious blooms.
- Taking a hog to the butcher in Taurus results in the tastiest cuts of meat.
- Building a house in the sign of Leo will ensure that it is filled with love.
- The sign of Aries is a bad time to wean a baby, whereas Sagittarius is ideal.

The human body itself is believed to be governed by the planets. The figure of the Zodiac Man (see illustration), dating back to the Middle Ages, represents the influence each planet has over areas of the body.

Here are the dates for the twelve signs, plus the parts of the body associated with each sign.

Aries (March 21–April 19): Head, face

Taurus (April 20–May 20): Ears, neck, shoulders

Gemini (May 21–June 20): Lungs, arms, hands

Cancer (June 21–July 22): Chest, stomach

Leo (July 23–August 22): Heart, spine, upper back

Virgo (August 23–September 22): Gallbladder, liver, intestines

Libra (September 23–October 22): Kidneys, lower back

Scorpio (October 23–November 21): Bladder, genitals, pelvis, rectum

Sagittarius (November 22–December 21): Thighs, legs, hips

Capricorn (December 22–January 19): Bones, knees, skin

Aquarius (January 20–February 18): Ankles, veins, calves

Pisces (February 19–March 20): Feet

Timing is therefore taken into consideration when treating bodily maladies. Pisces, for instance, rules the feet, and therefore foot issues are best resolved in that sign.

Signs are further considered in regard to the person your work targets. Say you plan to work against a Taurus (and God help you if you do). A poor time to target them is when their sign is most powerful, between April 10 and May 20. The best time is when your own sign is at its most influential.

Products related to zodiac signs are commonly available from spiritual candle shops and Hoodoo pharmacies. Items such as oils and incense are often named after a given sign and are used in a number of ways. A person may burn incense formulated for their sign as a means of dominating the atmosphere of a room, either to gain advantage over other occupants or simply to bask in energy complementary to their sign. Using a product in the latter way aligns a person with their given sign and, as we discussed earlier, sets them on a right-hand path consistent with God's design. Additionally, zodiac products are used to aid in representing the target of a spell; therefore, Virgo oil would be used for someone born in early September, perhaps by anointing the back of their photograph or by dressing a representative candle. (More about oils and their uses in chapter 8.)

Rarely do we have the luxury to plan months ahead for the most auspicious time to do a spell. There are, however, times when some workers eschew certain rites. Again, a good almanac can tell you when the moon is void of course or Mercury is retrograde, both of which are considered inopportune times for most magical work.

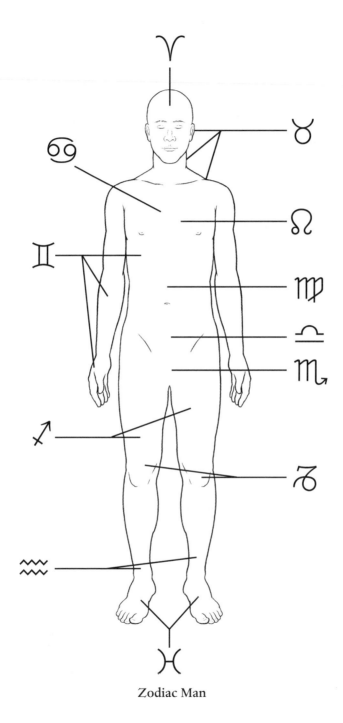

Zodiac Man

Days and hours are also ruled by astrological influences, though this is where we shift from the familiar zodiac to the Chaldean ordering of heavenly bodies.

Sun (Sunday): A day for blessing; for success, including wealth and notoriety; good for attracting a man and for works regarding fatherhood

Moon (Monday): A day for seduction, for working with spirits and for psychic work; good for attracting a woman and works regarding motherhood

Mars (Tuesday): A day for war, for competition, risk, and vengeance

Mercury (Wednesday): a day for justice, for communication and technical issues

Jupiter (Thursday): A day for luck, for money and gambling

Venus (Friday): A day for love, for spells concerning glamor and love

Saturn (Saturday): A day for protection, and for throwing curses as well

The purpose of each astrological hour of the day mirrors the associations given here for the days. While the days are set, the planetary hours require calculation, based as they are on the rising of the sun at your particular location. Older Conjure doctors, who tended to be more educated and eager to study occult technologies relevant to their work, had various publications and tools at their disposal, such as Professor A. F. Seward's *Planetary Hour Indicator*, a pocket-sized dial that could be turned to determine the astrological hour. Aids for calculating the planetary hours can be found in the resources section.

Herb Blends

The following are some of the more popular blessing herbs:

- Althea
- Angelica
- Basil
- Bay
- Blessed thistle

- Cornflower
- Frankincense
- Hops
- Life everlasting
- Myrrh
- Passion flower
- Rosemary
- Sacred bark
- Sandalwood
- Sweet grass
- Yerba santa

Some of these plants originate in North America, while others immigrated here recently or long ago. They are among some of the most well-known blessing herbs.

For me, herb blends are the starting point for whatever formula I am creating (assuming I am crafting a new formula as opposed to working with a traditional one passed down to me). Herbs find their way into bottles of conjure oil and are used to dress candles, added to baths, and ground for use in incense and powders. I first determine which herbs will best add their strength and special abilities to the condition I seek to achieve, drawing on my experience to determine if they are suitable for my formula. Often it is later that I will decide on other characteristics, such as scent and labeling (though the opposite has been true on occasion).

Your starting point for a formula is an individual process, assuming you wish to go that route at all. The tradition of crafting your own formulas is as equally rich as the history behind manufactured products, and neither is necessarily the weaker option, assuming you know enough to craft your own and also which merchants are reputable. If you are blending for yourself, then a good herb blend should be one of the first things considered; after all, this blend will find its way into a variety of products that may be ingested or applied to the skin, inhaled, or loosed into the environment. Consider how viable your herb blend will be given all the variables. Is it toxic? Can it be ground into powder easily? How flammable is it? Does it have a neutral scent? I prefer blends with no more than five ingredients, which I can buy in bulk and mix in a single act of labor.

....

BLESSING HERB BLEND

Use equal parts of the following herbs:

- *Hyssop:* Mentioned in the Bible, hyssop is an herb for purification and is believed to be the stalk used to raise a wine-soaked sponge to Jesus's lips during his crucifixion. It is part of this recipe because a good blessing begins with the removal of negativity. Cleansing, such as we will examine in chapter 5, is usually undertaken before a blessing, though not always. Should you see a car broken down on the side of the highway, you ought not wait until you have gone home and spiritually cleansed yourself before sending a blessing to the stalled inhabitants of that car.

- *Passion Flower:* Elements of the crucifixion are also seen in the complex structure of the passion flower, with its triple stamen (symbolic of the three nails), its five anthers (the five wounds), and its tendrils (the flagellum), to name a few of its attributes that correspond to Christian symbolism.

- *Rosemary:* This herb is protective. In this instance, it protects the blessings you are being given, providing peace of mind.

- *Cornflower:* Cornflowers are calming, enacting blessings by deflecting turmoil.

- *Angelica Root:* The lore associated with angelica root tells of the Archangel Raphael blessing humanity by teaching us about its medicinal benefits.

When devising herb blends, my advice is to create one that can also serve as a tea, which the previous recipe does. Keep in mind that an herb chosen for its metaphysical properties may not be the most flavorful. The most important thing to consider with tea is toxicity. There are many otherwise benign herbs that may adversely affect people with decreased kidney function or those who are pregnant or breastfeeding, or that may simply cause allergic reactions in certain individuals. Many herbs, especially those commonly used in Conjure for the purpose of spiritual cleansing, derived their associative mystical purpose from their medicinal use as a purgative or diuretic, so be sure to do your research for any herbs you intend to ingest. As for our Blessing herb blend, though not strong in flavor, it makes for a stimulating tea. Consumed in moderate doses, the ingredients in our Blessing tea should be suitable for most.

Herb blends can be used in a variety of ways outside the teacup. Here are some ways that you might use the aforementioned herb blend to draw blessings to you:

- Place in a bowl as potpourri, and allow its blessings to fill your home or office.
- Scatter some along the walkway leading to your front door so that visitors may be blessed.
- Place some beneath your bed or pillow to bless your sleep and dreams.
- Add some to a bath, to apply magical conditions to the body.

Many other uses for herb blends exist, such as adding herbs to mojo bags, oil blends, lanterns, and more, which we will explore in subsequent chapters.

Incense

The use of incense is a worldwide phenomenon most often associated with religious ceremony and intoxication. One theory holds that incense most often develops from plants that have psychoactive qualities. Myrrh and copal negro are of the same genus, and both contain opioids. From the Bible we see that the Israelites burned myrrh, often mixed with frankincense, which has no intoxicants but mixes well with myrrh, so as to dilute the anesthetizing effect; otherwise folks would simply fall asleep rather than have a stimulating spiritual experience. Copal negro was used by the Mayans as an offering; they did not use white copal (aka copal oro), which is more popular today and is not psychoactive. As-pand is popular in the Middle East, especially among Muslims, although it is not part of their religious tradition but a practice inherited from

Zoroastrianism. It can be somewhat hard to find in the United States and sometimes goes by the name Syrian rue (although it is not related to rue). Aspand is used for cleansing and is psychoactive; its smoke contains MAO inhibitors, which reduce stress. It is often used following funerary rites. White sage, used by Native Americans, contains thujones, which actually increase anxiety in people, and perhaps even more so in the spirits its smoke is said to cleanse a space of.

Various other popular incenses include dragon's blood, pine, gum arabic (acacia resin), white sandalwood (red sandalwood is its more environmentally stable substitute), camphor, palo santo wood, and others.

The use of incense in Conjure and its history varies according to region and religion. Its use was common in the Catholic areas around Louisiana, but less so in more Protestant areas. Protestants largely rebuked ceremony, and therefore incense largely went unused by them until the 1920s when A. A. Vantine & Company in New York began promoting its use in a secular context, to rid the home of unwanted cigarette smoke or to create a relaxing environment. The casual use of incense made it a perfect cover for magical acts meant to seduce or otherwise control those around you. The advantage of smoke is that one can see it rising heavenward, and therefore words are spoken into it so that wishes and prayers rise to higher realms.

If you wish to grind resins for incense, it is best to use a brass mortar and pestle. Otherwise the gooey resin will stick to the sides of mortars made of wood, ceramic, or marble, making cleanup rough and sometimes impossible.

....

TEMPLE INCENSE

- 1 part cedarwood
- ½ part cinnamon
- 1 part copal
- 1 part dragon's blood
- 1 part frankincense
- ½ part galangal
- 1 part gum arabic

- 1 part myrrh resin
- ½ part orris root

Making incense is an art, and should you get into it in a big way, there are amazing results that can be had by letting your ingredients soak in wine and oils. I do this in a crockpot, set low, sometimes over a period of several days. Diced dried fruits and berries, honey, essential oils, and other items may be added for scent, texture, or magical power. When the liquid has evaporated to the point that the mixture is thick and resinous, it can be worked into pieces small enough to set on a charcoal burner.

Smoke Blessings

The act of smoking someone, or something, involves using smoke from certain burning herbs or incense (or other burning items such as cigars or prayer papers) to cleanse away negative conditions or to apply positive ones. Herbs are placed in a fireproof container, such as an abalone shell, or a censer if you're fancy. To keep your herbs lit, you may need a charcoal, and perhaps a bed of sand to set it on, depending on your container. The charcoal keeps the herbs burning steadily. Additionally, resins may be added with the herbs or used alone.

If you are smoking yourself or another as a form of cleansing, then you begin above the head and move downward. When using smoke to bestow a blessing, you start at the feet and move upward. When working on a client, I prefer to have them stand with hands outstretched, myself moving around them, front to back. This work can also be done while a person is seated.

Here are some recipes for incense that may be used to apply blessings to someone in the form of smoke. All items should be ground into gravel or powder and are meant to be burned on a charcoal.

WARM BLUSH BLESSING INCENSE

This smoke will put some color in your cheeks. It evokes the feeling that is gained after a satisfying physical activity, be it the end of a morning jog or a kiss on the back of the neck.

- 2 parts myrrh
- 1 part rose hips
- 2 parts sassafras root

HOME BLESSING INCENSE

- 2 parts dragon's blood
- 1 part juniper berries
- 2 parts orange peel

PEACE INCENSE

- ½ part allspice
- 1 part benzoin
- 1 part frankincense
- 1 part jasmine flowers
- 2 parts spikenard

Blessings come when we align our actions with the natural movements of the universe. It is these actions that allow us to enter into a dialogue with both the natural world and its Creator, in order for their blessings to be received in our lives.

III
The Keys to Curios:
Unlocking Good Luck

WOULD YOUR TEAM HAVE won had you not worn their jersey, or rubbed Van Van oil on your rabbit's foot, or shouted "Go team!" a total of nine times? Who can say? But it might be best not to give up those practices, lest their failure be on you.

The definition of luck varies among cultures and may possess a variety of subtle meanings within a given culture. Luck is often seen as a force that stacks the odds for or against us. Even those lacking a strong belief in luck are often reluctant to do things that are considered unlucky, such as walk beneath a ladder, open an umbrella in the house, or clink a toast without making eye contact. From glitzy casinos to basement role-playing campaigns, we throw the dice with the wish that they will roll favorably, and in that brief moment as they tumble we hope that luck is on our side.

Belief in luck is an often criticized aspect of folk magic, decried by rationalist philosophers and psychologists alike for being a form of *magical thinking*. For those who view faith and thought as factors in directing our physical lives, magical thinking sounds like something to strive for, though in academic language the term is a negative one, irrationality being its connotation. Belief in luck is often considered to be a *post hoc ergo propter hoc* logical fallacy. For example, someone who believes that their winning the lottery was related to having found a penny and placing it in their left shoe is said to be exhibiting the false belief that the object and their action had a supernatural influence on their win. Although luck's domain is ruled by superstition and synchronicity, not science, studies have indicated that those who consider themselves lucky tend to actually be luckier, implying that the charm in your pocket does have a tangible effect on your life. On the mundane level, those expecting to find opportunities are more likely to look for and find them. Believers in luck are often more relaxed, and consequently suffer less from stress-related setbacks in physical and mental health. A placebo, a self-fulfilling prophecy, a prosperous delusion—those things are thought by some to explain the luck others attribute to their rabbit's foot. For those of us called to Conjure, however, our experiences run much deeper, so that we receive all the aforementioned benefits of our belief along with a relationship with our materials, tradition, and community.

Luck can be indistinct or intense. Sometimes simply getting home with minimal traffic makes for a lucky day. Other times our luck is even more evident, such as when we are winning at the tables. Communities with a strong concept of luck tend to encourage gambling, seeing it not as a moral vice or failure to conceptualize statistics but rather as a means to engage with luck—that mystical force that lands the ball on red or glares back at us from a pair of snake-eyed dice.

Luck is seen as an indicator that we are on the right path. When we are unlucky, we question what we might be doing wrong and become introspective about our shortcomings. While losing the lottery does not indicate that we are living our life wrong, those moments of loss are useful for forming strategies for how to improve ourselves. We all want to feel that we are winning at life, and sometimes those moments arise from a winning hand of cards.

Formulas for Good Luck

General Luck

Various products for achieving luck include Good Luck, Lucky 13, and Lucky Mojo. These may be utilized for a sort of generalized luck, such as the ability to easily locate a parking space or get a seat at a fancy restaurant. Or they may be mixed with other formulas, such as with Love Draw, in order to make one lucky in love. Of course, gambling luck is a concern they may be used for, or you may wish to use a more on point gambling formula like the following one.

Fast Luck

There are varieties of this brand name, such as Green Fast Luck, Red Fast Luck, and Yellow Fast Luck. There are also Double Fast Luck and Triple Fast Luck formulas available. Products sold under the name Fast Luck have been on the market for many years, with different formulas filling their bottles. While the most popular formulas are oils, which we will work with in chapter 8, we can look at these recipes to see how we might apply our knowledge from the last chapter in order to make herb blends. The color associations likely suggest the color of the condition oil, though they also suggest differences in their scent profile.

....

GREEN FAST LUCK HERB BLEND

- Patchouli
- Vetiver
- Mint

....

RED FAST LUCK HERB BLEND

According to Zora Neale Hurston's *Mules and Men*, this recipe consists of equal parts of the following three items:

- Cinnamon sticks
- Vanilla beans
- Wintergreen

....

YELLOW FAST LUCK HERB BLEND

Another Fast Luck recipe recorded from Hurston simply contains citronella, which is more often used as a cleansing agent than for drawing luck. For my Yellow Fast Luck I prefer the following herbs:

- Dandelion flower
- Lemongrass
- Yarrow leaves

Gambling Luck

Products for gambling luck are sometimes named for the type of game being targeted for a win, such as with 3 Jacks and a King, Bingo, Lottery, Lucky Dice, Wheel of Fortune, and others. To the extent that they aid in the dreaming of numbers, previous formulas used for psychic dreaming would also belong to this category of gambling luck formulas. Other products are less specific, such as Lady Luck and Black Cat, both of which work for winning in general.

Asian Good Luck

Prior to World War I, Asian influences lent a fresh exoticism to many Conjure practices, especially in the more urban coastal cities. The Buddha, often in his jolly, potbellied aspect of Hotei, appeared on many products espousing magical mysteries from faraway Asia. Among such products we find Lucky Buddha, Japanese Lucky 7, and others that work toward luck.

Next let's spend some time highlighting certain curios that are commonly used to draw luck.

Lucky Curios

The word *curio*, as it is used in occult circles, is the umbrella term for various types of mystically empowered objects. The word curio itself can be used without a magical connotation to apply to any object that is valued for its uniqueness, inspiring *curio*sity concerning its story. Spiritual merchants relied on this double meaning to evade anti-fraud laws, notably by adding the line *sold as curio* beneath otherwise high-flown descriptions of the magical uses of their products. As early as 1911, laws created allegedly to protect the public from false claims were used against the sellers of spiritual goods. Such laws were fueled by prejudice against the occult, and more so against merchants and clientele whose cultural and religious beliefs were held in contempt. Merchants were often portrayed as rip-off artists, despite the fact that many of them were philanthropists in their communities. The clientele for Conjure products, consisting mostly of African-Americans and Southerners, suffered from the misplaced advocacy of those who considered them to be superstitious fools in need of protection. That this clientele tended also to be of a lesser economic status meant that the manner in which they spent what little money they had was scrutinized by those with more, who were eager to insist that money spent on gambling charms was wasteful. As protection against allegations of fraud, all manner of materials, from lucky horseshoes to exotic fetishes, became commonly referred to as curios.

Charms are a form of curio, and commonly come to mind when thinking about luck. While the word *charm* has various definitions, what we are talking about here is symbolic imagery. Looking back at many of the graphic artists who illustrated the golden age of spiritual merchandising in the early to mid-1900s, such as Charles C. Dawson and Charles M. Quinlan, we see products and curio catalogues adorned with symbols of luck, such as four-leaf clovers, horseshoes, wishbones, and—prior to World War II—lucky swastikas. Such symbols embody power in their own right, making the advertising and packaging as lucky as the products they pitched. Ephemera can communicate much about a culture's beliefs and values regarding luck. Even images not intending to expressly convey the magical potency of a product hold a certain spell, such as cans of Underwood Deviled Ham (its logo of a lucky red devil from 1870 being the oldest trademarked image still in use in the United States at the time of this writing). Charms of this sort take the form of trinkets or illustrations. Both derive their power from, and conform to, the same magical concepts we will subsequently explore.

Similar to the doctrine of signatures discussed in chapter 2 is the concept of *sympathetic magic*, in which actions are carried out on an object in order to effect a change in another that corresponds to it. Sympathetic magic, as postulated by Sir James George Frazer in *The Golden Bough* (1890), is governed by two laws, these being the *law of similarity* and the *law of contagion*. Much of the work we will examine throughout this book will rely on a simple understanding of these laws.

The law of similarity rules through imitation. Like influences like. The image of a horseshoe, be it a similarly shaped pendant or a two-dimensional drawing, personifies the characteristic of luck, the same as an actual horseshoe is said to. We will explore this law more when we work with spells to influence others, for this concept underpins all practices of imitative magic, such as the proverbial Voodoo doll, which is made to correspond to another person and act on them in kind according to how it is handled. For now, simply understand that the symbolic expression of a horseshoe, be it an arrangement of flowers or a tattoo, bears the qualities of what it is modeled after.

The law of contagion states that, regardless of time or distance, a thing can be influenced by that which it has come in contact with. With some items this principle is obvious, as with animal curios, wherein the object contains the actual DNA of the body it came from. This concept can become more abstract in regard to such things as horseshoes or a bird's nest, as items that have been in contact with a creature continue to be linked to them through their shared history. Some people regard such a curio as containing something of its former handler's spirit, or, as it may be termed, *energy* or *life force*. When such an item is associated with a person, such as someone's comb, it is known as a *personal concern*, which we will explore more deeply and learn how to use later in chapter 7, though the principle of contagion is much the same.

With this understanding of how objects are believed to embody power based on the laws of similarity and contagion, let us take a closer look at the more common curios used in Conjure.

Botanical Curios

The plants we worked with in the previous chapter fall into the category of botanical curios. Each bit of plant matter can be defined as a curio, though smaller pieces tend to be referred to as herbs, with larger, individual items such as a root or seed pod being called a curio.

Books dedicated to the subject that provide longer lists than I can here are listed in the resources section.

Bat Nut (Devil's Pod)

This type of water caltrop is found in Eurasia and Africa. It is dark in color and double-pointed in a manner making it appear similar to a bull's head or the winged body of a bat. Chinese immigrants considered these lucky, just as the bat is lucky in China. Other folks associated the look of the nut with more sinister things such as the Devil, and utilized them in cursing rites. Much as gargoyles are used to scare away evil, bat nuts may be used as protective amulets in the home.

Buckeye Nut

Native to parts of North America, buckeye nuts are used for luck in gambling and money drawing, and are carried in men's pockets for sexual conquest, owing to their shape and size resembling a testicle. An application of oil gives them a nice shine, making it common to dress them with condition oils or with the oil that gathers on the sides of one's nose. They are also kept for health, to allegedly cure arthritis, headaches, and rheumatism.

Devil's Shoestring

This root is used for a variety of purposes, including to curse, protect, and win games of chance. It may be soaked in whiskey over a period of seven days, then carried to draw money, or the infused whiskey may be used to wash hands before playing cards or rolling dice.

High John the Conqueror Root

High John the Conqueror is an African-American legend. He was an African prince subjected to slavery in the Americas who never lost his pride or power. His powers were mystical, such as his ability to return to his continent by flight. To those suffering under slavery he was heroic, and toward slave masters he was a trickster, his stories reflected in those of Brer Rabbit. High John Root is carried for luck, alleged to aid with gambling. Its resemblance to a man's testicles supports its use in strengthening a man's sexual nature. As with its namesake, it is called upon for increased power. Much has been written about High John, such as by author Zora Neale Hurston, as well as other artists, including blues musician Willie Dixon in his song "My John the Conquer Root."

This root is not the only botanical curio that bears John's name. Others are Dixie John and Little John to Chew.

Lucky Hand Root (Salep Root)
We mentioned this orchid tuber in the previous chapter, noting how its hand-like shape is used to grab hold of good luck.

Mojo Beans (Saint Joseph Beans, African Wishing Beans)
Better known as fava beans, these are dried and placed on a table altar set out for Saint Joseph's feast day of March 19. After the service, the beans are taken to be carried in one's wallet to draw money, or placed in the pantry to ensure an abundance of food.

Nutmeg, Whole
To prepare these seeds for gambling luck, the tradition once was to drill them, fill them with mercury, and seal them with wax; however, this trick is toxic and no longer advisable. Even so, nutmeg seeds are still carried on their own for luck.

Queen Elizabeth Root (Orris Root)
This root brings good luck in affairs of love and marriage. Generally considered to be a woman's charm, it may be used to bring a man under control.

Rose of Jericho

This desert plant looks like a lifeless ball until you place it in a bowl of water, after which it quickly stretches out in all directions and takes on a green hue. There are a variety of ways, mostly regional, in which this plant is used to increase money. Most have you place coins in the plant's center. I use seven silver dimes. The water should be changed weekly, as it gets smelly and that is no good for what you are trying to accomplish. Rinsing it off is helpful too, as it limits fungal growth.

There are many more botanical curios, but let us move on to look at some of the more popular ones related to animals.

Zoological Curios

Some of these curios, such as alligator and rabbit feet, are byproducts of food production. Others are sought only by people with a mental illness and a penchant for abusing creatures smaller than themselves. While the ethics of humanely killing an animal for food or sacrifice is individual, we must agree that torturing an animal is an unjust and illegal act.

Alligator Foot and Tooth

In the northern United States, where there are no alligators, these curios are imported along with their dangerous reputation. Therefore, they are often used for vindictive spells, or for protection. However, down south, where an alligator is good eats and its hide worth a pretty penny, such curios are used to draw money or help with gambling wins. Feet with curled digits, as though grabbing for something, are most prized, as this is said to help grab the condition being sought.

Badger Tooth

A badger tooth is worn as a charm for gambling and comes to us from the Pennsylvania Dutch tradition, found in the book *Pow-Wows, or Long Lost Friend*.

Black Cat Anatomy

The infamous black cat bone was referenced in the previous chapter. Additionally, black car hair and imagery are used most often for gambling luck.

Black Dog Anatomy

Black dog hair was used for cursing in older accounts. A black dog is a familiar form for a faery to take, and is said to be the preferred pet of the Devil himself.

Black Hen Anatomy

Black hens, especially frizzled breeds, are said to be magical. From a practical standpoint, chickens in the yard will root out any tricks that have been thrown there, and thus their claws serve as protection. Their eggs are particularly powerful for cleansings, as they absorb negativity. Their feathers can be gathered and used to dust away bad energy from a person or object.

Cowrie Shell

The opening of a cowrie shell resembles a vagina and is therefore used to represent female energy. The opening allows for a tiny slip of paper with a target's name on it to be placed inside.

Crab Shell

Crab shells are used in reversing spells to send back bad energy that an enemy has thrown your way, because crabs scurry backward when fleeing.

Dirt Dauber's Nest

These wasps (also called mud daubers or mud wasps) build their nests from mud. The nests are used for a variety of spells, from cursing to fidelity. That the wasps sting certainly makes their nests appropriate for cursing work. The difficulty with which the nests are removed from the eaves of a home associates them with fidelity, keeping a partner stuck at home.

Human Finger Bone

The ability to purchase certain human remains is legal in most parts of North America, and human finger bones have a tradition of being used in mojo hands. (We will talk more about mojos in chapter 7, though now you have a hint as to why these are called *hands*.)

Porcupine Quill

These quills are used for cursing or protection. They may be used to carve names and symbols into candles for either purpose.

Rabbit Foot

For practical and spiritual reasons, humans try to utilize all parts of an animal that is being eaten, but with the rabbit there is little to be done with the feet. The gentry once fashioned rabbit feet with ornate handles and used them to powder their faces. Some believe it was this association with social power and beauty that made the humble rabbit's foot a charm for luck. For some, it is only the left hind leg of a rabbit caught in a graveyard that is lucky.

Raccoon Baculum

The raccoon is noted as having a particularly large penis bone (baculum), also known as coon bone. These are stroked with oil (such as High John the Conqueror) or with semen or vaginal juice in order to make a man sexually aroused. Work may be done with the bone to make a man impotent or to cure him of his impotence.

Snake Shed

In biblical terms the snake is often seen as the Devil, a torturer and tempter. Snake sheds are often added to cursing formulas as well as to spells that seek to tempt someone, such as with love or sex, much as the snake in the garden tempted Eve.

The word *medicine* is sometimes used to describe the spiritual power of an animal. The terms *spirit medicine* and *spirit animal* are part of the traditions of many Native Americans, and have been appropriated by non-Native traditions such as Core Shamanism, as well as certain regional lexicons. An individual's personal relationship to Snake might lead them to use a snake shed for a purpose such as road opening, symbolizing the sloughing off of old conditions and transformation, rather than what may be considered a more traditional use in cursing work. It is not one's intellectual relationship to a symbol that redefines its purpose, as may be the case in dream interpretation, although an individual relationship with the spirit of an animal or the curio representing it may yield individual results. While it is important to follow your own inspiration and wisdom, when working with tradition it is important that you yield to the wisdom of those who did this work before you. Using a shark's tooth in a love spell because you love sharks is unlikely to turn out well.

Lapidary Curios

Time now to move on to lapidary curios. We can see in King Novelty Company's *Curio Catalogue No. 45* from 1934 that tiger's eye and moonstone were being sold, along with more commonly used lodestones and pyrite. Thanks to the growing stone trade of the 1980s aimed at the then-growing market of New Age consumers, Conjure workers throughout North America gained access to a wider variety of lapidary curios. Some argue against utilizing such newer items as moldavite, aqua aura, angelite, and many of the crystals currently found in metaphysical shops, saying that their inclusion is inauthentic. Others argue that such stones would certainly have been used had they been available. What makes a practice valid, be it duplicating the ingredients and actions of an earlier time or governing modern means according to traditional precepts such as the doctrine of signatures, is one's individual call.

Like roots, stones and crystals are taken from the earth and underworld. They too have a history to tell, but a much longer and stationary one. Their consciousness is therefore much different than our own. As with herbs and animals, each stone contains its individual consciousness as well as that of its collective classification.

Citrine

Citrine is like sunlight in crystal form, a mood booster. It is a cleansing stone, which brings us to the topic of cleansing (discharging) stones. This is typically something that is done for stones purchased from metaphysical suppliers, but not for stones found in the wild. Said to absorb the energy that is around them, crystals are typically cleansed before being worked with. Stones are commonly washed in salt water (which for some stones, such as selenite, may be damaging). A practice that I do with my jewelry is to place those items in a bowl of dry rice that has a chunk of citrine in the center, and leave them there until I put them on again the next day.

Fool's Gold (Pyrite)

Pyrite's resemblance to gold cinches its use in wealth-drawing work. Small pieces can often be found in bottles of money-drawing conjure oils, or in mojo bags for the same purpose.

Lodestones (Magnetite)

Lodestones are helpful for drawing things to you, such as money. The magic of lodestones and other magnets is used to attract things to you. For example, placing a lottery ticket beneath the lodestone may help those numbers be chosen. Some workers create whole altars on which they do their lodestone work. Once a week you should take the lodestone and let it soak in a glass of whiskey for however long seems right to you. Some folks like to rub oils on their stone instead. After it is liquored up or oiled, it is fed with magnetic sand.

Lodestones constitute a distinctive type of magic that uses magnetism to draw favorable conditions, such as love, money, luck, or specific objects, including jewelry and people. Popular formulas for such drawing work, beyond the lodestone curio itself, include Lodestone, Mighty Magnet, and those named similarly.

Tiger's Eye (African Tiger's Eye)

Tiger's eye is carried for luck and to boost self-confidence.

Moonstone

This stone brings luck in money and love.

Of course, there are hundreds more varieties of stones and crystals that can be used in accordance with the doctrine of signatures, but those included here are used most frequently. Books describing the various properties of stones and crystals in more detail can be found in the resources section.

Manufactured Curios

Just as people who lived near woods or fields made a connection with the materials around them, so too did folks in industrialized locations. Every object, whether natural or humanmade, holds individual memories. Natural curios have experienced a life flowering beneath the sun or scuffling through the mud of the bayou, and often have more verve than manufactured curios. Same as it takes hardship to truly play the blues, it is the chipped guitar pick, not the unblemished one, that often has more to strum about.

Let us begin by harkening back to what we learned about animal curios, the essential concept being that part of an animal, such as its bones or feet, possesses something of that animal's skills and attributes. The concept that an animal's spirit continues to reside in its bones is simple to imagine. But what of the shoe worn by a horse, or the bell of a cow, or the hook that caught a catfish? These items, according to the law of contagion, possess qualities of the creature they came in contact with. Thus a dog's collar contains something of the spirit of the dog who wore it, and—assuming the individual dog that wore it was not ill-tempered—could have magical applications for matters such as loyalty, fidelity, and protection. Does your man act like a dog by rutting with every female in the parish? If so, then you could write his name on that collar and chain it to the porch to keep him home where he belongs, and douse it with your urine should you sense him thinking about some other tail. When it comes to using a curio that is associated with a living creature, it works best to use one that has actually been applied to its purpose. In other words, the horseshoe that has been worn by a mare or stallion possesses different qualities than one that comes straight from the blacksmith's anvil. Here is a list of some of the more common manufactured curios used in American folk magic.

Evil Eye Beads

These traditionally blue beads have a white center bearing a dot of black, resembling a blue eye. This is a Mediterranean tradition that fits well with Conjure due to shared perspectives on using the color blue to ward off spirits, such as Southern traditions of painting doors or the underside of one's porch a shade called *haint* blue.

Hamsas

Hamsas serve as protective amulets. They are made of varying materials in the abstract shape of a hand, decorated according to the artist's whim, often with an eye in the center or lettering in Arabic or Hebrew. Like the mezuzah, which protects doorways, this is one of many Jewish influences.

Horseshoe

This is most commonly used for luck, although protection is also ascribed to it. Debate over how a horseshoe ought to be hung—often above or beside a door—varies among cultures. Some conceptualize it as a vessel, like the Irish and English people who say it must be hung to capture luck as a bowl would collect rain, while others say its luck must be allowed to pour from its arms.

Keys

Keys are used for spells such as road opening and for learning secret things. The Master Key is a powerful symbol, found on candles and other paraphernalia. Skeleton keys, for their ability to open many doors, are often preferred.

Milagros

These are small figures that range from paired couples to singular body parts, and are used devotionally on altars or added to candles, mojo hands, etc. This is a custom prevalent in Mexican, Portuguese, and Spanish folk practices that has migrated to North America.

Mirror

A whole book could be written on mirror spells. They are often used to amplify a spell, the way a mirror would be used behind a candle to increase its light, and to reflect things back, such as in a reversing spell.

Spikes and Nails

Nails constitute a family of curios sourced for different purposes based on contagion. A nail can be used to "nail things down." Therefore placing one in your wallet is said to help you keep money.

- *Horseshoe nails* may be used to secure safe travel, as may wagon wheel nails (which are much less common these days).

- *Coffin nails*, in my mind, rely on contagion, or else they are simply nails. What you get from purveyors of occult supplies are mostly rusted nails, but there is an easy trick that involves burying them in wet graveyard dirt (which we will learn how to collect in chapter 12) until they rust. This method lacks the villainy of digging up a grave and wrenching the nails from a coffin, but it works nevertheless.

- *Railroad spikes* are used to nail down a situation. A popular spell requires four spikes, one to be nailed down in each corner of a property to protect the inhabitants from eviction.

Currency

Money printed during a leap year is considered particularly powerful. Popular coins include the following:

- *Indian Head pennies*, which are used protectively, are often nailed into windowsills or thresholds.

- *Mercury dimes*, which were coined between 1916 and 1945, bear an image of Winged Liberty, whose winged cap led her to be conflated with the Roman god Mercury. The silver in these coins made them great for detecting tricks, being how sulfur—often used in cursing magic—tarnishes them.

- *Paper money* has less influence. However, folks with access to Chinese markets—often in the Western United States—utilize faux bills called *hell money*, which are used by the Chinese to give as offerings to their beloved dead. When the Chinese immigrated to the area (as many did to help build the railroads), they needed such money printed to sustain their tradition. Some joker lost to history fulfilled their request but printed the name *hell money* on the bills. These bills are used by practitioners in money spells, and on some modern-day notes the word *hell* has been replaced with *heaven*.

The list of manufactured curios goes on and on, but these are some of the more common ones. All manner of religious paraphernalia is useful, every sacred thing—from crosses, to Buddhist mala beads, to pentacles.

Psychometry

Psychometry, also known as token object reading, is useful for our approach to curios, especially manufactured ones. This is a type of psychic ability that can be acquired through practice. The supporting paradigm states that each thing possesses an energy field that stores information about its history and can be accessed through psychic interaction. Psychometry was developed in the late 1800s from the writings of Kentucky-born author Joseph Rodes Buchanan, and became common practice among the spiritual church movement, a group whose magical practices contributed much to Conjure. In the hands of Spiritualists, psychometry sometimes serves as a step toward contacting the deceased owner of an item. Animism is not the supporting theory behind psychometry, but is not repudiated. Psychometry, as I practice it, involves connecting to the soul of an object and requesting its story. I find this personal relationship to be more evocative than the notion of *reading energy*. Also, since I work with curios in a manner leading to them being called into service as charms, I find that getting to know them one spirit to another makes for a more amicable working relationship.

Depending on the nature of your curio, you may wish to use some of the same techniques used for connecting with the natural curios that we have discussed, such as bathing an item in libations. You might knock on that martini shaker three times to awaken it, and learn of all the parties you were never invited to. Or fill a thimble full of whiskey to learn all the seamstress's gossip. Or fog the hand mirror with your breath to clean its surface, and then behold the preening faces of others who have been reflected in it.

Begin exploring your item through psychometry by holding it between your palms, or place your hands over it if the item is larger. Some people feel one of their hands is more sensitive to psychic perception than the other, or use one hand for receiving psychic energy and the other for projecting it.

Those who have explored their psychic abilities will have an understanding of how they best perceive psychic information, and focus their awareness on the area of perception they excel at. If you are new to this type of work, then just sit quietly and see what comes to you. My personal strengths are in vision and conception; therefore I close my eyes and look for images to appear within, or clear my mind and wait for insight.

You can use psychometry on anything, contacting the spirit of that thing and asking to learn its memories. Some things have lived more extensive lives than others, such as an old coin, which is a great item to practice on, retracing its steps and learning its story. Another way to practice is by having friends bring you items only they know the history of, and seek confirmation of your observations.

Places of Power

Earlier we saw how certain items acquire attributes according to the law of contagion. A foot spike from a utility pole, for example, contains the energy of that pole, which by holding up service wires for power and communication can be used for aid with those concerns. Some places are considered powerful in their own right, such as sacred sites, monuments, and even properties that service basic needs such as hospitals. Substances attained from such places, such as water, soil, rocks, and so forth, are linked to their previous station and contain the qualities of that place.

Though some places are ancient, such as the Blarney Stone in Ireland, which is said to grant good luck to those who kiss it, North America has its own treasured icons. Collecting materials from such places is often discouraged, owing to desecration and a desire for repeat tourism. More often visitors are encouraged to enact a minor act of magical contagion, such as by touching or rubbing an item. The nose of Lincoln's bronze bust at his tomb in Illinois, the Winged Fingers of the Republic statues at the Hoover Dam, the nose of Rachel the bronze pig at Seattle's Pike Place Market, and the testicles of the Charging Bull of Wall Street are all said to bring good luck to those whose hands touch them.

Not all places encourage ritual. The tradition of leaving love locks has been increasingly discouraged in public venues. Love locks are padlocks that are often inscribed with the names of a couple and locked onto a bridge, and the key thrown into the water so that none can tamper with what is intended to be a long-standing installation. Various municipalities, including Atlanta, Portland, and New York, have had to remove such locks, as edifices become damaged by the weight. Baltimore, Nevada, and Ohio have created specifically designed art installations meant to encourage the practice in a better engineered manner.

The nature of a place governs the type of magic that is deployed there. When we deploy a spell, we are placing it where it might best impact, or be impacted by, its surrounding environment. In chapter 2 we saw how working in the proper direction is important. This is something we consider when deciding where to place our spells, whether we place things in the front or back, underground or in a public venue. Here are some of the better-known places to deploy your spells.

Front Yard

The front yard is where you bury items intended to draw things to you, such as money, peace, and so forth. There is a long tradition of burying items beneath the porch, although modern architecture often forbids this, especially for those living in apartments. As an alternative, items can be buried in a flowerpot beside your front door.

Back Yard

The back yard is for keeping things close. This is where you bury or otherwise hide items to benefit your personal life.

Trees

Powerful spirits in their own right, trees connect the underworld with the heavens, and can serve as a great place to dispose of items. Water (that has not been made toxic) can be thrown against the trunk. Items may be buried at a tree's base, or placed in any holes or deep crevices within the tree.

Water

Running water, such as rivers and streams, moves energy away and works for getting rid of unwanted things in your life. Large bodies of water, such as lakes, hide spells and can cause another's endeavor to sink. Oceans carry things to distant lands, such as enemies and general woes. Tidal pools and estuaries have a rising and falling effect that influences mood swings. Toilets work well for cursing spells.

Railroad Tracks

These serve to crush enemies and make them move away. When I was a kid walking home from school, there were several railroad tracks I passed, and beyond the occasional penny that my friends and I would leave to be smashed, we would sometimes find photographs taped to the tracks, often surrounded by the remnants of burned candles and dregs we knew not to touch (though on a dare touched anyway).

Places are revered for a number of reasons, each valuing a certain type of work. Liminal spaces are especially prized, places in between, or where two or more places collide, such as shorelines, entryways, or crossroads. These are fluid places. Just as dusk and dawn are powerful times to do magic, in-between places similarly inspire change.

Doing ritual and deploying spells differs greatly according to the venue. Keep in mind that in public settings the discovery of your spell is always a possibility, and thus the spell might be broken. However, public places are ideally suited for certain types of work, such as notoriety spells working to increase a person's fame, or spells to encourage gossip.

If you want to influence a particular entity—say, the bank that owns the home in which you live—then going to just any bank won't do. You should visit their company headquarters, or the branch that services your loan, or at least a branch for that bank. However, if instead of targeting a particular entity you simply want to do money-drawing work, then any bank will do. Let's go over some of the more popular places of power:

- *Banks:* Great for workings involving money
- *Bridges:* For strengthening a connection
- *Churches:* For anything requiring blessing or protection
- *Coffee Houses:* For gumption
- *Courthouses:* For justice work
- *Crossroads:* One of the more powerful places, where various spells are deployed
- *Graveyards:* For working with spirits and for cursing work
- *Highways:* For movement
- *Hospitals:* For spells involving healing
- *Universities and Libraries:* For study

In later chapters we will visit the graveyard and the crossroads, and learn of the unique types of work that can be done in those places.

Through an understanding of what powers are contained in any given curio, you can forge a relationship with that item, awakening its potential, and put it to work in order to change your luck from bad to good.

IV

The Keys to Language: Unlocking Healing

THE FOLLOWING SPOKEN CHARM, the purpose of which is to rid a person or livestock of worms, comes from John George Hohman's 1820 book *Long Lost Friend*, also known as *Pow-Wows*.

> *Mary, God's Mother, traversed the land,*
> *Holding three worms close in her hand;*
> *One was white; the other was black; the third was red.*[5]

This book on the subject of Pennsylvania Dutch *braucherei* (or *brauche*), which even the Sears, Roebuck & Company catalogue carried in the late nineteenth century, was widely distributed and influenced many practices throughout North America, finding favor among folk magicians in parts of the Ozarks and Appalachia and among Hoodooists as well. Its popularity was due to its relevance to daily life, in that it contained charms to heal both kin and cattle, to quell fires, to win at cards, and to address many other practical issues. Beyond that, its Christian emphasis and familiar concepts spoke directly to the many spiritual practitioners who adopted its magical formulas. For this chapter's emphasis on healing,

---

5. John George Hohman, *Pow-Wows, or Long Lost Friend*, 10.

we will be examining how the spoken and written word is utilized for the purpose of helping cure disease.

While it cannot be over-stressed that in the event of illness one should first consult a licensed medical professional, we can utilize magic as a complementary therapy alongside whatever treatments have been prescribed by a licensed physician. Never use magic as the sole means to address an illness. Once you have been examined and diagnosed, then you will have the information that you need to properly address the situation using magic in concert with your doctor's advice.

Ethics are always a concern with healing. I've heard it said that you must get permission from the ailing person before working on behalf of their recovery. Others take it as their duty to pray and work for the wellbeing of those around them, and see God as the ultimate judge of a patient's fate. Something to consider when doing healing magic is when to focus on recovery and when to pray for the lessening of a terminal patient's suffering. Divination helps with such a determination, along with the will of the patient, who may be praying for their suffering to end. As we will learn in this chapter, the way in which you conceptualize a spell and articulate its execution is essential for manifesting the best outcome.

Techniques for healing magic abound, as do beliefs regarding the root cause of ailments. There is an aspect of healing work that deals with the removal of spirit attachments—that is, negative entities that cause disease. The white plate method from chapter 1 is one way to diagnose such an affliction. It becomes important to know when someone is suffering from a spiritual attack and when it is simply the flu (though some believe that every ill personifies a sickening spirit). Whatever the cause of an invading spirit, a ritual of spiritual cleansing is undergone to remove it, followed by blessing and protective work.

Popular Formulas for Healing

Angelic Healer
This is my Modern Conjure blend, which summons the power of the Archangel Raphael, famed for his miraculous healing work.

Broken Heart

This helps mend what love has torn apart.

Life Everlasting

Formulas often contain the flowers of the same name. The intent with this formula is to keep you healthy and active, more so than to repair damage.

Other formulas simply go by names such as Healing and Get Well Soon.

Of course, blessings are always welcome. Therefore, some formulas that we saw in chapter 2 apply, such as the ones for comfort, peace, and relief. Additionally, you could target a disease by banishing it. We will look more at banishing work in chapter 11.

The Spoken Word

To understand the significance of the spoken word, we must again turn to the Bible, which informed these folk ways. We see in the beginning of Genesis how God created the world by speaking it into existence, saying *Let there be light*. Furthermore, Mark 16:17 expresses the power believed to be commanded in Jesus's name: *And these signs shall follow them that believe; In my name shall they cast out devils; they shall speak with new tongues*. This latter part, known as speaking in tongues, evolved from the Holiness movement in the early 1900s, and grew to influence Spiritism, Pentecostalism, and Charismatic denominations with the belief that when possessed by the Holy Spirit one could speak the language of angels and, through such divine linguistics, produce miracles such as healing. It is believed that through our own voice we are able to become agents of divine change.

The practice of spoken charms predates *Long Lost Friend*, and indeed Hohman borrowed from earlier grimoires such as *Romanus-Büchlein* and Albertus Magnus's *Egyptian Secrets*, both of which focused heavily on verbal sorcery. In addition to the words themselves, ritual actions are often included. Spoken charms are sometimes repeated, with the numbers three and nine being most common. Spells are often punctuated textually, ending in three crosses (+++), which indicates that the names Father, Son, and Holy Spirit are to be invoked, often accompanied by hand motions that draw those crosses in the air. These physical actions are passed from person to person when the charm is being taught.

There are a variety of beliefs about how such charms may be taught. Even though the stated purpose of books such as *Long Lost Friend* is to teach these charms, some believe that they must be taught from one person to another, and furthermore only when the need is present. Some agree with the belief that certain charms—also called *tricks*—may be passed only across gender, from a man to a woman or vice versa, although as North American culture becomes more reticent to acknowledge and enforce strict gender identity this practice has become less favored.

The following are examples of spoken charms.

To Safeguard Against Burns

This "Against Burns" charm is from Hohman's *Long Lost Friend*:

> *Our dear Lord Jesus Christ going on a journey, saw a firebrand burning; it was Saint Lorenzo stretched out on a roast. He rendered him assistance and consolation; he lifted his divine hand and blessed the brand; he stopped it from spreading deeper and wider. Thus may the burning be blessed in the name of God the Father, Son and Holy Ghost. Amen.*

To Take Out a Burn

This is my version:

> *Three angels came from afar.*
> *One brought fire,*
> *One brought frost,*
> *One brought faith.*
> *Out with fire and in with frost.*
> *Faith be forever with you.*

There are many variations of this charm, and I've seen changes such as the number of angels, the directions from which they come, and the emphasis on faith or the Holy Trinity. While no specific angels are named, this is an intriguing narrative. This style of spoken charm is common, though for other forms of esoteric practice, such as Neopaganism and literary witchcraft, rhyming charms are more common. Pay attention to the charms spoken in such shows as *Bewitched*, *Charmed*, and so forth, and you will find that they almost always rhyme, a practice found in European literature, such as in this charm from Shakespeare's *Macbeth*:

> *Fillet of a fenny snake,*
> *In the cauldron boil and bake;*
> *Eye of newt and toe of frog,*
> *Wool of bat and tongue of dog,*
> *Adder's fork and blind-worm's sting,*
> *Lizard's leg and owlet's wing,*
> *For a charm of powerful trouble,*
> *Like a hell-broth boil and bubble.*

Rhyme embellishes language, giving it an uncanny quality more appropriate for acts of magic. There is likewise a tradition of utilizing words from dead or antiquated languages. Often the go-to language for this is Latin, largely because this was once the language of Catholic Mass.

Prayer and Petition Papers

In the tradition of Pow-Wow, the Bible itself is recognized as being a talisman in and of itself, its presence able to stave off a variety of threats. In addition to this belief, magical power may also be contained in a written spell called a *Himmelsbrief*, meaning "heaven's letter." A variety of these exist, purporting a variety of divine authors and alleged to have originally fallen from heaven. Copies of these letters are often placed in the home to prevent such catastrophes as fire, illness, and hunger. Less formal examples concerning the mystical power of scriptural documents are found in prayer papers and petition papers. There is little difference between these two types of papers, though in a strict sense a prayer paper constitutes a request, whereas a petition paper may be a command. Both address a higher power. The prayer paper is written in the form of a prayer and may contain biblical text, such as lines from a psalm.

Various types of paper can be used, though many prefer torn edges to machine-cut ones. Parchment paper is common, as are brown paper grocery bags. The size of the paper depends on the type of work being done. You would not want to use the entire back of a grocery bag for something you planned to fold and carry in your pocket. Small squares about three inches on each side seem to be a fairly common size.

Writing utensils also vary. Some workers have dedicated quills, whereas others use whatever is at hand. I have heard it said that the pen or pencil must be new. Pew pencils—the short kind without erasers often found in church pews for use in writing on tithing envelopes—are favored by some, the lack of an eraser being important in implying that the work is not temporary or open to change. One of these pencils "borrowed" from the church would thereby be imbued with sacredness and work particularly well.

Papers have a variety of uses that we will explore as the book progresses, and can simply be carried on one's person, in a wallet or shoe. For this purpose they are often folded, and this is where directionality plays a part. If a request is intended to bring something to you—say, blessings, money, love, or the like—then it is folded toward you. If the request involves sending something away, perhaps disease, a curse, or an abusive relationship, then it is folded away from you. Papers are also placed beneath certain types of items, such as lodestones and railroad spikes, to draw things to you or nail them down. For secretive work, papers face downward, as if you were lighting a candle to break two people up. (More on candle work in chapter 10.) When placing a paper in your shoe, which is done for such things as gambling luck, notoriety, and to attract a lover, it faces upward.

These papers can be deployed in a variety of ways. For healing, having a relationship with certain trees can be helpful, especially those that are old and in good health, such as a sturdy white oak, which serves as a place for healing prayer papers to be deployed. Some trees are known for their defensive qualities, such as walnut trees, and are most often used for protection, separation, and cursing, owing to the fact that such trees spread a toxin in the soil around them that discourages other plants from sapping their resources. The following charm is one that may be placed at a tree, buried at the roots, or tucked into a fissure.

....

To Stop Bleeding

On a piece of paper write this verse from Ezekiel 16:6:

> And when I passed by thee, and saw thee polluted in thine own blood, I said unto thee when thou wast in thy blood, Live; yea, I said unto thee when thou wast in thy blood, Live.

Beneath that verse, write the name of the person it is meant to heal, and place the paper in the tree.

To stop blood from flowing, you may wish for a more immediate option than using a petition paper, and so the same verse serves also as a spoken charm.

A tradition derived from Spiritualists is to write prayers or sacred symbols on a white plate, then ritually wash it, thereby transmitting the blessing to the water. This water can then be used as a spiritual cleansing agent for people or objects. (More about spiritual cleansing and waters in chapter 5.)

When writing your own petition, as opposed to using a verse, you may wish to keep in mind the axiom *words have weight*. This concept is especially relevant to workers who have adopted elements of New Thought into their practice. New Thought evolved from Theosophic ideas, and informed such religious sects as Spiritualism, Christian Science, and the New Age. This belief stresses that our thoughts shape our reality. Words being an expression of our thoughts, they have weight in the sense of creating tangible effects in our lives. Those who follow this belief choose their words carefully. Take, for instance, a petition paper. What is written on such papers often takes the form of an affirmation, such as *I want a job*. Although a job is the goal, desire is actually expressed by the word *want*.

A petition written in such words, one might argue, is more likely to manifest more want, rather than the job that was hoped for. It might be better written as *The job is mine.* Words direct the flow of your will through their precision.

Noting that prayers, often psalms, are used on prayer papers, we should explore the reasons why. What made this tradition of using psalms so prevalent was a book by Godfrey Selig titled *Secrets of the Psalms: A Fragment of the Practical Kabala, with Extracts from Other Kabalistic Writings.* This book, originally written in the 1700s, was edited and republished in the 1930s and distributed by Clover Horn and King Novelty, who sold various occult supplies through mail order. This edit of Selig's book included terminology specific to the contemporary nomenclature of Hoodoo, which made it right at home on the shelves of spiritual candle shops. The theme of the book, that there is power in words, remains unchanged. Selig's inspiration, the mystical Jewish practice of Kabala as expressed in earlier works such as the medieval *Shimmush Tehillim,* expresses the belief that psalms, especially those said to have been penned by King David, contain divine power that is released when they are read aloud, or in some cases written down, as with a prayer paper. This admixture of Jewish mysticism into Conjure came also from grimoires such as *The Black Pullet, The Sixth and Seventh Books of Moses,* and *The Eighth, Ninth, and Tenth Books of Moses,* which, like Selig's psalm book, were widely available through mail order and at candle shops.

This use of psalms is a well-established aspect of Conjure. I have been asked repeatedly, often by those whose religious persuasion or background makes the use of biblical text problematic for them, if other forms of writing could be used instead, such as verse from Shakespeare or *Aradia, or the Gospel of the Witches.* Although the poetry and prose of those works contain their own power, it is important to respect the distinct tradition of psalm use in Conjure.

Name Papers

Having seen that prayers, petitions, and psalms may all be written on papers and used in spell work, let's move on to the distinct category of name papers. A name paper, simply put, is a piece of paper on which is written the name of a person being targeted for a spell. It may contain a single name or more than one. My preference is to write out an individual paper for each person.

In her book *Paper in My Shoe*, catherine yronwode offers a variety of examples of how to create name papers. In magic, there is a tendency to favor actions that are hard-won. Because of this, some folks have created rules and difficult tasks to add to the value of their name papers. The example featured on the cover of yronwode's book is such an example, as it surrounds rows of names with an unbroken circle of text. This circle, which is written without lifting the pen, was popularized through her writing and is something I find value in, as it forces me to focus my attention while I struggle to connect letters in cursive. Yet as yronwode herself points out in her book, this manner of scripting a name paper is not the only way. At its core, a name paper simply contains a name, and any embellishment of it is a matter of what works best for you.

There is debate regarding the name itself. Does one use the person's legal given name, or the name by which they are commonly known? Again, the answer varies among workers. Those trained in numerology, a discipline that suggests that each letter has a number value that dictates a person's character and destiny, may prefer using a person's birth name. Others argue that it is the individual's common name that influences them the most. For my money, I try to do both. Perhaps Jane Doe married to become Jane Smith and prefers to be called Janey. I would write *Jane "Janey" Doe Smith*, thus covering all the bases. Other information can be included as well, such as the person's birth date. Also, if they have a strong preference for a prefix, such as *Ms.* rather than *Mrs.*, that too can be included, along with any honorific, such as *Dr.* or *Rev.*, or a suffix, such as *Jr.* or *the III*.

The question often arises of what to do should you not know the name of your subject. It may be the case that you do not know the name of those nasty neighbors or the drug dealer menacing your street corner. In such instances you would simply write *those nasty neighbors*, or *that drug dealer*. Whenever possible, add what little information you may have, such as *that drug dealer with the long blond hair*. Work with what you've got.

As with petition and prayer papers, you have choices regarding what the name is written upon, a neatly torn square from a brown paper shopping bag being my preference. Again, the size of the paper is determined by what you are using it for. Something to fit in your shoe will need to be of a small size, whereas a larger square will still fit nicely beneath a vigil candle. Some workers prefer using special ink, such as dove's blood ink or bat's blood ink—neither of which is derived from the blood of the creature bearing their name but whose names may be a source of inspiration when engaging in certain types of work, such as for blessing or cursing. I find that the following recipe for dragon's blood ink is suitable for all my tasks.

Dragon's Blood Ink

- 1 part dragon's blood resin
- 1 part gum arabic (acacia powder)
- 12 parts alcohol

I recommend starting with powered versions of your dragon's blood and gum arabic, as they will dissolve in the alcohol much more easily that way. Simply stir them into the alcohol. This could be simple rubbing alcohol, vodka, or even gin, so long as it has a high alcohol content. The dragon's blood and gum arabic being aromatic, they help take away the stringent smell of rubbing alcohol fairly well. I actually prefer to use gin, as it allows me to work with those herbal allies that went into making it.

You may wish to add some essential oils for scent or to resonate with your goal, such as clove, sandalwood, and frankincense. Dragon's blood is red, so spicy scents work better than those that bring to mind pastels, such as lavender. Because oil will not blend with your liquid ink, it is best to add it first to the alcohol, then add your powdered ingredients. Let this all steep for at least an hour, though I prefer a period of three nights. If you are unhappy with the color, you may add some powdered alkanet to deepen it. This formula should yield a useful ink that coats a pen nib well.

The Influence of Numbers

When creating a name paper, workers will often write a name more than once on a slip of paper. Not everyone finds this to be necessary; however, certain numbers are given added value. There are many spells that require actions to be taken a specific number of times. This repetition may also be applied to how many times a name is written on a name paper.

Some numbers are used more commonly on name papers than others, the numbers three, four, five, seven, nine, and thirteen being the most favored. The mystical meaning of numbers, as they are typically defined in Conjure, are largely based on esoteric biblical traditions, including the Jewish practice of Gematria and the Kabala, as well as by certain Native American influences. A worker from a cultural background such as Chinese, in which the word for the number four is nearly homophonous to their word for death, may avoid such a number in their work.

You have some flexibility when it comes to working with numbers. While some workings that have been passed down will clearly state how many times a certain action must be taken, there is no absolute rule regarding the meaning of a number. Even so, here are some meanings that are influential.

One

The number one represents the individual, and God, and it sometimes represents the individual's relationship to God, in that for some it is faith that is the primary influence in magic, and therefore there is no need for repeated actions. Indeed, repeated prayers and rituals represent a lack of faith to some, for if you have faith that your prayer will be answered then repeated requests only emphasize doubt.

Of course, others point to the Bible, and note that on several occasions persons are directed by divine authority to perform tasks in a certain number; so to them, faith is had in the completion of numbered tasks.

Two

The number two is often used to represent two individuals, such as lovers.

....

TO JOIN TWO LOVERS

Cut the shape of a heart from paper, and write the name of one lover on one side and the other lover's name on the other side. Fold the paper heart in the center so that the two names meet.

Find an appropriate tree, such as one in which lovers might carve their initials. Consider how the folded shape of this heart resembles a seed, and plant it at the tree's base.

Three

This is the number of the Holy Trinity. There is a tradition of knocking three times to complete a working to bless it in the name of the Father, Son, and Holy Spirit. Items may be placed in the center of three triangulated objects, such as candles, as a means of empowering them. For instance, an arm-shaped milagro meant to aid in the healing of an injured arm may be placed in the center of three candles lit for the purpose of healing as a means of strengthening its purpose.

Four

The number four protects, contains, and holds things steadfast. Conjure is influenced by the Native American relationship to the number four, which is powerful at keeping spirits of the dead at bay. Because rooms tend to be square, charms placed in each of the four corners affect the whole area.

Five

The number five is often represented by a quincunx, which is the pattern seen on the five side of dice, featuring a dot in each corner and one in the middle. This represents the crossroads, a liminal space where powerful magic is made. Four items plus one in the center create a symbolic crossroads that can be used for magic. Many petition papers are decorated in each corner with a symbol aligned with their purpose, such as dollar signs for money drawing, in which case the petition in the center becomes the work performed at the center of the crossroads. (In our final chapter we will visit the crossroads in earnest, and see what magic awaits us there within the quincunx.)

Six

The number six is seldom used in Conjure work, but it can represent sin, or the Devil seen in the number 666. Six is the number of days one has to sin before finding forgiveness at next Sunday's church service.

Seven

Seven is a lucky number and the number of completion, as it is said that God created the heavens and the earth in seven days. Spells are often done in runs of seven, once each day, covering the entire week.

In 2 Kings 5:10–11, the character Naaman, suffering from the onset of leprosy, goes to see Elisha, a prophet renowned for healing miracles. Elisha tells Naaman that to be healed, Naaman must bathe in the Jordan River seven times. This advice upsets Naaman, who speaks of his expectation that Elisha would simply heal him with a touch. A perspective on this scripture from certain spiritual Conjure workers is that certain actions are required to attain benefits. Much like Naaman, some folks expect that miracles will just be handed to them, without them having to take the required actions. Some believe that such tasks serve to test us, while others believe God has already provided aid by designing the world to respond to specific actions and words.

Eight

The number eight is not of particular importance in Conjure. Unless you are consulting a Magic 8-Ball or working a spell to win at pool, eight is not highly valued.

Nine

The number nine is significant for being the sum of three times three, so it triples the strength of something already triple-strengthened. For name papers, writing a name nine times in a row is common.

Ten

The number of digits on both hands, ten is used less often in folk magic. Ten can be used to grab on to things with all our might.

Eleven

Eleven is a lucky number, a winning number.

Twelve

Twelve is the number of months and disciples. It is used to represent the year in full.

Thirteen

Thirteen is often considered an unlucky number in North American culture, but Conjure flips the script, calling it *lucky thirteen*. Given there are thirteen moon cycles in a year, this number, like the moon itself, is associated with witchcraft.

Generally, I have seen odd numbers preferred in Conjure work. This may simply be because the numbers with the most popular meanings ascribed to them, such as the number seven, happen to be odd. The word *odd* itself connotes strangeness, which resonates with the often weird and transgressive nature of magic. Some workers are very particular about how many times a name should be written, whereas others are not.

Magical Seals

The term *seals* refers to various symbols regarded as possessing magical power. These come from European grimoires, which claim their spiritual authority through authorship by various alleged persons of magical renown, such as Moses and King Solomon. Though their influence was less pervasive than *Long Lost Friend*, many grimoires were available and had a notable influence on folk magic. Hoodoo, in its more urban setting following the Great Migration, became less dependent on earlier agricultural materials such as roots and bones, and adopted the more readily available seals published in grimoires. This admixture of ceremonial magic into Conjure was approached differently than the grimoires themselves often advised, as these seals were not engraved upon precious metals through arduous rites, but rather were printed on parchment paper and were available from the same vendors, such as *Standard O and B*, that promoted the sale of books from which they were copied.

These seals, which often featured sacred geometric symbols and Hebrew letters, were recognized as having power in their own right, independent of the complex ceremonies their initial authors intended. Through this innovative practice the seals were liberated from their haughty tomes and put to work for everyday needs. Today's workers may simply carry such a seal on their person, in their shoe or wallet, to draw positive conditions or repel negative ones. Additional script may be added to the back of such papers to direct the influence of the seal toward a specific target. Though some might consider the manner in which seals are used in folk magic to be a corruption or lower form of magic, compared to the haughty ceremonial shtick of their origins, these more modern methods have enhanced and expanded the tradition of working with seals in a way that keeps them relevant.

The most popular resources for seals among today's workers include the following:

- *The Black Pullet* by an anonymous author
- *The Book of Magical Talismans* by Elbee Wright
- *The Grimoire of Saint Cyprian* (*Clavis Inferni, Book of Saint Cyprian*) by an unknown author, attributed to Saint Cyprian of Antioch
- *The Key of Solomon the King* (*Clavicula Salomonis, The Greater Key Of Solomon*) by an unknown author, attributed to King Solomon
- *The Lesser Key of Solomon* (*Clavicula Salomonis Regis, Lemegeton;* includes the five books *Ars Goetia, Ars Theurgia-Goetia, Ars Paulina,*

Ars Almadel, and *Ars Notoria*) by an unknown author, attributed to
King Solomon

- *The Sixth and Seventh Books of Moses* by an unknown author, attributed to Moses
- *The Eighth, Ninth, and Tenth Books of Moses* by an unknown author, attributed to Moses and popularized by Henri Gamache

Several of these grimoires are centuries old. They have shifted in popularity throughout the years and will no doubt continue to do so as new translations venture into the market. Their presence and value in folk magic stresses the extent to which education on magical methods is sought and incorporated, debunking a prejudice against folk magic that relates its practice to a lack of literacy. Unscholarliness is praised by some as a virtue, the pages in a book seen as less valuable than the forest from which its pages were reaped. Book learning is looked down upon by some who would prefer to champion the intimate training that occurs between the elderly and their apprentice, or between a river and those who have come to fish it. On the flip side are those who emphasize too greatly their collection of rare occult books, disrespecting the simple wisdom of those whose tricks they seek to learn. The best education is a well-rounded one. It requires that you read as much as you can about a subject, learn from those who practice it, and practice it yourself in earnest.

In addition to utilizing commercially available seals, you are free to write them out yourself. This is usually done with a distinctive ink, such as those discussed previously in this chapter. Some instructions say to write these seals on parchment, although, as with name and petition papers, many simply use a paper bag. If you want real parchment you must recognize the difference between it and parchment paper. True parchment is made from animal skin, with the most prized being vellum made from calfskin. Keep in mind that many of the seals you will see have been copied badly over the years, sometimes being indecipherable to the eye. Add to that the number of Hebrew letters you will need to be familiar with and the task can be daunting. However it is meant to be challenging. As stated earlier, hard-won results are traditional in many areas of occult work, hence the often difficult instructions given in the grimoires.

Seals may be drawn on the ground or otherwise utilized to mark a space. Many feature geometric designs due to the belief that certain shapes generate power. Earlier we saw how the number three is used to represent a space and focus energy in its center, and this can be done with seals. Keeping with our theme of healing, you might choose to use the Second Pentacle of Mars, whose description in *The Key of Solomon the King* tells us it *serves with great success against all kinds of diseases when it is applied to afflicted parts*. Three of these seals placed in a triangle, with a photograph of the afflicted in the center, may be helpful in healing the person at a distance, if you are unable to place the seal on their body as instructed.

As jewelry, as tattoos, as decals you can peel and stick to the windshield of your car—all are methods I have seen employed for the use of seals.

Word Squares

Another magical symbol is found in the form of magic word squares. The most popular of these, which dates as far back as 79 CE in Pompeii, is the Sator Square (Rotas Square):

```
S   A   T   O   R
A   R   E   P   O
T   E   N   E   T
O   P   E   R   A
R   O   T   A   S
```

This magic square is displayed within the home and elsewhere for protection. Evil witches and devils are said to be confused by the repetition of letters. Many supernatural beings are said to suffer from a condition called *arithmomania*, which compels them to count the objects around them. Thus, a means of protecting yourself while you sleep involves throwing salt in front of your bed, or placing a colander above your headboard, as such beings will become distracted by having to count each grain of salt or hole in the colander, which might buy you some time. Similarly afflicted by palindromes, devils get lost and confused by the bouncing letters. The Sator Square is referenced in *Long Lost Friend* for such purposes as to be given to cattle to protect against witchcraft and to extinguish fire without water.

Word squares further influenced North American folk magic through a grimoire we have yet to discuss, that being *The Book of the Sacred Magic of Abramelin the Mage*. The author presented magical talismans, allegedly given to him by God and Abraham, in the form of word squares. True word squares require the use of actual words, and those of Abramelin are not strict in this sense, although words are contained among the many lettered squares.

In addition to word squares, magic squares (lines of numbers that add up to the same sum in each direction) yield a popular form of sigil design. Heinrich Cornelius Agrippa's 1510 treatise *De Occulta Philosophia* presented magic squares (*kameas*), one for each of the seven classical planets. For the purpose of commanding spirits (including angels and demons), the letters of the entity's name is converted into numbers, then those numbers are connected one to another across a kamea square to produce a relationship of lines to serve as a sigil for that being. From the Latin *sigillum*, meaning "sign" or "signature," a sigil stylistically represents a name or magical goal. Sigils may be penned on paper, carved on candles, drawn in the air with one's finger or a ritual tool, or simply visualized internally. The means by which a sigil is created are numerous.

Here is a chart showing how the letters of the English alphabet may be associated with a number:

1	2	3	4	5	6	7	8	9
A	B	C	D	E	F	G	H	I
J	K	L	M	N	O	P	Q	R
S	T	U	V	W	X	Y	Z	

To discover your personal sigil, write out your name and list the number beneath each letter. One example might look like this:

J	O	E	S	M	I	T	H
1	6	5	1	4	9	2	8

Now, based on the type of work I am doing, I will choose one of seven kameas to chart Joe's sigil on. As we learned in chapter 2, each planet rules a different part of the body. Let's say that Joe Smith has a bladder infection; we would want to work with Mars and its kamea.

I begin by drawing a circle in the square housing the number 1, which represents the letter *J* in Joe's name. Next, I connect a line down and to the left where the number 6 represents the letter *O* in Joe's name. Because the following two numbers are both 1, I have the choice of ignoring the duplicated number or marking the instance, such as with a triangle. On I go until I get the following:

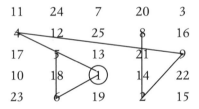

All of these are added up to find the quintessential number for Joe Smith's name:

$$1 + 6 + 5 + 1 + 4 + 9 + 2 + 8 = 36$$
36 is further broken down as $3 + 6 = 9$

Lastly, I take that quintessential number 9 and draw a square to mark its place:

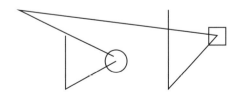

There are numerous other ways to create sigils. Not all folks fuss with numeric values or squares, but instead reposition the letters of a name to create something artistic, which is my preferred way of working. Letters can be drawn sideways, share and overlap elements, and be as stylistic as you fancy.

Perhaps the most popular written spell is the formula for *ABRACA-DABRA*, which descends in a decreasing manner and is therefore used for work seeking to reduce a certain influence, such as the authority of a judge or the heat of a fever:

ABRACADABRA
ABRACADABR
ABRACADAB
ABRACADA
ABRACAD
ABRACA
ABRAC
ABRA
ABR
AB
A

The most popular sigil is likely the *success sigil,* which consists of two dollar signs, two cent signs, and two more dollar signs. This is drawn from the word *success,* with the S's changed into dollar signs and the C's changed into cent signs and additionally rendered into a palindromic symbol. This is most commonly broken down to $$¢¢$$.

As we journey on through this book, we will see the many uses for both the spoken and the written word for summoning mystical power, as well as directing spells to their appropriate target.

V

The Keys to Cleansing: Unlocking Spiritual Purification

THE WATER IS COLD, a bit shocking as it pours down your back, but instantly you feel relieved. Perhaps you had felt the psychic grime that was covering you, or maybe it is only now, as it is washed away, that you feel lighter and can attribute this feeling to the removal of bad energy. Pouring the water on your front now, you feel as if your heart is unburdened, as though a window has been opened in your chest to let in light and fresh air. Rejuvenated, you take the cup from between your feet, filled as it is with water that has run off your body, and prepare to dispose of it, completing your spiritual cleansing.

While there is no microscope under which we might examine the toxins of the evil eye or the bacteria of bad luck, cultures share similar concepts about negative influences, understanding them to be forces that can be eradicated. Treatment often involves a process known as a *spiritual cleansing*, which commonly includes physically washing an individual and/or their home.

In defining the unseen forces that cause negative conditions to manifest in an individual's life and body, words such as *spiritual* or *psychic* are common qualifiers, often paired with other abstract terms such as *energy* or *vibration*. Sometimes this negative energy is thought to have been generated beyond the individual, such as a jinx thrown at them by an enemy. Other times this negativity is seen as having been generated by an individual's own desires and actions, the residue of wickedness. When a worker speaks of *washing away the sin*, it is with the understanding that sin is not only an event but also a condition brought about by the sinful act. Some speak of having a dirty conscience or even a dirty soul, and in either instance action must be taken to wash away the residue. *Sticky*, *dirty*, and *heavy* are words associated with being spiritually unclean, with negative energy sticking to a person much like tar.

Spiritual cleansing is undertaken at different times, most certainly when there is an evident need. Many workers additionally perform maintenance on themselves and their environment. One needn't be the victim of a curse or an ardent sinner in order to require a spiritual wash. The demands and emotions and chaos of daily life create their own effluvium that can stick and be in need of removal. Even a silver cross must be polished periodically to rid it of tarnish. Frequency of spiritual washing varies among workers, though a weekly cleansing is what I prefer even without evidence of pollution. The same goes for cleansing my house. I favor doing both on the same day each week.

It is common to do a cleansing before certain types of spiritual work. The degree to which I do a cleansing on myself varies depending on the type of work I am doing. If I am doing something to draw favorable consequences, such as love or money, then I will wash beforehand; however, if I am doing cursing work, then I would wash after that work is done to remove any negativity that may have resulted from my spell and stuck with me.

There are different types of spiritual cleansing that will be discussed in this chapter. They include the cleansing of your environment or your body (or that of another) as well as long-distance cleansing. Since these various modalities utilize many of the same products to achieve their goal, let us first look at what items you may want to have on hand. Although our theme for this chapter highlights cleansing, not every floor wash or bath has cleansing as its focus; many are used to draw in blessings such as wealth, peace, and protection.

Popular Formulas for Purification

Baptism

Acts of purification often precede blessings, such as with a good old river baptism. The dedicant is dunked under the water, which is said to symbolically wash away their sins, and this is followed by some words of liturgy to bless them and welcome them into the community of the church.

Chinese Wash

Originally produced as Young's Chinese Wash, this formula was popularized in the 1920s by Oracle Products. Chinese Wash is still produced by merchants and individual workers alike. It is used primarily as a floor wash, but also for other forms of cleaning, including laundry and personal baths, depending on the properties of the formula. Generally yellow in color, it often has the scent of oriental grasses, similar to Van Van, though with an added note of frankincense. Its purpose is to rid the home of whatever bedevils it and to thereafter deliver positive conditions, such as happy relationships, or to draw money into the home, especially if business is being done there such as hair dressing, gambling, or prostitution. Here is a simple recipe.

....

CHINESE WASH

- *Liquid oil soap:* Let's work with 4 ounces of oil soap. There are many commercial brands on the market. Go for something unscented or with a slight lemony scent. If you wish to use this as more than a floor wash—say, for personal bathing—then you will want an oil soap that favors the skin.
- *Essential oils:* Add ¼ ounce of any of the following oriental grass oils, or a mixture of them: citronella, lemongrass, palmarosa, or vetiver.
- *Frankincense resin:* Powder, and add ¼ ounce. Mix well.
- *Broom straws:* Some folks fuss over the number of broom straws to use. I favor thirteen, but add a number that seems sensible to you.

• *Bottle:* Use a bottle for storage. Add the broom straws first, followed by the scented oil/soap mixture.

When you come to the end of the bottle, scatter the broom straws around the exterior of your home, where they will attract good luck.

Four Thieves Vinegar

Folklore tells us of four thieves who concocted a special vinegar that kept them healthy even as they robbed graves during the Black Plague. Folk tradition utilizes this vinegar for the purpose of cleansing and protection, often adding it to a wash. There are many recipes out there for Four Thieves Vinegar ranging in complexity, though the most common include vinegar and an herb for each thief. In addition to use in a wash, a good recipe can be drunk or gargled.

....

FOUR THIEVES VINEGAR

• Vinegar: The variety is up to you. Red wine vinegar tastes good, though white vinegar shows the herbs well when placed in a clear glass bottle.

• Clear bottles

• Garlic

• Sage

• Rosemary

• Lavender

When I prepare this vinegar commercially, I like the herbs in the bottle to be selected for their appearance. I use a 4-ounce clear bottle, which easily holds a pair of garlic cloves, and 2 or 3 medium-sized sage leaves. In my region, my rosemary and lavender flower at the same time, so I add a short stalk of each to the bottle. Once I pour in the vinegar, it looks quite nice.

The vinegar I put in will have already been infused with the aforementioned herbs. For that I will have taken a gallon jug and filled it most of the way with 3 parts white vinegar and 1 part red, leaving room for about a cup of herbs. The herbs each equal about ¼ cup after they have been diced and smashed a bit with the heel of my hand to release their oils. I let this concoction sit for a full month before adding it to the bottles.

Road Opener

Road-opener formulas work similarly to those for uncrossing, though they are focused less on what is chaining you down and holding you back and are directed more toward what is in front of you, removing obstacles from your path, and propelling you forward toward your desired destination. This formula became popular in Conjure around the 1970s with the expansion of Afro-Caribbean spiritual products in the North American market. The herbal component is *Abre Camino* (*Eupatorium villosum*, aka *Koanophyllon villosum*), translated from Spanish as *Road Opener*. A good road-opener working will set you on the right road and clear that road of obstacles. Opportunities that might otherwise have been passed by unnoticed become illuminated so that they may be taken advantage of. Similar products to Road Opener include Blockbuster and others.

Uncrossing

A common term for a bad situation, such as a jinx or a bout of bad luck, is a *crossed condition*. Therefore, uncrossing work intends to remove that which inhibits desired conditions. In this manner, it is a type of cleansing. Products used to get rid of unwanted conditions of various kinds are sometimes applied to the act of uncrossing.

The following exercise was developed by my husband, Storm Faerywolf, to serve as an energetic uncrossing rite.

....

UNCROSSING RITE

Take a moment to consider everything that blocks you—the fear, the pain, the shame, the anger, what so-and-so did or said. All of it is symbolically manifesting in the form of a large black X that appears in front of you, with the crossmark of the X appearing at about your heart level.

Now, with three deep breaths, focus on how you feel about these conditions; get in touch with your emotions. With three more breaths cross your arms before you so that your forearms form the X in front of you. On the third inhale clench your fists, imagining that you now grasp the ends of the X in your hands. Take in another deep breath, then exhale forcibly and quickly while you thrust your hands outward to your sides, imagining an outward explosion of energy emanating from your heart, radiating outward in all directions, clearing away everything that has crossed you. Repeat this for two more breaths, each time returning your hands to the X position and thrusting them quickly outward again, maintaining the visualization of the explosive outpouring of energy from your heart. Imagine yourself light, happy, and free of any and all entanglements.

Washing Liquids

A variety of liquid ingredients are employed in washes used for both bodily and environmental cleansing. Despite our focus on liquid materials in this chapter, baths are often concocted from dry elements such as minerals and herbs. Popular minerals include ash, baking soda, gunpowder, laundry bluing, lye, salt, and saltpeter. Bluestone (aka blue vitriol or copperas) is mentioned in many older accounts; however, this is known today to be too toxic for use in baths. Herbs such as eucalyptus, hyssop, lemongrass, and others are commonly used for cleansing rites. Herbs can also cause skin irritation among those with certain allergies, so be sure you understand the relationship between you and what you are working with.

When using any item for a bath, it is important to keep in mind how your body, and tub, will respond. Many recorded formulas suggest using items that in large amounts can be damaging. They may remove your crossed condition—and your skin along with it. Research what you are working with, and always dilute adequately.

Alcohol

Some types of alcohol are used more than others. Be aware of how alcohol affects you mentally before deciding if it is right for a bath. I know tequila makes me mean, so while its astringent properties are useful, it is not something I would add to my bath water. More commonly used is whiskey. In his book on spiritual cleansing, Draja Mickaharic suggests a beer bath, which I have found to be quite effective. [6]

Ammonia

Not many people would think this strong-smelling cleanser appropriate for personal bathing, and indeed I recommend adding just a tablespoon to a tub of water, but it works well as a spiritual cleansing agent.

Colognes

Commercial colognes such as Hoyt's, Jockey Club, and Florida Water are among the most popular. There are a number of colognes derived from plant essences, such as Rose Water, Kananga Water, Rue Water, Notre Dame Water, and so forth. Sometimes these include actual matter from plants, including essential oils or hydrosols, and other times their scents are derived from synthetic fragrances.

Milk

Some associate the whiteness of milk with cleanliness, and milk is commonly used for beauty due to its association with youth.

Oils

Both essential and fragrance oils are added to baths as well as to the many oil blends familiar to Conjure. Such blends are referred to as condition oils, conjure oils, anointing oils, and other names as well, which we will explore in chapter 8. Oils are less often added to wash buckets, as their application leaves greasy streaks when applied to walls, furniture, and glass.

Turpentine

Just a few drops of turpentine may be added to a bath for spiritual cleansing.

---

6. Draja Mickaharic, *Spiritual Cleansing: A Handbook of Psychic Protection*, 19–20.

Urine

You mark territory with your urine, declaring dominance. Out in the woods, campers know to do this to discourage some forms of wildlife from approaching. Ammonia is often used as a substitute for urine in both baths and floor washes.

Vinegar

Apple cider vinegar and white vinegar are used more often than thick balsamic. Vinegar is known to sour people, and can be used against them in cursing work. Paradoxically, it is used for spiritual cleaning as well, which draws from its domestic and medicinal uses covering everything from cleaning window streaks to folk remedies for the removal of warts and fleas. The Four Thieves Vinegar mentioned earlier in this chapter is a popular form of cleansing vinegar.

Many other liquids such as birth water, coffee, kerosene, witch hazel, and others are used more obscurely. Some special waters gain their power based on when and where they are collected.

Auspicious timing can be a consideration, such is the case with rain or dew collected on certain days such as Easter, May Day, and Midsummer morning. These waters are considered especially powerful and are useful for helping with such varied purposes as contacting the dead, restoring beauty, and eliciting psychic vision. This includes time otherwise noteworthy to the worker, such as during an eclipse or when the cock crows.

In adherence with the law of contagion, water can be collected from various places, such as cemeteries, hospitals, and court houses. Water from a bathroom sink or drinking fountain is considered to have the attributes of its location. Sacred sites are especially powerful, with water from places such as Lourdes and Notre Dame being especially treasured by some. Some natural sources are equally respected, such as from reefs, rivers, and wells, each of which has its own associations.

Holy Water

The most powerful blend of holy water is said to be that which is combined from seven churches. The use of holy water is a practice that enters into Conjure from Roman Catholicism. Workers from that faith favor holy water blessed by their clergy, while others bless their own, citing various concepts concerning the role of divine authority in the process.

....

PEACE WATER

There are various formulas that represent themselves as peace water, with two being the most popular. The first is often referred to as Marie Laveau's Peace Water. Its ingredients are a combination of waters including the following:

- Ocean
- Rain
- River
- Spring
- Holy water

The more commercial peace water is typically blue in color, with a clear or white layer of oil resting on the top. It can be shaken, yet it separates back to its layered form, emphasizing how peace water helps return a sense of calm and order despite troubled waters.

....

QUENCH WATER

Blacksmiths wield a special type of power, which is the ability to extract metals from the earth and make them into the tools needed by civilization for industry and warfare. Each culture has their own myths concerning how the blacksmith came to know their craft; often it is a gift from otherworldly beings, while other times this skill is stolen from the gods. The water that is used to cool metal when forging it is known as *quench water*, and just as it cools hot iron, it can be used to cool a hot temperament. Few of us have our own forge, so water from the smithy's slack tub is acquired by request. However, if that option is unavailable to you, then you can make your own water. Here is what you will need:

- *A nail:* I prefer a simple zinc finishing nail.
- *An open flame:* I find that a candle works well; however, you could use the flame from a gas stove as well.

- *Tongs:* Use these to hold the nail so you don't burn your fingers as the flame heats it.
- *A vessel of water:* This can be a simple cup, although avoid plastic or anything that may melt should you unintentionally touch the glowing nail to it. Something with a wide rim is best, so you don't struggle to get the hot nail into the vessel.

The process is easy. Hold the nail firmly with the tongs and place the sharp end into the flame. As the nail heats up and begins to glow red, which happens swiftly, it is a good time to hold in your thoughts those things that are angering you, or to imagine the angry face of whomever you may be working to cool down. When the nail is glowing red hot, remove it from the flame and lower it into the water. Hear the sound of it sizzling, and know that as it cools, so will hot tempers.

This water may be used in baths, added to a wash, or simply placed in a spritzer to spray when tempers flare. You can bottle it for later use if you wish. The nail itself can be used as a charm in its own right, as something carried on you, or in other ways, such as for hanging a picture on your wall of a family member you wish to make calmer.

Bar Soaps

Soaps are often favored for their scent. Sandalwood soap is good for happy homes. Lemongrass, such as is found in Colgate's Octagon Soap, is prized for its spiritual cleansing properties, as is Fan Medicated Soap with its camphor. Some have familiar smells, such as Florida Water soap, which is based off the cologne, and similarly is used for cleansing and blessings.

Spiritual suppliers offer a variety of soaps, some with the names of saints reputed to aid certain work and others aimed at conditions. Many of the popular formulas discussed in this book have been compounded into a soap, though unless a soap is being given to someone as a trick, the more negative formulas are less common.

African Black Soap

This soap is used to cleanse and protect.

Black and White Soap

Given its name, it should be apparent why this soap is used to attract and support cross-cultural relationships, most often for love.

....

PURIFYING LAUNDRY WASH

Some folks like to add a magical agent to their laundry to target negative energies, or else to empower what is washed with qualities such as good luck. How this is achieved depends much on the method of washing, as well as the fabric being washed. You will need the following:

- Mason jar: A pint-sized jar works well.
- 5 peppermint leaves: Fresh, not dried
- 3 rosemary sprigs
- A camphor square: These are commercially available in little squares, meant to be placed in the yard to keep away deer.
- Unscented liquid laundry detergent

Fill the jar with the ingredients. After leaving it in a sunny window for one week, strain out the herbs.

Herbal Baths

If you are using herbs and want to avoid having your shower or tub filled with debris, you can brew the herbs into a tea, strain out the herbs, and pour that into your bath or over your body while standing in the shower. If you dislike bathing with particulates, you should consider placing your herb blend in a muslin bag or large tea strainer. Professional workers prescribing herbal baths for their clients often offer blends with a specific number of ingredients, the most common being seven, nine, and thirteen. Clients are sometimes directed to pour the water over their head as many times as the bath is named for, or to take that number of baths for as many days.

....

SEVEN-DAY HERBAL BATH FOR PEACE OF MIND

Use about ¼ cup of each of the following:

- Balm of Gilead buds

- Flax seeds
- Heather

Best Practices

As with all things, timing, directionality, and disposal are key. The most traditional time for a cleansing bath is before dawn or during sunrise, to take advantage of the newness of the day. Since we are discussing a cleansing bath, designed to remove negativity from you, our movement will follow the direction away from us. If you are simply pouring a pitcher of special water from your neck down, then gravity will do the bulk of the directional work. A hand cloth can be used for this; rather than pouring the pitcher over your body you could soak the cloth in the prepared water, gesturing downward on your body. Whatever method you choose, the important part is that when covering parts of your body with your hands or cloth your motions carry the bad energy away from you—say, from your shoulder down to your hands—rather than the other way. Move down your body and limbs, not up. If this were a bath taken to put something on you—say, a solution to help you win in court—then you would motion the opposite way, from your feet and on up to your hips, from your stomach up to your neck, fingers to shoulders, and so forth.

When finished, many people say it is necessary to air-dry, believing that the magic is otherwise wiped away.

Whereas the water remaining from a spiritual bath was once disposed of by tipping the tub in the appropriate direction, proper disposal methods have evolved. In modern times it has become common to collect a sample from the bath, since a built-in tub cannot be moved, and that remnant is taken and thrown to the east. A similar procedure is used with shower water, which is often collected in a cup or bowl of water placed between the feet when washing.

....

THE WATER RITE

The *water rite* is a particular method of internal spiritual cleansing that comes from the Feri Tradition. Though it is considered a tradition of witchcraft, its founders, Victor and Cora Anderson, were trained in rootwork and mystical Christianity. This particular rite, also referred to by some as the *Kala rite*, is a simple and powerful way to cleanse yourself from within through the consumption of blessed water.

For this practice you will need a glass of water, no more than you can drink in a sitting.

Begin by concentrating on whatever negativity surrounds you, from mundane annoyances to the larger life issues that cause you stress and the negativity that accompanies it. Having full awareness of this negativity, hold the glass of water near your lips. Take three deep breaths, and with each exhale imagine this negativity passing from inside you and into the glass. Picture it like tar or soot, black and thick and nasty. The glass may even feel heavier as you fill it with the negativity.

Now feel yourself connecting to the divine source above you, which many picture as the white dove of the Holy Spirit. Sense this powerful spirit enter into you from above. Breathe it in. With your next exhale feel this divine energy pass from your lips into the water in the cup. Sense it transform from the toxic sludge you relieved yourself of into crystal-clear water. Much as bee, scorpion, and snake venom have been transformed into cures for various ailments, the alchemy involved in this trick transforms something negative into something beneficial.

Drink this water, and feel yourself filled with cleansing, life-giving water. This is a great way to rid yourself of various anxieties. It is said that the effects will last as long as it takes you to urinate next, at which point you are free to perform the rite again.

....

A FOOT WASHING

Having learned how to care for ourselves, we can now explore how to care for the needs of others. Conjure is largely a community practice. Assisting others with their needs, whether you do so in a professional paid capacity or as a service to your family and friends, is the traditional role of the Conjure worker. Explained here is how to be of service to someone in need of a spiritual cleansing by administering a foot wash. Be sure to do a cleansing on yourself prior to working on someone else.

In the book of John, Jesus washes the feet of his disciples at the Last Supper. Akin to that act is the tradition of foot washing. This rite serves various needs, both physical and spiritual. Often it was the case that the Conjure doctor was as close to a physician as many folks had access to, and a proper examination of the feet serves to help diagnose physical maladies such as ingrown toenails, as well as signs of diabetes, such as sores, poor circulation detected by the coldness of the feet, and a lack of sensitivity. While we must be certain not to offer medical advice, noting possible health issues and suggesting examinations with medical health professionals informs others of issues they may not be aware of, especially if they are unable to examine their feet themselves due to physical limitations. Beyond this practical need is the spiritual one, and here I must briefly mention the role of foot-trafficking as it relates to specifically cursing the feet. We will delve deeper into this practice in chapter 11 when we discuss powders. For now, simply know that a traditional way of cursing someone is through the scattering of material that has been tricked—that is, designed to hex the victim who steps upon such matter. For this reason particular attention is given to feet, and the cleansing thereof.

Though you may certainly do a foot cleansing on yourself, it is often done for others as a humbling spiritual service. I offer this service, preceded by a reading for diagnosis. My listing for this service helps sum up the experience:

Foot Washing is a traditional remedy for the removal of jinxes and maladies of the spirit. My practice includes a reading at the start of our session, so that we may better understand the cause of the negative energy you have come to be cleansed of. The rite itself is literal to its name; you will be seated in a chair, having both feet washed in a small tub prepared for this service. Please dress appropriate to this endeavor, with pant legs that can be lifted past your calves, sans pantyhose.

To perform this rite yourself you will need the following:

- *A basin:* Use one that is large enough to place both of a person's feet in.

- *Water:* From a clean and natural source, such as a river or well, is preferred. Store-bought spring water is a fair substitute.

- *Holy water:* You can get this from a church, or bless your own if you feel you have the spiritual authority to do so.

- *Bar soap:* A new bar of soap is needed for this rite. Many choose one of the many soaps common to spiritual work, such as Florida Water soap, sandalwood, African Black Soap, or rue.

- *Olive oil:* Pour the oil into a small bowl. There are many commercial condition oils that can be used for blessing, but since we have yet to explore them I suggest for now simply using olive oil. You may pray over it first if you wish to transform it from being a mundane cooking ingredient into a spiritual salve.

- *A towel:* A white towel is preferred for this rite.

- *Facial tissue:* Always consider the emotional needs of those on whom you do work.

To get started you will want these tools near your basin, which will be filled with water and placed in front of a chair. The chair is for your participant to sit in, with enough room for their feet to rest between the chair and basin. Position yourself with the basin between you and the person being worked on. You may assume a prayerful position, or use a short stool depending on your need.

Prior to setting up this ritual, you will have had correspondence with the participant, who from here on we will refer to as your client (whether or not you are doing this professionally). Depending on how many details you received about the client's condition, once they are seated it is a good time to discuss the matter that has brought them here. Are they suffering from a curse or from some action that has left them feeling unclean, or are they preparing for a new beginning that warrants the removal of old energy?

Following this talk, I have the client remove their shoes and stockings if they have not already done so. I tell them briefly the order of things to occur, not assuming that they know the mechanics of how I do a foot washing. Be aware that clients may have different ideas of what is to happen. I had one client be disappointed that I was not using a singing bowl, as the worker she had previously gone to had first played a large crystal singing bowl and used that as his basin. Given the different ways in which Conjure doctors work, it is always good to gauge a client's expectations, as you never know what their prior experience has been.

At this juncture you will have the client place their feet in the basin, by moving their chair forward or sliding the basin toward them.

A prayer is offered, either before, during, or after the holy water is added to the basin. Something heartfelt is fine, such as "We ask that (client's name) be cleansed of all evils and impurities and step into a blessed life." Consideration is to be given to the religious beliefs of your client, as well as your own. Being that the praxis for this rite is Christian, as are the majority of adherents of Conjure, you should be wary of invoking the names of deities unfamiliar to the client, as this rite is meant to speak to them and strengthen them in the standing of their faith.

The further mechanics of this rite may vary. Essentially you will take your clean bar of soap and wash from the client's lower calf down to their toes. This is where we consider directionality, in that we wash downward to remove the negativity from the feet and into the basin. The most effective way I have found is to place their heel in my one hand while my other hand engages with the soap. You may rub the soap along their wet skin, or you may create a lather and apply it with your hand or a white wash cloth if you prefer. Wash both feet and rinse them by submerging them in the water, or if your water is shallow you may rinse by cupping water in your hand or using a cup.

After the client's feet are washed, they are dried. I place the white towel across my thighs and place one foot followed by the other in my lap and pat the feet dry. I then have the client place their feet back in front of them, between their chair and the basin. If outside, I would at this point tip the basin away to the east, but most often I am in my office and will therefore pull the basin aside and dispose of it properly after the client has left.

Next I work on each individual foot. I have no preference for the order. Kneeling beside either foot I dip my fingers into the olive oil, rub my hands together to distribute the oil, and rub it onto their feet, my hands moving upward on their foot, from toes, to heel, to ankle.

I mentioned that this was a humbling rite to perform, and the experience of clients tends to be emotional, hence the need to have facial tissue handy.

Long-Distance Cleansing

Performing a hands-on cleansing is not always possible, so let's talk about what it takes to do a cleansing at a distance. This form of work is designed for working with individuals who are immobile or far away. Distant cleansing is one of several cleansing services offered by many professional rootworkers, myself included. Here is how my listing reads:

> *Distance and mobility are factors that keep some people from seeking the spiritual cleansing they require. Yet the power of Spirit is boundless, a truth long recognized by Conjure workers, who developed the practice of cleansing a client at a distance through the use of a doll. Such a doll will be named and ritually baptized for you, then cleansed on your behalf. At the time you schedule for me to perform this cleansing, you will be required to sit for as long as it takes you to read the King James version of Psalm 145 a total of 7 times. Following this cleansing the doll can be mailed to you or ritually buried by me, according to your preference.*

In addition to cleansing individuals by proxy, spaces can be worked on as well. With an address and a floor plan, one can create the semblance of a place and utilize the law of sympathetic magic (like affecting like) to direct cleansing energy to the place in need. Personally I feel that a hands-on cleansing is best, but again, some circumstances prohibit that. In addition to written maps, dollhouses can also be used. Mimicking architecture is not essential, nor is using a doll whose features perfectly match the person being worked on. My preferred way is to draw the floorplan on a white plate with markers, then wash it all off with Florida Water soap. The plate comes clean, and I am left with a basin of water to work with, which I can dispose of at a crossroads or dilute with more water and throw against a nearby camphor tree I work with.

Cleansing Your Environment

Unwanted forces can build up in places as well as people. When you encounter hostile emotions or bouts of bad luck in the home, office, or elsewhere, it is a good time to do a thorough cleaning. My advice is not to wait until such rancor occurs, but to do routine cleanings of the spaces you frequent. These can be done each day, week, month, or year. While there are many ways to spiritually clean a home, floor washes, such as Chinese Wash, fit best with both the theme and the methodology of this chapter.

Floors are swept and then mopped, with motions that direct negativity toward the back door. Doors and windowsills are also areas that need attention, as well as any spaces that are open to the outside, such as fireplaces and air conditioning vents. A solution of white vinegar is useful for cleaning window glass.

Cleansing a space does not always involve the application of a formula. Striking the walls and ceiling with a broom and then sweeping outside your door is one way. After the negative energy is removed, it is customary to bring positive energy back into the space. Just as many folks take probiotics after having taken antibiotics, the concept is similar. Any of the methods we examined in chapter 2 to invite blessings may be applied here.

I have hopefully imparted the importance of keeping your person and surroundings spiritually clean, and provided some techniques for achieving this. Be aware that it is possible to go overboard with cleansing. If you are doing work to put positive conditions on yourself and your home, you do not want to wash all of that away. Too sterile of an environment can impede your work. Be sure to follow your cleansing jobs with blessing work.

~ VI ~
The Keys to Knots and Stitches: Unlocking Protection

IT IS HERE WITH you now, a presence you cannot see. Your skin can sense it, a chilling feeling, something like cold breath on the back of your neck. Too late for tricks. No red brick dust lines your threshold. No circle of salt contains you. Your skin crawls but not from any familiar form of fear, for you realize the crawling is inside you, wriggling up from within your meat and muscle, a hundred or more mouths yawning awake now beneath their blanket of your skin, gasping into the fullness of their strength, and preparing to devour you.

This is an example of having *live things in you*. The method of deployment is said to come through one's food. How easy it is to hide a nest of spider eggs inside a humble dumpling. It is said that magic aids those eggs in remaining alive so that they may hatch inside someone. Beyond the obvious precaution, which is to avoid food offered from a potential enemy, or any manner of gift really, there are magical precautions and protections to employ against this and other attacks.

Attacks can be waged by other people or by spiritual forces, or through the cooperation of both, and may take the form of physical threats or unseen jinxes. Protection may be gained by deflecting, reversing, binding, or transforming a hex. The tactic is determined by the quality of the hex and the state of its source. Petty jinxes can often be deflected and brushed away, while sometimes a taste of their own medicine by way of a reversing is what is required to stop an enemy from throwing one at you. Should you feel reluctant to curse a foe in kind, a binding done on them may be the preferred treatment. The truly skilled worker can see the quality of whatever negative form surrounds them, and is able to channel it into a positive purpose. Spirits sent to do harm can sometimes be bargained with and turned into allies. That big ball of stress that someone has thrown at you can be contained, even utilized, as a certain degree of stress can be helpful for certain projects (more than a bit fuels me now as the deadline for this book looms close, and is effective at keeping me here at my desk and alert to inspiration). Anger and outrage, while considered by some teachings to be unspiritual, sometimes referred to as *low vibrations*, are a natural response of the human condition and can be harnessed to enact personal and social change.

Apotropaic magic is the term for spells and talismans deployed to protect against attack, such as how *nazar* amulets (aka evil eye beads) are used to deflect evil. Apotropaic magic is used to repel both physical and supernatural attacks.

Let us first explore the subject of physical attacks. Of course, when physical danger is present then precautions beyond magic must be considered. While responsibility for violence sits solely with its perpetrators, defensive measures safeguard our wellbeing. Woman are particularly vulnerable to violence in the form of sexual assault, and consequently amulets to protect against rape are common in many cultures. A *palad khik*, a penis-shaped Thai amulet, is one example. Such items are often carried close to one's sex, much as a protective mojo bag is, beneath a belt or in a bra.

In this chapter we will consider ways to ward our space and bodies against attack, with an emphasis on the magic drawn from threads and cords. First let's look at some of the better known formulas for protection.

Popular Formulas for Protection

One could argue that it is difficult to address protection as a singular category, as many formulas assist with a degree of protective need, such as how Stop Gossip protects against gossip or Money Stay with Me protects money. If we were to look at protection in the abstract, then this chapter would be never-ending. Instead we will focus solely on those formulas whose main purpose is protection against attacks, physical and psychic. Formulas to rid oneself of bad conditions, such as Uncrossing, often go hand in hand with protection. Getting rid of the dog that is biting you is always the first step in stopping injury; however, protection work is necessary to prevent the dog's return.

Fiery Wall of Protection

While this formula may be useful for any kind of attack, it is said to be especially effective against a personal enemy who is harassing you.

Free from Evil

This formula aids in releasing a person from the bondage of a curse and from threats of all kinds. It is especially effective in guarding against evil, such as by anointing protective talismans and entrances to the home.

Guardian Angel

The belief that each person is appointed a guardian angel at birth, tasked to guide and protect them, is the basis for this formula. While angelic products vary in their purpose, those especially useful for protection often invoke Archangel Michael. He can often be seen on various labels with his iconic sword and shield, sometimes with the Devil's head under his foot.

Jinx Killer

Known by similar names, such as Hex Breaker and Jinx Destroyer, this formula does what it says, stopping all the bad luck that occurs as the result of a jinx.

Keep Away Hate

Although this formula protects against all forms of hate, actions and negative emotions born of prejudice—especially those aimed against individuals due to their race, religion, sexual orientation, and economic status—are of special concern.

Law Keep Away

This particular formula is one that I have worked with and produced for years, and it sometimes draws comments. I find it interesting that some assume it is made for criminals, while others understand how some people require protection from the law because of their racial or economic status. As it is crafted, it addresses both purposes. It intends to shield protestors and minorities from police brutality, while hiding the affairs of moral renegades.

....

LAW KEEP AWAY PATCH

For this trick you will need the following:

- A small square of red felt
- A needle
- Black thread
- Scissors
- A prayer paper

To be left alone by the law is what the prayer on your paper must address. Feel free to pen a prayer in your own words, or consider something like the following, which comes from the back of the Law Keep Away candle I produce for my Modern Conjure brand.

> *Eyes of the law are turned away,*
> *Their prying eyes becoming blind.*
> *My tracks are covered night and day,*
> *This person they will never find.*

The prayer paper should be smaller than the patch of felt. The rest is simple, and involves sewing the patch over the prayer. Red felt was chosen because it is associated with mojo bags, of which this patch serves as a creative variation. You could instead use a manufactured patch, such as one that comes in a style such as skulls, angel wings, crosses, and so forth. If you require a specific type of protection—say, from homophobic cops—you should be able to find a rainbow flag patch, for example. Such fancy patches may be worn on the outside, but if you are using the red felt patch then I suggest sewing it somewhere inside your garment where it will attract less attention. In sewing it on, I like to make my stitches as little x's, as that seems most protective to me. The patch itself may shrink somewhat, so be sure to stitch it tight. Laundering the garment will cause the prayer paper to disintegrate over time, but this does not affect the magic; rather, it is believed that the prayer further infuses the garment, much as prayer written in ink on a white plate infuses the water it is cleansed in.

Protection from Envy

Watchful Eye of Protection is my formula for Modern Conjure, based on elements of older products such as Evil Eye. Mothers are known to sew nazar beads onto their children's clothing to protect them from the evil eye, which often occurs when their child is complimented, a sign that the person giving the compliment is envious of such a precious child.

Reversing

Reversing is a specific type of work that seeks to send a curse back to the person who sent it. Other names include Return to Sender and Turn Back

Rose of Crucifixion

According to Lewis de Claremont, author of *Legends of Incense, Herb, and Oil Magic,* this formula is said to safeguard against crossed conditions.

Safe Travel

Physical protection while traveling is a common concern. A lot can go wrong when you are in an unfamiliar locale. Confusion caused by strange settings and customs decreases attention to safety and opens folks up to scams. Con artists are rampant in tourist towns, with theft and violence being a common result.

Textile Magic

With distaffs, spindles, and sacred looms, characters throughout many mythologies emphasize the importance of textiles to human life. Joseph was envied by his brothers for his coat of many colors. Sleeping Beauty was bewitched by an enchanted spinning wheel. Flying carpets, magical top hats, even a simple sock gifted to set free a house elf all hint at the magic inherent in textiles. Such magic is often woven therein by the seamstresses and tailors of these stories, memories stitched into quilts, blessings braided into cords, hatred secretly knit into lace doilies. It is believed that emotions and intentions can be directed through the actions involved in spinning, sewing, knitting, and braiding, and thereby contained within the fabric of a thing.

These days few of us spin our own yarn or weave our own fabric, let alone shear wool or hackle flax, but once upon a time these chores were charmed with familiar songs, the implements of textile craft serving as cunning allies. Take the fairy tale *Spindle, Shuttle, and Needle* by the Brothers Grimm, in which the arts of spinning, weaving, and sewing are bestowed upon a young woman on her godmother's deathbed. A king comes to town searching for a bride, and after their brief encounter the lovelorn young woman sings to her spindle:

> *Spindle, my spindle, haste, haste thee away,*
> *And here to my house bring the wooer, I pray.* [7]

Having thusly commanded her spindle to fetch the king, it jumps from her hand, out the door, dancing along the road to where the king is found, leading him back to the woman's cottage. While waiting for her king, she again sings, this time to her shuttle:

> *Shuttle, my shuttle, weave well this day,*
> *And guide the wooer to me, I pray.*

---

7. In *Grimm's Household Tales* by Jacob and Wilhelm Grimm.

This next part is my favorite: the shuttle springs out the door and weaves a carpet in her front yard, complete with flowers, a tree growing from it, as well as deer and birds that can move but have no voice. With work still to do, the woman turns from this miracle and sings to her needle:

Needle, my needle, sharp-pointed and fine,
Prepare for a wooer this house of mine.

Know what that needle does? It sews her a tablecloth, reupholsters a chair with velvet, and fashions drapes.

Fast forward... The King and the woman are wed, and the spindle, shuttle, and needle secure a place of honor in the royal treasure chamber. I like that the story tells the fate of the tools, who I see as strong magical allies and characters in their own right. Although we may not expect results as miraculous as what that woman conjured, we too can sing to our tools, with songs meant to manifest our wishes. Spiritual work is often engaged in side by side with physical work, making the mundane more sacred and grounding the ineffable in a physical task.

With the understanding that an item retains the energy with which it is made, newly obtained items, especially clothing and bedding, benefit from cleansing work. Consider the harsh conditions of many sweatshops. Beyond the obvious suggestion of purchasing union-produced and free-trade items, you may wish to add some spiritual cleansing agents to your washing machine, dryer, or iron. We see the inherent value of those who place their energy in the work they do, which is why students in the United States are still taught that Betsy Ross sewed the flag. When respect is not given, an example being the horrible conditions of American textile factories in the first half of the twentieth century, new songs must be chosen and sung into the work. The brutal history of protests in America and the violence surrounding them returns us to our topic of protection.

THIMBLE SPELL

Here is another bit of apotropaic magic. A thimble is used to protect one's finger when sewing, but we can think bigger, imagining how the wee thimble might be made into a mightier charm. Begin by turning the thimble upside down so that it resembles a cup, and place the following inside it:

- 3 hairs from the person it intends to protect
- A small rose thorn
- A pinch of salt
- The head of an unburnt match

Light a black household or chime candle. (You can use any size you wish; what matters is the quality of wax, which needs to cool hard, making wax such as soy impractical.) Roll the hairs into a ball and place them in the bottom of the thimble. If they are unruly and will not roll together, you can roll them in a drop of wax to help them stick; basically you just need to avoid having hairs sticking beyond the rim of the thimble, which can also be avoided by cutting them shorter.

Choose a small rose thorn that takes up as little room as possible. Add the salt and cut the match head from the stick. Now fill the remaining space inside the thimble with wax by holding the thimble in one hand and tipping the candle above it with your other hand. You may wish to put paper down if you are afraid you might not be nimble with the wax. Once the wax fills the thimble to the rim, wait a few minutes for it to cool, then press it down with your thumb. You may need to do this a couple more times. When finished, the wax should be compact and flat at the rim.

This charm would work poorly in extremely hot climates or if left in a car in the summer, but generally it can be carried in a pocket for protection or placed somewhere significant such as near the entryway. A variation less subject to heat requires using hot glue from a glue gun to fill the thimble. It works well, but lacks the mystique of a black candle and the magic it engenders.

Spiritual Attack

Spiritual attack comes in different forms. It may be the result of negative energy emanating from a person or an environment. It may entail an entity sent by a foe.

This notion of negative energy is something that many believe they fall victim to. Those who identify as *empaths* often say they are especially affected, often negatively, by the energy of people or places they encounter. Too often folks approach me expressing how they are so empathic that they can barely tolerate being in public. It seems that such conversations are meant to express how psychically powerful they are, although I am usually left thinking that they are merely unable to cope with their alleged abilities. On more than one occasion I have screamed inside my head for them to stop talking; however, their empathic abilities seldom relate to the person they are standing in front of, and furthermore seem to distract from obvious social cues directed at brushing them off. Nevertheless, many of the aforementioned formulas can help folks protect themselves from feeling overpowered by the energy around them.

Other times it is an entity in spirit form that is responsible for spiritual attacks, such as a ghost, hag, or demon. Atmosphere affects how we are haunted. I do not mean merely that spooky places are more likely to be haunted or to heighten our sense of the spirit world, as much as that may be so. Rather, the quality of the air itself is believed to affect the spirit world. Spirits are often blamed when someone steps into a cold spot.

Dark and stormy nights are considered good weather for spirits to move in; indeed, damp and foggy places are often favored for hauntings. It is said that water helps spirits manifest, though some waters repel them. Salt (and salted water) is said to disrupt the ether, making it more difficult for spirits to manifest. *Asperging* is the term used to describe sanctifying a space with water, which often contains salt and maybe herbs or oils depending on what traditions a worker favors. Fingers may be dipped into a bowl of such prepared water, then flecked about the room to asperge it. Or one might dip and shake something like hen feathers, or the sprig of a protective herb such as rosemary. Spray bottles also work well.

....

ASPERGING SOLUTION

- 1 camphor square
- ½ cup distilled water

- 3 tablespoons table salt
- ¾ cup Florida Water
- 1 rosemary sprig

Place the first four ingredients in a bowl, letting the camphor dissolve, then stir with the rosemary. Use the rosemary sprig to disperse the water by dipping it into the bowl and snapping the sprig in the direction where you wish water droplets to rain.

Smoke is also enjoyed by spirits, especially incense and cigar smoke, but not all types of smoke. Sage, for example, is said to repulse them. Strong and bitter-smelling herbs are used to send unwanted spirits away.

Light also disrupts the atmosphere of the spirit world, which is why spirits favor dark places. Brightness drives them away, and dulls our psychic senses from tuning into them. That may sound like a vulnerable position; however, spirits are said to use our attention as traction to keep them from slipping out of the realm of the living. Some rely on our fear to help them manifest.

A Trick of the Light

A modern trick is to write on a bulb using a permanent marker. With newer LED bulbs this is made easier, as they do not heat up in the same manner. The point of this trick is to make it so that the light must pass through a mystic marking before illuminating the room, thus giving the light a magical intention, in this case protection. For this trick, draw three crosses in the shape of a pyramid on the curved glass face of the bulb, like this:

Hag Ridden

Sleep is a risky state, wherein one is prone to physical and psychic attacks. One of the most fearful experiences to be had at this time involves what is referred to as *hag riding*. The hag in question is most often imagined to be a woman in or near one's community who is a witch. Such a witch is understood to shed her skin at night in order to take possession of another body, whom she rides throughout the night.

Frequent nightmares and exhaustion are attributed to one who is being hag ridden, and there are various solutions. Supposing you could find the hag, you could wait until she peels off her flesh and flees her bed for the night, after which you would salt her skin so that upon her return it will have shrunk too small for her to crawl back into. As mentioned in the section on the Sator Square in chapter 4, many supernatural beings, hags included, are said to suffer from arithmomania and become distracted by having to count various items. To keep from being hag ridden, you must rely on the hag's obsession with counting, distracting her by means such as scattering rice at the foot of your bed, or with a broom whose straws she must count, or by displaying a colander whose many holes the hag is compelled to number. Knots work well toward this end, and a knotted cord tied to a bedpost will compel the ghoul to stop and count them. Better hope she does not count quickly, or your body may become her costume for the night!

Spirit Possession

The belief in possession is prevalent in Conjure. A good number of clients seeking Conjure doctors like myself do so with the understanding that an evil spirit is manipulating their life or possessing their body. Negative life experiences and ill health accompany this condition. This is where the diversity among practitioners becomes more noticeable, as there are widely different views on what a demon is and what it is capable of doing, according to religious traditions such as Pentecostalism, Palo, Neopaganism, etc. In all of these, faith aids in the cure, and in keeping oneself from becoming reinfected by infernal powers. Such faith may be held for a religious authority, or the advocacy of one's ancestors, or simply one's own autonomy. While I do not believe that bedevilment is a wholly psychological phenomenon, I find that mental health is a large factor in attracting negative spirits, and hinders one's ability to be rid of spiritual attachments and prevent them from reoccurring. Individuals experiencing spiritual attacks should be asked the following questions:

- Does the experience fill you with a sense of purpose?
- Does it excite you?
- Does it entertain you?

The evidence of any of those factors will make it more difficult to resolve any type of spirit manifestation, be it a haunting or a bodily possession. I have had to approach situations where one or several of these were a factor.

The effectiveness of such cures relies on a true understanding of the entity's nature. Much as folktales tell us that we must know a creature's name in order to control and be free of it (consider Rumpelstiltskin), we must understand where an entity came from and what drew it to the victim, then name it and send it away. Remedies for uncrossing and spiritual cleansing are applied to conditions of spirit attachment, followed by protection.

Ahead of chapter 11, which explores cursing, I present the following insight. An effective curse includes an element of love magic. Just as some folks thrive on the drama of an unhealthy relationship, others relate to curses and hauntings in much the same way. Some people fall in love with their demons, and will call them back again and again like a lovelorn sophomore drunk dialing their ex. A good degree of counseling best accompanies any type of work involving exorcising spirits.

Prayer Cloths

One way to ward against spiritual attack is with the possession of a prayer cloth. These cloths are often made from handkerchiefs—made in the sense that a plain white hanky is prayed over to sanctify it, changing it from a simple snot rag or affectation into a sacred object able to protect against evil and bestow blessings.

There are various ways to sanctify a prayer cloth. Some anoint it with blessing oil. Pentecostals may anoint it with their sweat while possessed with the Holy Spirit, believing that the powers of Spirit are thus transferred to the cloth. I have heard that tucking the cloth into your sleeve when you take communion results in it being sanctified, as does wetting it from a church font. If those options are not available to you, place your cloth between the pages of your Bible where Acts 19:11–12 appear, and say a heartfelt prayer asking the Holy Spirit to sanctify your cloth, that it may be used to purify and transfer blessings to all that it touches:

11. And God wrought special miracles by the hands of Paul:
12. So that from his body were brought unto the sick handkerchiefs or aprons, and the diseases departed from them, and the evil spirits went out of them.

Prayer cloths need not be unadorned white handkerchiefs. Prayers and psalms can be written on the borders, and some sold at sacred sites or by church merchants come adorned with scriptural verses or sacred imagery. More modern variations of the prayer cloth have developed to incorporate color magic, with colors associated with specific types of prayer, such as blue for peace and green for money. Some spiritually minded knitters are known to stitch their prayers into the cloths they create, which is a wonderful way to do it if you have the time and skill.

Prayer cloths can be carried on one's person to deflect wickedness and, some would say, to promote healing as well. I use them when praying over certain objects, such as protective amulets, which I cover with the cloth to add strength to my prayer. Prayer cloths are especially useful for those times when you are not feeling as connected to the divine as you wish you were.

Binding Knots

Bindings are a popular form of stopping an attacker, especially among those who do not wish to engage in cursing work. They can be used on either a person or a spirit, provided you have a name for them that you can use. The general concept behind this form of knotwork is that things can be contained within the knot. This might be a wish, a prayer, or a person or spirit. Generally this entails the name of the thing or person being spoken into the knot as it is tied and tightened.

In volume 1 of Harry M. Hyatt's *Hoodoo, Conjuration, Witchcraft, Rootwork*, an informant from Charleston, South Carolina, talks about catching a spirit in a knot of cotton string. The process is as simple as calling the person's name, and tightening a knot when they answer. Handkerchiefs are used for this also, according to another informant. We might consider that a person's voice serves as a personal concern, since its sound waves are capable of being captured in a knot and used to influence them. Their voice over the phone, though less directly tied to them, serves as a second option. With personal concerns, that which comes from one's body is considered strongest, but lacking that you would say their name and tie it into a knot.

> *I bind you, Nancy … from doing harm*
> *against yourself … and harm against others.*

This line, from the 1996 film *The Craft*, is the most popular example of a binding spell to date. In this instance, the protagonist, Sarah, seeks to stop Nancy, which has the effect of landing Nancy in a psychiatric institution. This demonstrates the ill effect that can result from a binding. The person who is bound, should they continue to generate negativity, is unable to release it, thereby causing a toxic effect in themself.

There is much folklore regarding knot magic, for which we will look again at Hyatt's material from *Folk-Lore from Adams County, Illinois*:

- When your thread knots while sewing, you will have a quarrel.
- To get rid of pains in your stomach, make seven knots in a cord string and tie it round your waist.
- Pick a wart with a needle, and having made a knot on a string, rub the knot in the blood. Throw the knot away and the wart will be lost.
- To prevent a broody hen from sitting, tie a red string around her leg.
- If you don't want your husband to have any nature for you,[8] when he is sleeping measure his privates with a cord string and tie three knots in it. Then hide the string in the house and he will not have any desire for you.

---

8. The term *nature* in this context refers to a man's sexual potency.

Witch Ladders

A witch's ladder is made from a length of braided cord (string or yarn) into which curios have been entwined. The Wellington Witch Ladder is perhaps the oldest. In 1878 it was discovered hidden between the roof and upper room of a home being demolished in the region that is its namesake, along with a chair and broomsticks. Several feathers pierced the length of cord, which garnered the attention of various folklorists. Among them was Charles Godfrey Leland, who claimed to have spoken to practicing witches in the area who similarly made what they called a *witches garland*. Leland's witches crafted their garlands for cursing, knotting feathers plucked from a living black hen into their cords, along with the hair of the potential victim. A hen figure shaped out of cotton, pierced with two crossed, blackened pins, added further embellishment. These were to be hidden in the bed of the cursed, and the curse could be lifted only by discovering them and throwing them downstream.

....

Witch's Ladder for Protection

Leaving that dastardly cord to float away now, we turn our attention to a witch's ladder made for the purpose of protection, for which you will need the following:

- A length of black yarn, a yard long
- Holy water
- 9 broom straws
- 9 black hen feathers
- A dried chicken foot

First wash the yarn in the holy water. Pull it tight to remove the wetness. Tie a loop at the top that will later serve to hang it. Pair each straw with a feather, and knot these along the length of yarn.

With each knot recite the first verse of Psalm 91:1: *He that dwelleth in the secret place of the most High shall abide under the shadow of the Almighty.*

At the bottom tie the dried chicken foot. This cord is to be hung somewhere high, such as in the attic of your home, or over your bed if goth decor suits your style.

Similar cords can be constructed for a number of purposes utilizing a variety of curios. Coarse twine or butcher's string works well for rough jobs, whereas softer work such as for love or healing benefits from silk or macramé cord. These of course can be chosen in a variety of colors to correspond with your purpose. All manner of things may be hung from a cord, including bones, bottles, charms, dolls, and basically whatever you can find a way to tie on. Aesthetically these cords can appear creepy, to ward away trouble, or bejeweled and lacy, to inspire enchantment.

Since humans first began wearing clothing as protection against the elements, the materials we knot and stitch together have kept us from harm. As a warning regarding this type of work, be sure you can let your guard down enough to enjoy life. Too strong an emphasis on protection can lead to paranoia.

～ VII ～
The Keys to Personal Concerns:
Unlocking Influence

WHY WERE YOU SO resistant to the idea? It seems so silly now that you would have felt so strongly about it. And what was it about her that always rubbed you the wrong way? Why, she is perfectly delightful. A great friend. And that new shampoo she bought you—enchanting.

Situations over which we have little influence are the concern of Conjure, through which we seek the magical keys to better control our life. A matter of survival for many, enchantment is often the only recourse for ensuring that those in charge do not call all the shots. From the domestic maid who pours Essence of Bend Over into the mop water to the maligned employee sewing shut a cow's tongue stuffed with his gossiper's personal concerns, spells to influence another's actions are abundant. In a land as disparate as the United States, is it any wonder that we find such a wealth of magic targeting those who wield social, economic, and legal control over us?

Influencing work brings up philosophical and ethical interests. New Age spirituality and Neopaganism have contributed to the magical dialogue in North America, and common to both belief systems is a value placed on a concept called *free will*. The nature of free will has been explored by minds such as Aristotle, Hobbes, Hume, and Voltaire. Theological elucidations of how factors such as fate, divination, and an omniscient deity function under free will (or negate free will, according to metaphysical determinism) vary greatly among faiths, and most people possess vague or contradictory notions of how destiny and choice relate.

Tenuous as the concept of free will is, it is often used to condemn traditional Conjure practices designed to influence others. Any attempt to subjugate another's perceived free will is seen by some as unethical, as black magic. Even spells with positive goals, such as certain love spells, are deemed unethical if they are believed to compromise another's alleged free will, a standard that would condemn Cupid himself for bringing lovers together. No matter how destructive a person's behavior may be to themselves or others, setting things right by magically influencing another's decisions or desires is believed by some to be taboo.

The fierce and protective individualism expressed through the concept of free will taps into a strong American cultural value: that of freedom of choice. In the shifting attitudes over magical ethics we see two Western concerns at odds: equality and individualism. As is often the case, one's perspective is influenced by social status. Those lowest in society live with considerably less control over their economics, receive less legal representation, and are held captive through servitude or relationship status, and therefore are often less resistant to the idea of doing magical work to control those who control them. People who are more privileged experience a world in which others exert less control over them, and they have more luxury to entertain their ethical biases.

What it means to influence another person, and what the mechanism for achieving compliance consists of, varies. While there are some who believe that a person can be made into another's obedient slave through magical means, others disbelieve that a person can have their will manipulated magically—tempted perhaps, but not fully controlled. Some therefore consider influencing work to be more of a nudge than an act against consent. Just as one might pray that God persuade a prodigal child to abandon their reckless ways and return home, prayer in the form of ritual action is believed to encourage divine intervention such as may influence another's thoughts, feelings, and resulting behavior. According to such a mindset, the effectiveness of any influencing work is seen as an affirmation of divine will and therefore is morally sound. When discussing spells with another worker, it is always important to understand their worldview before judging the type of work you perceive them to be doing.

In this chapter we will look at tricks for bringing others under your influence, with a focus on personal concerns and container spells. Such work is foundational for various spells, including those seeking more intimate relationships. For the sake of focus, we will suss out work that aims to alter the emotions of another toward you in an intimate manner, namely spells for sex and love. It is one thing to bewitch a meter maid to avoid a parking ticket and quite another to bewitch a crush to fall madly in love with you, or a parent to acknowledge you as their child, or a prodigal child to return home to you. Humans want to be desired and loved, and sometimes want those feelings from a specific person. Our sense of self-worth is tied to our ability to gain another's love through the merit of who we are, not how many pins we can poke into the heart of a doll. This subject will be addressed more thoroughly in chapter 8 when we explore love magic. For now, our focus is on those people who would compromise your autonomy in such spheres as governance (police and judges), economics (bosses and bankers), and associates (coworkers and neighbors).

Popular Formulas for Influencing Work

Differences are seen in the variety of formulas for influencing work, each of which is understood to exert its power differently. Popular formulas for influence go by many names, including the following.

Bend Over

This formula is especially useful for getting others to reverse their prior decisions and to get them to do your work for you. Sometimes called Essence of Bend Over, the name hints at its earlier formulation as a cologne. It is especially favored by domestic workers eager to see their employers do the bending over to scrub floors and toilets.

Boss Fix

This formula is for fixing problems with your boss, in whatever manner you specify, although it often involves getting them on your good side.

....

BOSS FIX HERB BLEND

- Galangal root
- Pipe tobacco
- Patchouli

These can be ground together with a mortar and pestle, and the blend hidden somewhere near your boss, such as with a plant in their office or behind the headboard of their bed, depending on what you have access to. While this blend may be burned as an incense, the smell of pipe tobacco is not as common as it once was, and so it serves less as a sneaky trick.

Commanding

This formula gives you the authority to direct someone's behavior, to tell them exactly what you want them to do and have them do it. Similar formulas include Do as I Say.

Compel

This formula urges another to take certain actions, bringing them around to your way of thinking.

Control

This formula seeks to leash someone. It is restrictive.

....

CONTROLLING TEA

- Bergamot leaf
- Calamus root
- Licorice root

Court Case

In regard to influencing work this formula is used to target lawyers, judges, juries, and anyone involved in a litigation. In a manner not targeting individuals, Court Case works to bring a favorable outcome to your case by whatever means is most effective.

Dominate

Variations of this formula include I Dominate My Man and I Dominate My Woman, which have the familiar characteristics of Commanding but often with a sexual connotation that involves the desire for the target to be sexually submissive.

Follow Me

Variations of this formula include Follow Me Boy and Follow Me Girl and are a bit passive-aggressive in my experience, manipulating a lover into making a show of being sensitive to your needs. The emphasis is on the person working to prove that they belong in your lap, like a good lap dog.

Stop Gossip

This formula is used to control another's tongue, specifically to keep them from spreading rumors about you. An alternative formula is Speak No Evil.

Additionally, there are many formulas whose goal is love, reconciliation, marriage, and fidelity, whereby influence plays a part in securing the desired condition. Since influence is just a particular element in their overall methodology, I will save these formulas for later chapters.

Such products may include several of the same ingredients to achieve their goal, but the intention of whoever makes the formula, and that of whoever deploys it, informs its operation. This is why it is important to form succinct affirmations or recite specific psalms—not because the magic is solely a result of your will, but rather because the spirits your practice conjures need strict direction.

When we discuss influencing work in the context of Conjure, we are generally talking about influencing people rather than situations, although some workers will target a situation by personifying it and using influencing products to manipulate it. This allows practitioners who are opposed to influencing people to utilize the wealth of formulas and practices that are available. For instance, Run Devil Run, which aims to chase away whatever is bedeviling you, may be used in work aiming to get rid of a malicious person, but it can also target abstract devils such as addiction, indecision, and bad luck. By naming such things as devils, they can be targeted and sent running. There are many ways in which you can treat a condition as a person, forcing it into a context in which you can better influence it.

Personal Concerns

An item that contains a person's biological matter or has come in physical contact with them is known as a *personal concern*. These items adhere to the law of contagion introduced earlier. The term personal concern is also applied to items that have captured something of a person, such as an image in a photograph, their written name, or their voice captured in a knot. A personal concern need not possess a person's DNA, although many workers prefer that.

The personal concern used in a spell often works best when it corresponds with the type of work being done on the person. For example, if you wished to make a man impotent, you would want personal concerns associated with his penis, such as pubic hair, underwear, or a condom he has owned (all the better if he has worn it, though one from his wallet or dresser drawer will do). However, if you were trying to do a spell to help him concentrate for his college midterms, then pubic hair would be less appropriate, and would most likely cause him to focus on sex and distract him from his tests. Some personal concerns are better suited to certain types of work than others. With this in mind I have compiled the following list of personal concerns according to which area of the body they are associated with and, by extension, what type of work they are best suited for.

Feet

Personal concerns related to the feet are often used for controlling jobs, and include foot-track dirt, shoes and laces, insoles, socks and stockings, toe rings, anklets, foot bath water, skin, toenails, and toe hair.

Sex (Male)

Personal concerns associated with the male sex are often used for arousing or limiting sexual activity, and include semen, smegma, pubic hair, urine, a worn condom, a cock ring, piercings, underwear, a photo of the man's penis, and the measurement of his penis.

Sex (Female)

Personal concerns related to the female sex are also used for arousing or limiting sexual activity, and include vaginal secretions, menstrual blood, tampons or pads, urine, a diaphragm, used sexual devices, jewelry, underwear, a photo of the woman's vagina, and the measurement of her vagina.

Buttocks

Personal concerns associated with the buttocks are often used for cursing (except when the butt is of erotic interest), and include excrement, hair, used sexual devices, and underwear.

Breast

For men, a bit of chest hair is nearest to the heart and is related to love. For women, a bra relates to the heart, to nurturing, and to sexuality for some.

Clothing

Again, we see what area of the body these correspond to and can be used to act upon. For example, underwear relates to sex, as it is hidden and is closest to the body.

In addition, there are a number of useful personal effects, such as a person's handwriting, glasses, rings, wallets, etc.

Obviously some personal items are easier to collect than others. There are many sneaky ways to procure certain items, and to learn these I encourage readers to make contact with other workers within magical communities where such discussions often take place. (Some folks love to talk about how devious they can be!)

Make certain that what you are collecting actually belongs to the person you are targeting. If you are plucking hair from someone's drain, be sure that it actually is theirs, and not some innocent family member's. It is good not to rely on a personal concern alone but to also name the person and picture them in your mind's eye when using the item. That hair extension you stole will have some of its wearer's energy on it, but if it is natural then it may contain the essence of whoever sold it to the wig manufacturer. This is one of the reasons why I call upon Spirit in my work: to guide my magic and act only in a manner that is justified, as well as to ensure that my spell has not been thrown at some poor woman in a distant land whose income relies on having to sell her hair.

Container Spells

A container spell utilizes some type of receptacle, be it a box, pouch, bottle, or the like, to contain the magical items that have been selected to work toward the magical goal. Many examples can be given, such as a paper envelope containing herbs, prayer papers, or other curios. Another option is a cowrie shell, into which small objects such as herbs, dirt, or tiny slips of paper can be placed and then sealed in using wax. The thimble spell described in chapter 6 is considered a container spell. Certain containers are more in line with certain goals, such as using an empty perfume bottle for a love or attraction spell or an old ipecac bottle for cursing.

A witch bottle, mojo bag, conjure ball, jack ball, mirror box, and stuffed beef tongue are all examples of container spells.

The ability to contain a person or situation within a vessel places them in your control, allowing you to better restrict and influence them, which is relevant to our topic of influence spells.

Besides simply holding the objects related to your spell, the container itself can be manipulated, altered, or adorned to amplify its power. Painted bottle spells not only are effective but can be beautiful as well. Some are elaborately painted, depicting people, saints, or symbols that pertain to a magical goal. Sometimes the bottle is painted opaque, leaving only a window to see the contents inside. Some bottle spells are meant to be shaken regularly to activate or agitate the contents, such as with an Inflammatory Confusion bottle spell, in which herbs and curio (such as black mustard seed and vinegar) are added to a bottle along with the target's personal concerns. Once sealed, the bottle is shaken each day to rile up the target of the spell, bringing about the desired state of confusion in the target. As with all spells in Conjure, bottle spells are deployed and disposed of according to their goal.

Witch Bottles

Perhaps the most well-known bottle spell is the witch bottle. Relics of these can be found in England from the Elizabethan era and in North America dating back to colonial times. They are usually found hidden within walls or beneath fireplaces or else buried on one's property. Witch bottles are created for protection and are typically filled with sharp and distressing items. The items included in the following witch bottle spell are typical.

....

HARMLESS WITCH BOTTLE

We will take the notion of a classic witch bottle and the protection it provides, and apply it to someone who may have an issue with self-harm. While psychiatric treatment is key to helping such individuals, we can apply magic while at the same time encouraging them to get medical help. Included in this witch bottle are the following items:

- 12 pins
- 12 thorns from a hawthorn
- Spanish moss
- 2 aspirin
- Hair from the target's head

If this spell can be deployed near where the target lives, all the better. Keep in mind that such bottles need not be large. If placing it on their property will not work, then bury it at a crossroads.

Bottles on their own are sometimes used for protective purposes, as is the case with bottle trees. Bottles are hung from trees or skewered onto dead branches. The belief is that these bottles trap bad spirits, which are eliminated with the rising sun. While any type of bottle can be used, blue bottles (reminiscent of the haint blue color used to protect doors and porch ceilings) are the most popular.

Mojo Hands

Mojo hands go by a variety of names, such as conjure bag, jomo, nation sack, root bag, toby, and others. Though many cultures share the concept of a bag filled with meaningful items and carried for magical purposes, the term *mojo* is African-American, and similar items are found throughout Africa and the Caribbean, known by such names as *gris-gris* and *wanga*. Whether to increase one's spiritual development, repel or protect oneself from negative conditions, or draw love, health, or prosperity, a mojo bag serves as a simple method of formalizing a spell, with the added benefit of creating a physical object that can be carried or worn to help maintain its magical presence. The word *hand* emphasizes the ability of the mojo to reach beyond the limitations of its bag and grasp that which it has been made to attract or threaten. *Hand* also carries the connotation of a gambler's hand of cards. Human finger bones, lucky hand root, and five-finger grass, all of which may be found in a mojo, may also have led to the term *hand*.

The most common material for a mojo bag is red flannel, sometimes referred to a *southern style*. Some will say that this is because red is the color of blood and life force. Flannel is a natural cloth, and as such is thought to be more conducive to magic than, say, an acrylic blend. While these may be elegant explanations, the likely reason is more practical, as historically red cotton flannel was an inexpensive and widely used fabric. Any good worker can utilize whatever is close at hand to achieve results. Contemporary workers commonly use various colored bags, such as green for money-drawing mojos, black for protective mojos, and so forth according to color associations.

Among workers who sew, it is common to find bags sewn up the sides, with the top folded and sewn around string that serves to draw the bag closed and tie it shut. This variety is often seen in old curio catalogues. Those who do not sew tend to favor taking a square of fabric about 4 inches by 4 inches, placing the items in the center, and then cinching the fabric at the top and tying it shut with string. That is how mine are fashioned.

Just as a mojo is more than what type of fabric holds it together, it is also more than the individual objects placed inside. Each individual object is prayed over in order to align its spirit with the overall goal of the work. When used in conjunction with prayer, each herb, root, oil, paper, bone, stone, and other curio unite in purpose, together serving as the organs of a body. Combined with the will of the Conjure doctor, a mojo hand becomes a potent magical force to help bend the fates in our favor. Once constructed, a mojo is considered to be a living being.

DOMINANT HAND MOJO

This mojo is made to dominate those around you, to lend you confidence and cause others to defer to you. It includes the following items:

- Fingernail clippings from the pointer finger of your dominant hand
- High John the Conqueror root
- Licorice root
- Calamus root
- Tiger's eye stone
- From *The Key of Solomon the King* include the following seals: the First Pentacle of Saturn, the Fourth Pentacle of Saturn, and the Seventh Pentacle of Saturn.

Once your bag has been assembled, you will choose a name for it. Since it is an extension of the maker, some folks like to include their own name. So if your name is Joe, you might call it something like *Little Joe*, *Joe's Mighty Hand*, or *Joe's Command*.

Take a few deep breaths, feeling your life force build within you. Then blow into the bag, saying its name as you exhale. Do this a total of nine times, pulling it tightly closed at the end of your last exhale.

Light a purple candle and, holding the bag by its string, far enough above the flame to prevent it from catching on fire, let it hang there while you express the function it has been created for. Considering what we learned about affirmations in chapter 4, address your mojo by name, then affirm such things as *I dominate my enemies / I command the room / I control others / I am obeyed / I am in charge.*

When your bag begins to swing, it is said to be dancing, a sign it has awakened and become animated with life.

After it has danced for just a short while, wet the bag with whiskey. (Do this at a responsible distance from the candle to avoid a fire.) Whiskey in this instance is used to give the mojo energy, and the act itself is referred to as *feeding* your mojo. This is done in a quincunx pattern, a five-spot on a die. You can hold the bag up to the mouth of the whiskey bottle and tip the bottle briefly, in this way wetting all five points. I start at the upper right and move clockwise, ending in the center.

I suggest feeding the bag weekly—or more often if you prefer—giving it whiskey in this manner, or cologne or oil instead. If using an oil, choose one whose name serves your goal, such as those mentioned earlier in this chapter. The drawback to oils is that they do not evaporate in whiskey or cologne like alcohol does, and so over time your mojo will be soaked in oil and become too messy to carry around. I prefer to feed my mojo with Hoyt's cologne.

Beyond the metaphysical purpose of giving your mojo such libations, feeding it guarantees that it will stay active and not forgotten in the back of a drawer. While there are certain spells that are deployed and then walked away from (such as witch bottles), others die if unattended, and your power dies with them. It is much better to have just a few well-cared-for charm allies than it is to have items forgotten in pockets and beneath beds, where in their final days they command nothing but lint and dust bunnies.

Your mojo will get messy over time no matter what you anoint it with, and will eventually deteriorate beyond use. I've never had one last much longer than a year, although I am told I am rough on stuff, which the state of my shoes and clothes confirms.

It is a common magical practice never to allow anyone to see, and especially never to touch, your mojo. For this reason they are often kept out of sight, hidden discreetly beneath undergarments. Should such a mojo be tainted by the handling of another, it is customary to ritually deconstruct it, in which case you should open it carefully to reveal its contents, contemplating what each is for. All soft herbs should be buried or tossed into a fire or moving water, along with the bag itself. If you have a relationship with your compost heap, such that you recognize its work as being sacred, then decomposable items can be placed there and aid the cycle of nature. Any larger roots or curios may be washed with Florida Water and repurposed.

Conjure Balls

If you had candles burning in your home as a child, as we always did around the holidays, chances are you poked your finger in the wax to coat your fingertip. It would harden, and could then be popped off and rolled into a tiny ball, perhaps freeing your fingertips to then menace a bowl of pitted olives. A conjure ball is simply a ball of wax within which reside ingredients for a spell. It can be any size, the width of a quarter or a golf ball being common.

Conjure balls are deployed in a number of ways, though they are rarely carried on one's person, as their wax is prone to melting. They can be buried in the yard or added to fuel a fire. They can also be thrown onto your roof, preferably on a hot day so that they melt. When throwing a conjure ball on your rooftop, it is good to go small, about the size of a quarter, and to have it be flatter than a ball so that it does not simply roll off the roof. This can be a great way to enact a cleansing or blessing on your home. Additionally, while I do not condone acts of property damage, this technique has a history of being used for controlling and cursing work. Having a spell deployed above a person's head works particularly well for influencing them, as positions above a person are ideal for dominance. One might imagine that such a conjure ball would include a mixture of powdered herbs and perhaps the ash of a petition paper.

CONJURE BALL TO INFLUENCE SOMEONE

- *½ ounce wax:* We will be making a conjure ball about two inches in diameter. I find that if I have a seven-day vigil candle burning (and I always have several), and I pour out some of the wax, I often have the needed amount. For influencing work, wax from a purple candle is ideal, as purple is the color most commonly associated with this type of job. Some waxes work better than others, depending on their density. Lacking a vigil candle, you could cut a chunk off a taper candle and melt it. There are several ways to accomplish this. A double boiler works but is larger than what you need for this task. If you are in the habit of burning essential oils, it may be that your oil burner will work to melt this wax. Most ceramic oil burners that are heated with a tealight candle work fine for this, and there are some burners that are especially made to heat scented wax disks, which can be used as well, provided their scent and color do not detract from the work being done.

- *Work surface:* I like to use a white plate upon which I have placed a sheet of wax paper, and pour the melted wax onto that.

- *Controlling Tea blend:* This recipe is from earlier in this chapter. Of course, instead of adding these ingredients to hot water, you will be putting them on top of your wax. You could grind the ingredients into a powder, or it might be easier to use a few chips from each of the three ingredients.

Sprinkle the powder or chips onto the puddle of wax. Do so in a manner that spreads the herbs across the surface so they will blend more easily into the wax, as a clump of herb matter in the center makes for a less stable conjure ball.

The wax shouldn't be too hot to handle, so lift the corners of the wax paper so the contents are weighted in the center. When the wax has cooled enough to be handled but not to the extent that it has hardened, pinch it into a compact shape, then roll it between your hands, compressing it gently with your palms, until it is the shape you need.

Deploy your conjure ball someplace above the target to control their head.

About Jack Balls

A jack ball (sometimes called a luck ball) resembles a small red ball, similar in look to that used in a game of jacks though with the addition of a tail, from which it may dangle to be used as a pendulum. Much like a mojo hand, a jack ball contains personal concerns along with herbs and curios that are aligned toward a magical goal. Here are the steps for making one, beginning with a list of what you will need.

. . . .

JACK BALL

- Strip of paper
- Pen, pencil, or other writing instrument
- Urine
- Melted wax, about ½ ounce worth
- Hair
- Red thread, such as embroidery or crocheting thread (I find that yarn is too thick)
- Needle: a good long one with an eyehole large enough to threaded

Begin by creating a name paper, using the name of the person the jack ball is being made for—in this instance, you. (We will discuss how to make a jack ball to control someone else at the end of this section.) Write your name on the paper. This paper ought to be small, like the size of one in a fortune cookie.

Next, urinate on your name paper. You wanted to practice Conjure. Well, this is how it's done.

For the next step, you will work with the melted wax in the same way you did with conjure balls, adding your name paper and hair to the wax and working it into a ball about the size of a quarter. Don't worry if your name paper disintegrates as you are rolling it in the wax, as its purpose and potency will remain intact.

You could also add herbs to this as well, or even a piece of lodestone if you have one that is small enough. Some folks prefer using fingernail clippings or other small personal concerns.

Next, begin wrapping the thread around the wax. Rather than cutting a specific length of thread, I just give myself some slack to work with and keep the thread attached to the spool. It's good to do this when the wax is still a bit malleable, so that the thread digs into the wax slightly. Continue wrapping it while turning it, overlapping threads, until the wax is completely covered with thread.

At this point I judge how much thread I may need to finish the task and then cut it from the spool. About three feet is usually good to work with, and I often end up trimming a bit of that at the end.

Thread the needle, and use the needle to dig under the strings wound around the wax. This will help the thread remain secure. You needn't dig in far enough to pierce the wax, just enough to go under and over the existing threads. Do this a few times at different spots until the ball feels secure. Doing this too tightly will squish and distort your sphere; however, it shouldn't be too loose either.

Lastly, remove the needle, and you should have a good length of string remaining. Since this ball will be used as a pendulum, you will want a decent length for it to hang. You can cut the end at the desired length, knot its end, and be done. Or, as I prefer, you can knot the end of the thread at the point where the thread emerges from the ball. This creates a cord that you can slip around your neck if you choose to wear the jack ball. I like mine to hang so that I can hold it in my armpit. Decide how low you want your ball to hang before finalizing the knot.

Some folks tie off the ball after it has been stitched tight, cut off the excess thread, and then use another length of thread with the needle to tie on a cord. There is no rule stating that the jack ball must be made with one continuous length of thread.

Naming the jack ball, just as we saw with mojo hands, is important. A jack that is an extension of you should be named appropriately, and one made to influence someone else should be named after them. As with the mojo hand, your jack ball will need to be fed often, such as with whiskey, cologne, or oil. You can feed it with urine as well, which is more often the case when it is being engaged for the purpose of gambling, much as a man has his female companion pee on his hands before hitting the casino.

Additionally, you could add some herbs, though too many ingredients will make the ball too big. Don't worry if it's not the exact size of a classic rubber ball from the game of jacks; it can be a bit smaller or larger.

Unlike other container spells, a jack ball is an active tool. Like a pendulum, the ball can be swung by its tail in order to do divination, usually in the form of a yes-no question. A jack ball goes a step further than simple dowsing, however. It can be deliberately swung in certain ways so as to conjure forth energies and events. For example, to draw something toward you, you might make prayers while swinging your jack ball to and fro, focusing strongly on the inward swing of the ball and concentrating or vocalizing the desired condition you wish to draw to you with each swing. For example, you might say *Money, come to me* each time it swings toward you. Or to repel a thing the reverse would be employed, such as by saying *Trouble, move away from me.*

The jack ball is a personal representation of the practitioner and as such should be treated with great respect. Since it contains personal concerns, there is a very real connection between the person and the magical object. The ball is considered to be synonymous with its namesake, so certain things may be done to it in order to influence the person it represents. Because of this, it is vital to keep it away from others, lest they use it against you.

Jack Ball Trick to Influence Someone

You can make a jack ball from the personal concerns of another to influence them. Write the person's name on the paper, or better still get their signature somehow. Douse the paper in your urine, since this implies dominance over them. Using their hair, their nail clippings, their chewed gum, or any personal concern small enough to create a jack ball around, construct the ball in the same way as just described. Because jack balls can be manipulated on their string, they serve as a way of keeping someone leashed. Pulling another's jack ball toward you serves well for such things as getting a lover to return. Swinging it counterclockwise can influence someone to reverse their decision.

Dolls

Dolls are used in folk magic to represent a person who is the object of a spell. According to the principle of sympathetic magic, it is believed that any action affecting the doll will similarly influence the object it represents.

The term *doll baby* is most prominent among practitioners of Hoodoo, where there is a tradition of acquiring manufactured dolls, such as those that are marketed to children and can be purchased cheaply at dime stores and elsewhere. These may be made of ceramic, though plastic is more common nowadays. Often their heads or limbs can be removed and their insides stuffed with personal concerns taken from their target, along with other curios that lend power to controlling work, such as licorice root. If the goal is to cause the target to fall in love or to experience a curse, then curios related to those endeavors will be added. The degree to which their physical attributes resemble the person being worked upon varies. Some try to match eye, hair, and skin color, while others are less concerned about that, or else paint the doll to match accordingly.

Poppets and Voodoo dolls are similar to doll babies, though most often these refer to dolls crafted by the practitioner. These can be fashioned from a variety of substances such as wax, cloth, or clay, or even carved out of fruits, vegetables, and roots. As with doll babies, these are stuffed with personal concerns and relevant curios. Some workers have their own peculiar tricks for crafting a doll, such as placing magnets inside its hands, or a graduation hat tassel in its head, or a rose quartz heart in its chest.

The presence of personal concerns gives the doll life force. Dolls are given the name of their target, sometimes in an act symbolic of a christening. This may be done through the use of prayer and holy water, though given that such an act places a blessing on the doll, this may be avoided if the end goal seeks to curse the person. My training curriculum called *A Course in Modern Conjure* suggests using the following words to name a doll for influencing work:

Into this form I conjure thee,
(Name the person, and repeat three times).
Your body is this body.
Your spirit herein resides.
As I hold you in my grip, you are subject to my will.

If you were creating a doll for more benevolent purposes—say, for healing—then your verbiage would vary.

In addition to naming the doll, methods for bringing it to life are common, such as giving it breath. Some folks blow on it, or into it, or in the region of its mouth. I prefer not to give my own breath if it is meant to represent someone else. A better option is to pass the doll through smoke as a representation of breath. You can choose smoke from a source aligned with your work, such as sulfur for a doll destined to be cursed, or tobacco for a boss to be dominated.

Because I like to sew my own felt poppets, my final act in crafting the doll is to sew through its stomach to form a belly button. As it is tied and severed, I become aware of how this act mimics that of a child's umbilicus being cut at birth. I'm also fond of giving the doll a spank on the butt like a newborn.

Once any rituals related to the doll's activation and association with its namesake are complete, it can then be manipulated accordingly. When it comes to sticking it with pins, traditions differ. We are all familiar with the idea of sticking a doll with pins to cause someone pain, but that is not always the goal, as pins are also used to direct positive energy. Pins of this nature are often more decorative, with fancy hairpins being popular. For someone undergoing treatment for a hip injury, a pin may be placed in that area to send healing to it. One is reminded of acupuncture. Some conceptualize this as being something like an antenna, absorbing waves of positive energy sent to it through prayer. Like cupid's arrow, a pin might pierce the area of the heart to stimulate love.

Mirror Box

Dolls are frequently used in mirror boxes as a way to bind someone.

The mirror box itself is so called because its interior is lined with shards of mirror glass or other reflective material. The concept is that a troublemaker can be contained therein, their negativity reflected back on them. The box can be any size or shape, though small coffin-shaped boxes are favored. Some consider the reflective surface of aluminum foil to serve well enough, while others will break apart a mirror and glue the pieces inside the box. A prohibition I have heard states that a mirror used for such a purpose should never have contained your reflection. This can make things tricky, as you will need to avoid catching your image in it when you purchase it from the store, smash it, and glue its shards inside the box, but such an arduous task can enhance the spell. To keep your hands from being reflected, you should wear gloves, which given that you are handling glass is a good idea anyway.

Bury the mirror box in a graveyard if you wish the person to be dead to you, or keep it in your freezer to immobilize them.

....

Beef Tongue to Stop Gossip

Another spell that utilizes your freezer is the infamous *beef tongue spell*, in which a beef tongue is sliced open and filled with a name paper and the personal concerns of its target. For this, something that has had contact with the person's mouth would be best, such as a straw, a piece of chewed gum, a cigarette butt, and so forth. Peppers are commonly added, the idea being that the tongue of the gossiper will be set on fire. Alum, vinegar, and controlling herbs are popular additions as well. The tongue is sewn shut after being stuffed. Some accounts call for pins to be pierced into the tongue. It is then wrapped up, in plastic wrap or a brown paper bag (freezer burn would be a desirable result), and placed somewhere in the freezer where it is least likely to be disturbed. It can be kept for as long as the gossiper remains a concern.

Whether you use a person's personal concerns to heal or control them is up to you. When I do work on behalf of my clients, I include a personal concern that they have willingly given me. I feel this greatly helps me connect with them, and gives their scent to the spirits that I conjure so that they may be found at a distance.

ᴄᴇ VIII ᶕᴐ
The Keys to Scent:
Unlocking Sexual Enticement

IT'S EASY FOR HER to sneak out of bed now that he's spent and snoring, but first she reaches for the length of red yarn she hid beneath the pillow and takes a measurement of his penis. Off to the bathroom, she is ready to complete her nation sack. Already it is filled with nine dimes, a Queen Elizabeth root, and a paper with his name written on it. She cuts the yarn to the size she measured and then coats it with his semen, which she secreted beneath her fingernail. She calls out to him, and as he hollers back she ties the knot. "Forget it," she replies, as she places his measure in her sack and cinches it closed. His manhood belongs to her now. She will caress the sack, kept hidden near her hip, when she wants him to become turgid for her and will squeeze it when his lust needs to be tamped down.

The nation sack, other times known as a *nature sack*, is a special mojo for women to use on their men. Its mechanics recall the last chapter's lessons, but its purpose has everything to do with sex.

Sex, whether it is exalted by poets as proof of God's love, condemned by churches as the temptation of the Devil, or paraded on television to sell products and drive economies, is a primal human concern. Sex magic ranges from practical needs, such as improving appetite, increasing potency, and securing sexual partners, to the more esoteric, whereby sex serves as a bridge to understanding death, connecting with the divine, and producing energy to fuel metaphysical goals. Sex magic is a means for fulfilling both our physical and our spiritual desires.

Early trailblazers in the development of sex magic include Dr. Paschal Beverly Randolph (1825–1875). Randolph fits well with our subject matter, being a free man of color who lived at times in New York, New Orleans, and San Francisco. A Spiritualist medium and Rosicrucian, Randolph had knowledge of Hoodoo and was a major contributor to the larger field of ceremonial occultism. He authored various works on the subject of sex magic, his most influential being *Eulis! The History of Love*, published in 1874.

While there are various techniques and applications explored throughout *Eulis!* and Randolph's companion works, the most influential teaching stressed that a man and woman through their sexual congress are able to access higher dimensions of divinity. By asserting one's will while in such a state, a magical intention can be expressed to higher spirits who aid in producing change. Though esoteric in approach, Randolph's works claimed such magic could manifest the sort of everyday desires that folk magic tends to be most interested in, such as keeping a partner sexually faithful, increasing wealth, and even creating amulets.

To many modern readers, some of Randolph's assertions seem outdated, especially his sole focus on heterosexual coupling. Influenced by the concepts of magnetism and polarity popularized by Franz Mesmer, Randolph viewed males as holding a positive electromagnetic charge and females the opposite, the act of sex being an interchange of electrical currents. This emphasis on gender polarity is stressed in several branches of magic. Many Wiccans strive to balance both masculine and feminine energies in their magic in order to honor both God and Goddess. Many North American folk traditions favor cross-gender practices, as we have seen with how spoken word spells are often taught only to a person of the opposite gender. To Randolph's credit, unlike other writers on the subject, he stressed the importance of both the male and the female orgasm.

Early sexual mystics adopted principles they claimed were derived from the Hindu practice of Tantra, most notably the idea that a man's ejaculation was to be avoided lest it further trap him in the cycle of rebirth and deplete his vital energy. Female sexuality was seldom addressed, though this was corrected with the work of Dr. Alice Bunker Stockham, author of *Tokology* (1883) and *Karezza* (1896), Karezza being the name she used to identify her system of sexual practice. Bunker encouraged female orgasms, while believing male ejaculation should be contained and limited to consensual spousal congress. Both genders were said to be empowered through sexual activity that remains beneath the threshold of orgasm. Stockham was the first to remove much of the mysticism and cultural trappings of Tantra, and explore its scientific and medicinal value. Another female sexual mystic was Ida Craddock, author of many books including *Heavenly Bridegrooms* (1918) and *Psychic Wedlock* (1899), who went so far as to encourage having sexual relationships with non-human entities, such as the angel Soph, whom she declared was her paramour. *Psychic Wedlock* describes a three-degree system of initiation into the sexual mysteries leading to a sacred communion with deity.

The concept of building, storing, and releasing *sexual energy* to be directed toward a magical goal is at the core of most methodologies of sex magic. Sexual energy is often described in terms of it being an abstract force, one that although invisible is undeniably felt. Procreation depends on it, and so sexual energy sustains all life. It is a creative force sought by artists and magicians alike. This power is generated through arousal and often released through climax, or else stored by abstaining from orgasm. Either way, magicians use this energy in various ways, such as to create spirit helpers, to bring objects to life, and to manifest their focused will.

The difficulty comes when you endeavor to impose your will on this energy. At that time, you are called upon to concentrate on something other than the sex act you are currently indulging in, which often interferes with your ability to orgasm. This is where a technique suggested by Austin Osman Spare becomes important, for he suggests that you craft your desire into a sigil that represents the condition you wish to manifest, and hold that in your mind's eye throughout the orgasm.

The folk magic approach to sex magic places less of a demand on one's mental faculties and isn't afraid to be dirty. Participants are free to fully indulge in sexual acts, unencumbered by internal chants or other feats of mental focus. It is the movement of the bed that rubs together the coon bones beneath the mattress, and the fluids of intercourse that will later be rubbed on them.

The personal concerns particular to sex magic contain bodily excretions, which include bath water, breast milk, menstrual blood, pubic hair, semen, smegma, spittle, sweat, urine, and vaginal discharge. Undergarments are useful as well, along with almost anything that has been used in a sexually fetishizing way. The practice of hiding such personal concerns in food to be consumed by a targeted individual is off-putting to some, though it has a long and well-documented history.

Scent in the form of colognes and oils plays a key role in Conjure's approach to sex magic. Here are some of the blends known to be associated with sexual concerns.

Popular Formulas for Sex

The following formulas all address various ways of enticing prospective sexual partners, getting them to succumb to your wiles, spicing things up, and regulating sexual promiscuity.

To Get Attention

Glamor and notoriety constitute a type of magic concerned with getting attention and projecting a desired image of oneself. Dominating the room with an intoxicating scent is one strategy to accomplish this.

GLAMOR OIL

- 1 part clove
- 2 parts lavender
- 1 part sandalwood
- 1 part vanilla

Kiss Me Now: Many of the blends used to get sex are also used for love and romance. It you want your partner to kiss your neck, then rub a drop there, and if you want the space between your legs to get attention, then you may wish to rub some close to that area or on the garment that is closest to it. Be aware that few oil blends are suitable for genital areas; indeed, many formulas that intend to spice things up or add heat include things like cinnamon, which you wouldn't want anywhere near your more sensitive areas.

Look Me Over: This formula is suited for the work of standing out and being attractive, whether that be physically, mentally, or professionally.

LOOK ME OVER OIL

Combine the following essential oils:

- 1 part honeysuckle
- 1 part neroli
- 1 part jasmine

To Seal the Deal

Bewitching: This formula fulfills the wish of being able to seduce another so thoroughly that they become your willing sex slave.

Cleo May: The purpose of Cleo May is to attract clients to sex workers, encourage generous payments, and aid in the type of protection needed in a profession too often prone to violence.

CLEO MAY OIL

Combine the following essential or synthetic oils:

- 1 part bergamot
- 1 part cinnamon
- 1 part myrrh
- 2 parts jasmine
- 2 parts neroli

You may wish to give your finished product some color. Pink works wonderfully for Cleo May. This can be achieved naturally by adding alkanet chips to the oil, then straining once it turns the desired color. For Cleo May the presence of alkanet serves as a protective element, along with the myrrh. Other items you might add include jezebel root, sugar, lodestones, and orris root.

Desire Me: Also called Flame of Desire, this formula is used to arouse another so that they desire you. It can also be used to induce romance, although the emphasis is less on love than desire.

....

Desire Me Oil

Combine the following essential oils:

- 1 part cardamom
- 1 part ginger
- 2 parts patchouli
- 2 parts sandalwood
- 2 parts ylang-ylang

The formulas Cleopatra and Jezebel can be used similarly, and aside from helping get the bills paid, they can be used by ladies to ensure good times in the sack.

To Heat Things Up

Goona Goona: Goona Goona first appeared on the market in the 1930s, when it became a popular slang term for sex. This arose from the 1932 sexploitation film *Goona-Goona: An Authentic Melodrama of the Isle of Bali*, which relied on stock footage of topless Balinese women. The racism of that period deemed the exhibition of nudity acceptable when demonstrated by native peoples. The film was advertised as featuring "witchcraft, sorcery, and the sensuous charms of savage sirens." The plot of the film involves a magical powder that orchestrates a sexual act, so it seems obvious that someone would try to make such a thing.

Such products had become popular by the time they were seen in Anna Riva's *Golden Secrets of Mystic Oils* in 1978 as well as volume 1 of Herman Slater's *The Magickal Formulary* in 1981. We see that both of these publications describe Goona Goona as being used to *create an atmosphere of trust and understanding*—a far cry from the inspiration that is its namesake. Most published recipes for Goona Goona are floral and spicy, that spiciness suggestive of its true purpose for seduction and sex. To avoid confusion, I have named the product I make for my Modern Conjure brand Lusty Goona Goona, so that its intention is understood. While the recipe I use for my brand is proprietary, it features some of the more popular ingredients found in various published recipes.

GOONA GOONA OIL

For this recipe you can choose to work with either essential or synthetic oils, or a blend of both. Combine the following:

- 2 parts rose bouquet
- 1 part ylang-ylang
- 1 part allspice
- 1 part juniper
- 2 parts patchouli

Q: This oil was popularized by Herman Slater (1935–1992), who crafted it for his clientele of homosexual men to get them laid. The *Q* stands for *Queer*, a term for homosexual men. This term was used by some to rebelliously self-identify and by others to degrade. The reason why Slater likely named it Q rather than Queer had to do with the need for homosexual men to be secretive, lest they face various forms of persecution. Homosexual acts were often described with euphemisms, such as the phrase *the love that dare not speak its name*. That phrase comes from Lord Alfred Douglas's 1894 poem "Two Loves," which describes the love between two males and was popularized following Oscar Wilde's trial for indecency. Q is in a family of conjure oils blended specifically for gay men that includes many proprietary blends, such as Lavender Love Drops by Lucky Mojo Curio Company and Hot Fucker by Dr. E. Products. According to Slater's own formula, Q oil consists of carnation, myrrh, and peppermint. For those who wish to make this without having to use synthetic oils, the carnation will need to be replaced, or you may use the following essential oil blend to approximate the scent of carnation.

....

CARNATION OIL

Combine the following essential oils:

- ½ part clove
- ½ part lavender
- 2 parts palmarosa
- 1 part jasmine

Satyr: This oil is used to attract sexual attention by both gay and straight men alike. Deep, woodsy, hot, and flirty are all words that could be used to describe a well-rounded Satyr blend. Of the many recipes out there, the following includes some of the more common scented oils.

....

SATYR OIL

Experiment with different amounts of the following oils:

- Cinnamon
- Musk
- Oakmoss
- Patchouli
- Vanilla

As recipes for a good Satyr oil vary according to how many parts of each ingredient are used, I will leave you to experiment with the amounts. By the end of this chapter you should have the know-how to determine which of these ingredients you wish to smell a little or a lot of, how these scents change according to how they are applied, and also what substitutions could be made.

Seventh Heaven: This formula gets a good description from Anna Riva, the professional name of Dorothy Spencer (1922–2003). Her book *Golden Secrets of Mystic Oils* celebrated the use of scented oils in magical work. While that volume contained no recipes, it did give brief descriptions of many popular formulas, leading us to an understanding of what her customers were being encouraged to use such products for. Here is her description of Seventh Heaven: *When used on the body before engaging in sexual relations, it is said to bring satisfaction and gratification never before experienced.*[9]

To Fix Nature

High John the Conqueror Root: This oil is derived by soaking chips of jalapa root in oil until the masculine smell of the root is transferred. This formula is good for things like increasing power and wealth, and is also used to restore a man's nature, as defined in the following listing.

Nature: The term *nature* in regard to a man refers to his sexual potency and ability to achieve and sustain an erection.

Because men, unlike women, are unable to perform sexually if their nature is lacking, there are far more formulas to boost a man's abilities than there are for women. Lucky Mojo Curio Company strikes a balance with two types of massage oil created by the owner, catherine yronwode: Lucky Swastika Penis Oil for the men and Lucky Clover Vulva Oil for the women.

History of Conjure Oils

Magical oils came to be an integral part of North American magic, thanks largely to black skin, Jewish chemists, Prohibition, and an occult trade in magical formulas that were later adopted by many metaphysical and Neopagan practitioners.

There was a time when folks had to fulfill their needs with what grew around them, soaking herbs in whiskey to concoct medicines. As commercial products became more available, they were put to the task of magical work, everything from kerosene to bluestone finding a use. From interviews such as Hyatt's, we learn that older workers used a variety of commercial products, Hoyt's cologne (which Hyatt misinterpreted as *Hearts* cologne) being chief, along with Florida Water and others. That

---

9. Anna Riva, *Golden Secrets of Mystic Oils*, 140.

magical products created solely for the purpose of magic would evolve seems a given, and in places like the Algiers neighborhood of New Orleans we see the rise of essence of Van Van (whose name derives from the French pronunciation for *vervain*, though recipes most often use the more stable essential oil of lemongrass). As the population of North America moved away from the country, and events such as the Great Migration moved once rural African-Americans into urban environments, the needs associated with magic changed, as well as the means by which workers acquired the tools and ingredients for their practice. Pharmacies, which in the South had long catered to the needs of workers, became a major resource, as did stores dedicated to the sale of occult supplies.

The prominence of colognes gave way to oils following Prohibition, when alcohol for perfumery became more difficult to come by and less cost-effective for manufacturers. Scented oils and pomades became more popular, and their applications proved more varied, such as by taking advantage of the growing interest in candle magic in the form of dressing oil. These utilized all manner of oils, essential and synthetic. The use of oils for blessing and anointing was well documented in the Bible (usually olive oil served for this purpose), and therefore these new perfume oils were easily put to spiritual use and perceived to be part of biblical tradition. Oils could be added to certain cosmetics, such as creams, shampoos, shaving soap, etc.

While the use of oils for magic was not unknown—such as Abramelin oil, whose recipe could be found in the medieval grimoire *The Book of Abramelin*—their popularity in American folk magic is the result of merchants, mostly of Ashkenazi Jewish heritage, who catered largely to African-American communities and designed their products to suit the needs of their clientele. Why simply sell plain old pomade when one could sell lucky Van Van pomade? Why not sell a room spray that not only freshens the air but also makes your home more peaceful? Many of these customers were sought out through catalogue distribution, and there are some amazing catalogues full of descriptive artwork and copy that have served to preserve an otherwise largely oral tradition. Suddenly folks were able to purchase their spiritual supplies through mail order, and these same companies supplied wholesale products to candle shops and independent rootworkers, as well as hairdressers who often purchased both beauty supplies and magical ones to sell to their clientele.

Glamor

When you get down to it, humans are rather manipulative animals. Mythology tells us that fallen angels taught humankind magic, along with arts such as cosmetics and perfumery, meant to manipulate the eyes of others and to intoxicate them with scent.

Culturally we live in an ad-driven world, in which every billboard and pop-up is trying to make us want this or that product. We have come not to mind it so much, and are generally proud that we as individuals are enough of our own person not to succumb to such control. If anything, these constant attacks reinforce our belief that we have the will to resist the majority of temptations being broadcast to us. We feel in control. But that is one of the revelations that comes from doing this type of magic: you start to see all the many ways in which your perception of things is an illusion, and how controlled by other people and institutions you truly are.

Glamor is closely associated with acting. Just as an actor steps out on stage embodying a character, you must learn to do the same. This does not mean you must aspire to be a classically trained Shakespearean actor, but you do need to be able to project a crafted image of yourself. Others may inspire you with their wit or style. Consider keeping their quotes and magazine shots in a journal, something to turn to when you may be feeling dull and unattractive. Never be a fake version of some one else, but identify what traits you wish to possess, and find examples of people who express them.

It is important to take a realistic look at yourself. Gauge how your attributes relate to current standards of beauty, or else the standards of a specific person whose attention you seek. Your own standard of beauty may not be in line with the consensus; however, it is important to know what is commonly considered attractive, and where you are in relation to that. Your understanding of yourself may be unrealistically positive or a negative condition of low self-esteem, or you may actually be ugly by most standards. Knowing yourself will help you determine if you have a few attributes you could improve or if you need the entire Pygmalion treatment.

If you are focused on attracting the attention of a single person, be sure to know what they find sexy before getting too involved, emotionally or magically. Also, beware of any baggage associated with what they are turned on by. You may find yourself stuck with a gravelly voice, just like your lover's mother has. Magic is said to take the least resistant path, and sometimes that means that you are the one who gets changed, not them. Such permanent change is not the objective of glamor magic. It's that aura of confidence you carry into a meeting and the sass in your step when entering the club.

Magic Mirror Spell

While too much mirror gazing is narcissistic, it is healthy to see yourself clearly. Procure a hand mirror and wash its surface first with milk, then with fat, and lastly with whiskey.

When the moon is at its fullest, take the mirror outside to catch the moon's reflection.

Gaze into the mirror by candlelight for twelve minutes, seeing your true self.

Close your eyes and imagine yourself with finer attributes. Rub the glass against your forehead and give the mirror a kiss. As your lips pucker and touch the glass, move the mental image you have of yourself into the mirror. With mouth smiling and eyes shining, behold your reflection to see the beauty you are.

The Secrets of Scents

Let us take a look at the role scent plays in gaining attention. Scent by its very nature demands intimacy. Invasive, it gets inside of you. Manipulative, it awakens memories, moods, desires. Its magic has been exploited by religions to elicit visions and quell desires, and by Conjure workers to cast love spells and turn antagonists into advocates.

Aromatherapy utilizes scent for such purposes as sharpening one's focus, improving cognition, elevating one's mood from depression, and lessening anxiety and overstimulation. Although there is a medicinal component to the practice of aromatherapy, the use of such therapy to cure disease lacks scientific oversight and is beyond the scope of this book. Nevertheless, we can take note of the changes in brain function that aroma can inspire, whereby the limbic system governing emotions and memory is influenced through olfaction.

Scent represents the spirit of a thing, and what is strong in scent is therefore believed to be strong in spirit. The smell of jasmine or angel's trumpet on a warm night is so seductive that one can hardly help but breathe deeply of such scents. Woe to the prudish who is courted in such a garden, as the atmosphere is steamy with the spirit of sensual abandon. Alternately, the smell of such things as sulfur and asafoetida curl the nose but serve well to drive away unwanted spirits or send spite to an enemy. A bottle of War Water made with lavender and lemon zest would have less impact when thrown against an adversary's door. Scent is an important component of many types of work.

Given our focus on sex work, consider how certain scents might play together as bedfellows. You may think you know rose, but consider how it would receive a drop of cinnamon. Now there is heat, and a relationship begins to develop, floral and spicy. Vanilla, normally so comforting, so wholesome, when invited to swing with our other scents becomes downright slutty, a bottom note that holds its own while making everything else warmer and sweeter. Those three on their own might compose a good oil for exciting the arousal of your beloved. (Be careful how you use it, as cinnamon will sting skin.) I will leave it here for you to build on, to consider what other scents you might invite to such a bacchanal.

When blending, it is important to consider what note an individual scent is so that you will have an idea of how it may work with others. Notes are described as being top, middle, or bottom. A well-rounded blend contains all three. Expect the top notes to fade away the quickest. Top notes are floral and sharp. Blends that are too top-heavy become unrecognizable after their notes fade and give way to whatever is underneath, unless you have blended only top notes.

Some scents will arouse more of a wrestling match than an eager mingling, dominating the whole affair. (Perhaps that's what you're looking for—no judgment.) It is important to know which scents complement one another and which ones stand alone.

The previous suggestions were for essential oils (though that rose would cost you, its high price determined by the large volume of rose petals it takes to extract an essential oil). Fragrant oils are another option, to work with exclusively or to mix with essentials. In the vernacular of the perfumer, *fragrant* does not equate *synthetic*. Rose fragrant oil may itself be a mixture of essential oils that together mimic the scent of rose. At the same time, an oil labeled as fragrant may indeed be entirely synthetic, a mixture of chemicals combined in a warehouse rather than in nature.

This brings up the contentious subject of synthetic oils and their place in the tradition. If we are approaching this work with the understanding that all the items we work with are possessed of an indwelling spirit whose power we seek to utilize, then we must ask if synthetic scents also contain such spirits. Some adamantly declare the answer to be no, while others insist that even unnatural things have a spiritual essence. Some value the alchemy of creating the smell of a rose from unrelated sources. Your relationship to the elements you are working with will largely dictate your practice.

Personally, I admire a balanced approach. First determine the herbal allies you want to work with, and find a way to include them. A bath mixture might therefore be scented with cinnamon fragrance oil that is safe for skin, yet contain cinnamon chips to engage the spirit of cinnamon. Many recipes also include such things as roots, sugar, and stones, which are added to the oil's container. The 32-ounce glass jar that holds my Chuparosa stock oil, for example, includes the nest of a hummingbird that contains two sugar cubes, and it is from there that I fill the individual bottles that I sell, which themselves contain an herb blend.

For colognes, which we will explore at the end of this chapter, you would not want to add herbs, as the water causes them to deteriorate over time. I make a mild tea with whatever herbs I wish to work with, and later add that when making the cologne. While many prefer to use waters from natural sources such as wells and rivers for their work, I do so only with my personal supplies, as there is too great a risk of contamination for waters that will sit on the shelf for unknown periods of time, despite preservatives. Even with something like our smudging spray, which contains sage and lavender, both of which are astringent, I don't risk it and I use distilled water for all merchandise.

Before committing expensive oils to a project, you are advised to use the perfumer's trick of applying your oils to a strip of paper. Scents change according to their condition, having a certain smell when sniffed from a bottle and another that comes from their interaction with acids and other oils on skin or their warm release from an aromatherapy burner. Different notes burn off at varying rates; typically floral notes are most fleeting, while woodsier smells linger.

Many recognized formulas, such as Van Van, Fast Luck, Fiery Wall of Protection, and others, were originally made by local pharmacists or occult proprietors. Some of these have formulas that can be found in various old drugstore formularies, though changes were common, with chemists or perfumers putting their individual touch on popular formulas and sometimes substituting fragrances for reasons such as accessibility and cost. Many older recipes call for items such as civet (the glandular secretion taken from the civet cat) and ambergris (produced in the digestive tract of sperm whales), which are unattainable and therefore require substitutions. While synthetics may be an option for some, I have never found a commercial version of civet or ambergris that I felt was comparable enough to serve as a substitute. People new to the craft of blending scents for Conjure often worry about the authenticity of a recipe, believing that there is only one absolute formula for any given condition oil, which is a fallacy. At the same time, no one will recognize your attempt at Van Van oil if it smells like sweat and strawberries.

Van Van

Van Van is the most well-known conjure oil, so it is well suited to our topic, although it is not what first comes to mind for acquiring sex. Nevertheless, Anna Riva writes of Van Van, saying that wearing it on one's arms and shoulders attracts interest and love.

Van Van is known for smelling lemony. That citrus scent may come from within a woodsy vetiver or a much stronger lemongrass. A sophisticated blend may include both of these, and then some. Popular recipes employ a variety of other Asian grasses, such as citronella, gingergrass, and palmarosa. Based on its name, many have assumed that Van Van contains vanilla. This seems to have been the case with Herman Slater (credited earlier with promoting Q oil). Slater was a prominent figure in the promotion of Wicca in the United States, and along with his partner, Eddie Buczynski, was owner of an occult store named the Warlock Shoppe in Brooklyn Heights, New York, which later closed and moved to Greenwich Village under the name Magickal Childe. Slater was the author of several books, including *Hoodoo Bible* and *The Magickal Formulary*. Both of the recipes for Van Van incense in his writings contain vanilla, though also vetiver, to his credit. We see that many of his recipes bear names familiar to the shelves of Southern drugstores and catalogue distributors, although many of Slater's concoctions appear to be more the result of guesswork on his part. It seems plausible that customers came looking for these items, described certain aspects of them, and Slater did his best to create similar products.

This early appropriation of products traditional to Conjure into the Wiccan framework Slater promoted has also added to confusion. Too many times I have heard Neopagans proclaiming that the likes of Van Van hearken from the British Isles or even Egypt. They do not. As a newly created religion, Wicca didn't have a broad history of magical supplies to draw from, so North American practitioners took what was available from Hoodoo and other folk traditions, too often with a disregard for the original character, cultural significance, and spiritual context of such products. This practice was passed on through the works of Cunningham and others, causing some confusion among more traditional Conjure workers and Neopagan practitioners.

Extracted from their original cultural and religious origin, some products become unrecognizable, as products used for controlling and cursing are reinterpreted to satisfy prohibitions against such work. For example, reversing products, which are traditionally used to reverse the course of a curse by directing it back to the person who sent it, become reimagined as something meant to simply reverse the course of bad luck. Depending on how the reversing product was formulated, the elements involved may not support this innovation. While the intention of the worker is of much value, it is not the only factor, or the most dominant one.

That said, it is important to recognize that formulas may be applied differently in different time periods and regions. Although the citrusy ingredients of Van Van speak of cleansing and uncrossing work, this oil has been recommended for almost everything under the sun. I sell Van Van packaged with a rabbit's foot, which the oil is used to feed, much like a mojo hand. On a base level, the Asian grasses in a good blend repel insects such as mosquitoes. Sometimes a worker will develop a certain trick that allows for an oil to be used for a different purpose, such as we saw with Anna Riva's application of Van Van on her arms and shoulders. Be experimental but mindful in your approach.

....

Van Van Oil

- 1 part citronella
- 1 part gingergrass
- 1 part lemongrass
- 4 parts palmarosa
- 3 parts vetiver

Those ingredients alone make a fine Van Van, a bit woodsy due to the vetiver and somewhat flowery if the palmarosa is of good quality. It is similar to what I craft for my Modern Conjure brand Van Van. When using natural ingredients, be aware that their characteristics are subject to change, the extraction from one year's harvest perhaps being more astringent than floral, which is often the case with lavender and others. While most recipes for Van Van go heavy on the lemongrass (by Zora Neale Hurston's account, lemongrass and alcohol were all one needed to make Essence of Van Van [10]), the only two of those five scents that appeal to me are palmarosa and vetiver. The others remind me of bug repellent and therefore are not as useful for my purpose, though this recipe keeps with tradition by including them in small amounts. Consider variables

---

10. Zora Neale Hurston, *Mules and Men*.

when deciding on a recipe, such as ensuring you will be able to procure the sometimes difficult-to-find gingergrass oil.

Colognes

The process for blending for scent with oils is the same whether you are making a cologne or an oil blend. Start with your mixture of essential or fragrant oils. Many recipes are written to say *one part this* to *two parts that* so that you may scale your blend accordingly.

To create a cologne you will need some type of alcohol. Oil and water do not mix; however, alcohol extracts elements of scent, and may then be dispersed into water. Start with one ounce of your stock oil, and add that to one ounce of alcohol. Some alcohols are better than others; for instance, Everclear works better than vodka, I find. Perfumer's alcohol and neutral grape spirits are the best options if you can acquire them.

Swirl the oil and alcohol together in a closed bottle, and do this daily.

After nine days, add sixteen ounces of distilled water.

Swirl the container to stir daily for nine more days.

You will likely wish to filter the oils out of your mixture. If this cologne is being added to a wash, such as for the floor or laundry, you will not want oil that can stain fabrics or leave streaks. A simple coffee filter is called for. I place the filter inside a medium-sized sieve, which happens to fit in the mouth of a pitcher (a rustic auburn-colored glass piece originally intended for margaritas) that I repurposed for the dark arts. After giving the mixture a final swirl, I pour it into the filter-lined sieve to filter it. When it gets to the point where it is dripping only about once every three seconds, remove the sieve, which carries the filter, which should contain oil. If it filtered well, then there should be about an ounce of oil in the filter. If there is still water in the filter, then pour it into a container, empty the filter and replace it with another, and pour the remainder of your mixture into the filtered sieve. Some blends that contain thick oils take longer to filter and require multiple changes to the coffee filter. Most blends filter in a single shot.

The other way to make colognes is to blend hydrosols. Also known as *distillates* and *floral waters*, hydrosols come from the distillation process whereby steam collects and becomes scented water. These may be blended on their own to create a water-based scent or added to recipes such as our Cleo May (given earlier in this chapter) in place of some or all of the water.

Here is a recipe from *Fenner's Complete Formulary* for a Hoyt's-style cologne.

....

Hoyt's German Cologne

- Oil Bergamot 1 ounce
- Oil Lemon 1 ounce
- Oil Neroli ¼ ounce
- Oil Santal Wood ½ ounce
- Camphor 20 grains
- Cologne Spirit 7 pints
- Rose Water 1 pint

Mix and let stand a month, then filter.

Scent can be a powerful ally. For myself, dabbing on a bit of Hoyt's cologne immediately puts me in an enchanted mood that is ideal for many types of work. Scent serves as a powerful trigger for shifting your consciousness. The more you utilize scent toward a specific purpose, the more powerful a trigger it becomes. As with all things in Conjure, this is a personal relationship between you and whatever scent serves as your ally. It is a relationship that deepens over time.

～ IX ～
The Keys to Sweetening: Unlocking Love

WITHOUT EMOTIONS, A KISS is nothing more than the touch of two lips. Flowers seem superficial when given as part of an insincere apology, whereas those offered with heartfelt remorse appear more vibrant, better able to elevate previously tense moods. Actions divorced of sentiment have less impact.

We have acknowledged the belief that God's creation is mechanized to respond to certain actions, this being a reason why Naaman had to wash himself in the Jordan River seven times before being healed of his leprosy. Opinions vary as to whether the universe works like a computer program, executing outcomes based on input, or if there is more, if faith and feeling play a part in the resulting magic. When thaumaturgic directives are given in scripture, faith is often the theme, with the protagonist struggling to understand why God would make such demands. While magical work does not rely on belief alone, faith may well be a factor. Similarly, love magic is said to be given added power through emotional involvement. Effective magic requires more than actions, it requires desire. Words of power and finely executed rites can work wonders on their own, but when performed with deep care for the outcome, their power is magnified. For potent love magic, strong emotions are key.

Emotions, love especially, cause physical change, which is immediately evident in a person's body, wherein chemicals including cortisol, dopamine, oxytocin, phenethylamine, and vasopressin are released, changing our chemistry, proving that love truly is a drug. Those butterflies in your belly result from blood being drawn away from your stomach to swell your rapidly beating heart, which treats love with the same fight-or-flight response as one experiences in any dangerous situation. Perhaps our body understands the peril we put ourselves in when we succumb to love. Flushes of adrenaline can cause us to act outside the confines of our better judgment. Our pupils widen, our hands sweat, our voice rises, and our magic is amplified.

Being how love is a broad subject, and types of love magic diverse, let us first define some popular terms taken from the Greek language.

Philautia

Self-love. Its positive attribute is self-esteem; its negative is narcissism.

It is often said that a person cannot attain the love of another until they have learned to love themself. Negative feelings of self-worth can be uncrossed, and many formulas designed to elicit another's love may be used on yourself.

Storge

Familial love. This is the love you experience with parents, and siblings, and those who are part of your family unit.

Beyond your own emotional desires, it may be necessary to elicit the love of certain family members. Sweetening a hostile and meddling mother-in-law is a discipline of love work unto itself. Relationships between family members are often subject to wounds in need of healing, hurt better replaced by love.

Philia

Platonic love. This is the love you share with friends and have for people you admire.

This category covers magic that is done to draw friends, or find the right social group to fit into, as well as to mend broken friendships.

Eros

Lustful love. This is the love that can manifest for a person who arouses you sexually.

It is this category that sees an intensity in jealousy and possessiveness, often with the fear that what brings us pleasure may be lost. (Sex magic is covered more fully in chapter 8.)

Pragma

Matured love. This type of love develops and strengthens over time.

Marriage has not always centered around love, but was often undertaken for more practical concerns such as wealth and alliances, especially in societies that favored arranged marriages. Amidst such pragmatic arrangements an abiding love often developed over time, prompted by shared experiences, struggles, offspring, and such. Even today, many relationships exist out of convenience more so than passion. Products such as Happy Home and Peace in the Home seek to strengthen such love.

Agape

Unconditional love. This is love for all of humanity and creation.

Such love for all things leads to a sense of unity, an esoteric understanding that everything is one. This state of oneness can greatly enhance spiritual work, connecting you in a deep way to the people, things, or conditions you desire, allowing you to more directly influence them. The problem with this temperament is that you are likely to sense the desires of others and give them weight equal to your own, and therefore not get much done according to your individual will. Serenely or ecstatically, this form of love seeks to connect you to everything around you. Agape love can be felt simply, like when the wind kicks up and suddenly you are connected to the air brushing your cheek and to the sky from which it blew. Such a state of ecstasy can be reached in many ways, touching you through a stunning photograph or musical symphony. It is awakened in those moments when you are filled with great appreciation for being alive, when you connect to Spirit, and Spirit is there to experience beauty through your eyes or pleasure through your skin. Through drugs, through great sex, through the experience of licking an ice cream cone, and through many other means are found the keys to understanding how you and the universe are one, and to unconditionally loving yourself beyond the boundaries of your skin.

As distinct as the various forms of love just described are the types love spells:

- *Attracting Love:* The act of bringing love into your life
- *Sweetening:* Getting another interested in you
- *Commitment:* Defining your relationship
- *Loyalty:* Limiting your lover in the relationship
- *Reconciliation:* Getting back together after a breakup
- *Romance:* Adding excitement to your relationship

We will explore all of these various themes of love individually.

Popular Formulas for Love

Coming from our last chapter on sex, it should be easy to see how many of those formulas might also apply to love.

Attracting Love

By far the most sought-after type of magic, love-drawing formulas come in a variety of dramatic styles.

Adam & Eve: In addition to the famous couple from the Bible, this formula gets its name from the now endangered Adam and Eve orchid root. It serves as an example of how formulas must change over time as ingredients become unavailable. Despite the lack of true Adam and Eve root in modern blends, they nevertheless serve as a strong love formula for heterosexual couplings.

Dixie Love: The main component in this formula is Beth root, known by such regional names as Dixie John and Southern John. In addition to the root, try the following scents.

....

Dixie Love Oil

Combine the following essential oils:

- 1 part cinnamon
- 6 parts jasmine
- 3 parts patchouli

Sweetening

Chuparosa: This formula gets its name from the Spanish word for *hummingbird*. It helps build friendships, but may also be used to bring around a friend whom you would rather have be your paramour. Its scent is floral, much like the flowers favored by hummingbirds.

....

Chuparosa Oil

Combine the following scented oils:

- 2 parts honeysuckle
- 2 parts rose
- 1 part jasmine

Commitment

Bridal Bouquet: Just as she who captures the bridal bouquet is said to be the next to get hitched, this product saves you the trouble of having to knock several reaching bridesmaids out of your way.

....

Bridal Bouquet Oil

Combine the following scented oils:

- 1 part gardenia
- 1 part heather
- 1 part lilac
- 1 part palmarosa
- 1 part rose

Marriage: This formula is used to get someone to propose to you, or to urge them to accept your proposal.

Loyalty

Stay with Me: Elements associated with influencing work go into these formulas. Indeed, you might just as readily mix Commanding with Love to create a blend to keep your lover from straying. Loyalty often means fidelity, but it can go deeper than that, as some feel that their lover is unfaithful not simply when they bed another but also when they form intimate feelings for someone outside the relationship.

Keep Me: With some lovers you can only ever expect so much by way of loyalty, and therefore Keep Me serves as a plea for them to continue their relationship with you, even if they are incapable of keeping their trousers up in the company of mistresses.

Reconciliation

Return to Me: You want them back, God help you. Hopefully they are worth wanting. We will look deeper at the particulars of reconciliation work later in this chapter.

....

RETURN TO ME OIL

Combine the following essential oils:

- 1 part bergamot
- 2 parts lavender
- 1 part myrrh

Romance

Fire of Love: The version I craft for my Modern Conjure brand is called Fireworks of Love, and it comes with a warning for those who would try to use it as a general love-drawing product. The emphasis of this formula is on heat and excitement, which may help revive a humdrum relationship but may exacerbate existing hostility and contention.

Blue Sonata: This formula has a horribly cloying scent. Although it is said to inspire romance, it is my opinion that anyone who wears such a fragrance deserves to die sad and alone.

Hold Me: This is formulated to encourage cuddling, but be focused in your application of it, lest your lover end up having to hold you because a new tragedy compels them to do so.

....
HOLD ME INCENSE

- Amber resin
- Rose hips
- White copal

Passion: This is an overall good formula for arousing romantic feelings and inspiring action to be taken with them.

Attracting Love

Attracting love into your life begins with fortifying the love you have for yourself. If you don't think you are worthy of love, ain't no one else gonna. That devil of self-doubt may be removed through methods we have visited in previous chapters, such as with the aid of uncrossing work, or with formulas like Run Devil Run, Banishing, and so forth.

You can do attracting work for several types of love, such as for drawing new friends, new erotic partners, or a potential spouse. If there is already someone in your life you wish to sweeten toward you, then move on to the next step, for attraction of the sort discussed here focuses on bringing someone new into your life, or else opening your eyes to someone you might never have considered having in your arms.

It's best to have some idea of what you want in a lover, within the bounds of what is realistic. There simply are not enough rich supermodels in the world to suit everyone; however, wanting someone who is gainfully employed and takes care of themselves is not asking too much. Make a list of ideals you want in a mate. If your list reads as too shallow, then it's time you had a conversation with yourself; if the items on your list are too vague, then you must ask yourself how you will recognize Prince Charming when he arrives. Consider creating a charm, such as a mojo hand, to act as your wingman. Include your list in the charm, and consider adding some of the following love-attracting curios:

- Beth root (Dixie John, Southern John)
- Catnip
- Cubeb berries
- Damiana
- Gentian root
- Lavender
- Rose petals
- Juniper berries
- Vanilla beans

All of these draw love in different ways. Because folks doing love work are often particular about their gender identity and that of their desired partner, some of these herbal curios are considered to work on behalf of a specific gender, which is why Queen Elizabeth root is traditionally called a woman's root and High John a man's. Develop your own relationship with an herbal ally to understand what help it is willing to give you.

Another method of attracting a partner utilizes a jack ball. Lacking a specific name, you might write on the name paper something like Mr. Right or My Miss. Place the jack ball a distance from you, then pull it closer on its string while asserting your will with such words as *lover, come to me.*

Sweetening

Having attracted a suitor, the job of making them your sweetheart begins. We continue by looking into sweetening spells, so named both for their ingredients and for their ability to sweeten someone's response to you.

Different types of sweeteners are chosen for their various associations. An example of this is seen in the choice between brown and white sugar, which may be made in accordance with a target's skin color. We see the same choices being made in relation to name papers, with white copy paper being chosen for works affecting light-skinned folk, and brown paper—such as can be torn from a typical brown paper grocery bag—being the choice for spells working with darker-skinned folk. The emphasis on integration in North American culture has led to a decrease in this practice, so that either type of sugar or paper is deemed appropriate regardless of a person's skin tone.

Brown Sugar

This granulated sugar is distinctive for its molasses content. Something common to varieties of brown sugar is their tendency to harden, which is not ideal for sweetening work. *Hardened* in this context refers to emotions that have become less loving, resulting in actions that lack sensitivity. Softening the brown sugar counteracts this.

Although we are exploring sweetening spells for new lovers at this point in the chapter, consider nonetheless the following trick for when times get harder.

....

To Soften a Hardened Lover

- Hard brown sugar
- A bowl, the wider and shorter the better
- Scissors
- A brown paper bag
- A permanent marker
- Water
- A clean towel

Place your clumpy brown sugar in the bowl. Sometimes this has hardened into pebbles and other times into larger shapes. The larger the clump, the longer it will take for moisture to get deep within it and soften it. If possible, break up any larger pieces.

Cut a heart shape from a brown paper grocery bag, no smaller than the circumference of the bowl. Cut from an unprinted area on the bag.

Use the marker to write the name of your hardened lover three times across the heart, as we might do for a name paper.

After that is done, wet the paper. The thickness of a grocery bag is helpful for this, as it will absorb more of the water. Don't worry if the writing on your paper runs; it will still be understood by Spirit. At the point where the heart is wet but not dripping, hold it over the bowl of sugar and speak the following charm:

Like this sugar before me now,
Lover whose heart has grown too hard,
Soften to me and make a vow
To be ever mindful of my regard.

Give the heart a kiss and lay it on top of the brown sugar.

Wet your towel and wring it out so it is damp but not dripping, then lay it over the bowl.

Depending on factors such as the quantity of sugar, the depth of the bowl, and the temperature and humidity level of the room, the sugar should begin to soften after a few hours—and the temperament of your partner along with it.

When finished, the heart can be used in numerous ways. You could slip it under your partner's side of the bed, throw it in the washing machine with their clothes until it disintegrates, or bury it in the back yard to secure their gentle love.

Colored Sugar

Sometimes called screened sugar, this sugar comes in various colors used for decorating confections. The same color associations generally employed for magic apply here. Thus, pink sugar could be used in work pertaining to friendship, red for love, and so forth. This may be done decoratively, like on a cupcake or cookie you have prepared, or used more slyly, such as dissolved in your sweetheart's coffee.

Molasses

Molasses is the primary ingredient for gingerbread, and there is something so delicious about breaking and biting the limbs off a gingerbread person. It is satisfying on the level of sticking a pin into a Voodoo doll, though eating a gingerbread person as a magical act is done much more sensually, letting each bit melt in your mouth before consuming it. Here is a recipe for making your own sweet effigies.

....

Gingerbread Effigy

- 1 cup molasses
- ½ cup shortening
- 1 tablespoon ginger
- 1 tablespoon baking soda
- 2 tablespoons warm milk
- 2 cups flour
- ½ teaspoon salt

Mix the ingredients together and chill for 2 hours. Then roll the dough to ¼-inch thickness, cut (with a cookie cutter or freestyle), and bake at 350°F for 10 to 12 minutes.

Unless you plan to entice an entire football team (and *go you* if you do), it is better to enchant individual cookies rather than ritualize the whole production.

Decorate your gingerbread person however you wish, then name it after the one whose affection you intend to sweeten, saying:

> *Straight to my lips*
> *Then past my tongue,*
> *Ready my hips,*
> *Our affair has begun.*

By sucking on the cookie and gently nibbling at its body, you consume it—a delicious act of domination.

If you don't care for the taste of gingerbread, then this isn't the job for you. It would be better perhaps to use another type of cookie dough.

Molasses, unlike other sweeteners, is often used for matters of controlling magic as well, given how its stickiness binds things to it.

Powdered Sugar

This is also known as confectioners' sugar or icing sugar. Chapter 11 will focus on the use of various powders, but carry into that lesson the knowledge that powdered sugar on its own constitutes a throwing powder used, of course, to sweeten your target. When mixed with pumpkin spice or even saltpeter, powdered sugar can be tossed into a fire with the whisper of your beloved's name to fire up a relationship.

Table Sugar

Known also as white sugar, this granulated sugar is common and has many uses. At its simplest, it can be added to a bath to both remove negativity and sweeten your outlook on life, which is ideal after a tough day.

If you have a sugar bowl, it can be as magical as a witch's cauldron. A name paper can be kept at the bottom. Every time you place a spoon in to remove some sugar, stir the sugar a total of nine times clockwise, saying the name(s) of whoever you wish to sweeten.

Rock Candy

You can create your own magic wand with this technique.

....
Rock Candy Wand

Start with a thin stick, no thicker than a pencil. Write a name paper for your love interest, then wrap it around the stick, using three pieces of thread or string to tie it tight. (Thicker strings with natural fibers work best for this, as the crystals grow more easily on them.)

Next, bring to a boil 1 cup of water, and while stirring slowly pour in 3 cups of table sugar. To this you may add food coloring, again using basic color associations. Pour this into a jar, such as a basic mason jar. Then suspend your stick, papered side down, into the jar, but only after coating it first in sugar by rolling it toward you on a sugar-laden dish. I find it best to tie the stick to another stick, so that the one is submerged in the jar but not resting directly on the bottom. Set this aside to be undisturbed for two weeks, then break through the crystal layer on top with a spoon and wiggle the stick until it comes loose (You may have excess crystals at the bottom or possibly need to heat the bottom of the jar in hot water for the stick to release.)

Now you have a sweetening wand. You can use this to sweeten your lover's beverage, focusing on your goal as you stir clockwise. Or you may simply point it in your target's direction and feel your desire for them to be sweet for you move through your arm and out the wand to strike them with your intention, wherever they may be.

Sugar Cubes

These little squares can be used as building blocks or placed beneath a plate or another lightweight surface. If you are looking to sweeten your landlord, get four sugar cubes and four Indian Head pennies, and place them in the four corners of your property. This will mean burying them on your property, or else placing them in the four farthest corners of your apartment. To keep ants away, these may be placed in plastic bags.

Syrups

Syrups come in many varieties, from the thin sugar water used in cocktails as simple syrup to the thick Karo brand. Unlike honey, Karo syrup is clear, and is preferred by some for honey jars in which a photograph has been placed.

Simple syrup is handy for when you wish to give your beloved a drink that you have bewitched. It is a widely available mixer; however, here is a recipe, should you wish to make your own.

....
SIMPLE SYRUP

- 1 cup water
- 1 cup table sugar

Bring to a boil.
That's it, and that's why it's called *simple*.

In the following cocktail recipe, the simple syrup sweetens your target, while the blackberries are meant to snag and hold them as brambles do.

....
BRIAR TRAP COCKTAIL

- 2 parts gin
- ½ part simple syrup

- ½ part blackberry liqueur
- 2 whole blackberries

Fill a glass with crushed ice. Add the gin and simple syrup and stir. Float the blackberry liqueur. Garnish with the blackberries.

Chocolates

Chocolate can also be used in sweetening magic, often of a more sensuous nature. Chocolate can be complex, sometimes bitter, so be mindful of its character before using it. Stale, bitter chocolate will do no good in sweetening anyone.

Chocolate Powder

To increase passion in your sexual relationship, take a picture of your partner and hold it flat, with your partner facing you. Sprinkle chocolate powder on the photo and speak your desire, saying something like *kiss me more on the backs of my knees*, or whatever you are into that you also want them to be into. Use the sort of language you wish to hear in bed, be it suave or dirty. Blow the chocolate powder from your lover's face, facing east when you do this.

Chocolate Syrup

You can use a squeezable container of chocolate syrup or else a stick dipped in the syrup to write and illustrate your wishes on the ground. This is best done right before a spring rain, lest your magic be overrun by ants or the concrete stained. Something as simple as your initials and those of your lover will do, such as *NS + EW*. Draw a heart to contain those initials.

Chocolate Chips

To answer yes-no questions, take a checkerboard and five chocolate chips. Place the chips in a cup. Blow into the cup three times, and between each breath repeat a succinct question, such as *Does he want to be with me?* Upend the cup a foot or so above the board, then note which squares the chips have fallen on. A predominance of occupied black squares predicts a negative response, while mostly white spaces denotes a yes.

Candy Debris

Empty sugar packs, popsicle sticks, soda bottle caps, and so on can all be put to use in creative ways, serving as curios in their own right. Candy wrappers and foils can often be used for name papers.

Apples and red onions also have a tradition of being used in this type of magic, hollowed out and filled with honey and the name of your target. These are often then placed in a jar or tin, to allow for a candle to be burned on them. They may also be buried beneath a plant. The best choice of plant for this purpose is one that has leaves that stretch out in all directions, such as many palms and ferns.

....

Honey Jar to Sweeten Someone

Honey jar spells are said to work their magic slowly, for honey is thick and slow to pour. Patience is required for this work, but the payoff is well worth it. For extra boosts of energy, such as when you need to ask the object of your spell for a special favor or when reunions are inevitable, simply burn a candle atop the jar shortly before your encounter.

Besides the obvious ingredient of honey, you can add to the jar curios, a name paper, and ideally a personal concern. Regarding curios, many of the aforementioned herbs for attracting love may be stirred in.

You may also stir in a favorable conjure oil, such as Chuparosa. Its purpose is not only to encourage a particular person to love you, but also to foster a relationship rich in honesty and communication. Since secretly putting a spell on your romantic partner goes against those values, this spell is best used candidly. Oftentimes people wanting to strengthen and deepen their love will willingly participate in shared magical actions to achieve that goal.

Once everything is assembled, simply place all your ingredients in a jar and tighten the lid. Then place a tealight candle on top, light it, and state your intention.

Here is a rhyme I use not to sweeten a lover, but to sweeten those whose good side I wish to be on:

Honey jar, so sweet and golden,
To me shall (name of person/persons) be beholden.
Sweeten every disposition
That acts toward me in opposition.

Concerns Regarding Love Spells

Once you have found someone who suits you, the next step is to get them interested if they have not yet come around. To the degree that it is working on the will of another, such a spell falls in the category of the influencing work we considered in chapter 7. This leads to the issue that many have with love magic, the question being *Can I be happy knowing they love me only because I have bewitched them?*

Beyond that, you may wish to question the character of your love. I would question any person who admitted to putting a spell on me. Someone who truly loves me will respect my values, including my desire for autonomy. *Does this person really love me*, I should ask, *or do they only wish to own me, loving me as a possession?* Everyone deserves more "love" than that.

When I first began working as a professional worker, I was very picky about the type of love magic I was willing to do for clients. I was fine with doing magic to nudge and influence someone toward the arms of another, but could not understand why anyone would want to be with someone who at their core felt love only because of a spell. Over time, however, people came to me with different needs concerning love work. One of the first spells I did to make a man fall back in love with his wife came after he had taken their children to a foreign country and refused to return. She was not a citizen of the United States and had no access to legal recourse. She wanted her husband to fall back in love with her so that he would return with their children. Furthermore, she needed him to remain in love with her until those children reached legal age. Since she had no love for him—certainly none left after what he had pulled—she also requested that his nature be diminished so that she would not have to sleep with him. Did I have a problem doing that work? No, none whatsoever. Good thing, as this is not an uncommon request, especially from disadvantaged women who face loss of residency, income, and child custody should their men become disinterested. Such love spells are seen throughout sources on folk magic, as in days gone by a man leaving a woman meant she was likely to become destitute. Ensuring the love of her mate was essential to survival.

Sometimes the easiest and most effective route to get what you need is through love work. Here are other situations in which love may be the answer:

- When a partner threatens to tell the immigration department that your marriage is a sham and you should be deported
- When your inheritance is in jeopardy should Nana's dementia prevent her from embracing you again
- When your caregiver has stopped caring for you

Although you might choose to utilize love magic for these types of situations, we should discuss the limits of love magic. For as many spells as there are promising to make someone fall head over heels in love with you, love magic that aims to change another person's feelings and behavior is difficult. Some say it is impossible, that an individual's psyche will always be stronger than a spell. I believe that individuals vary. Some have a strong enough will that no amount of magic will change them, and others less so. Even if you do succeed in making a person love you, spells can be broken. People can go for years living in a spell-induced haze, then suddenly wake up, lucidly assess their life, and break free of your spell. This is something to always keep in mind.

Commitment

Now that you've got 'em hooked on your honey, it's time to get that ring.

What many people want is lasting love. While there are many spells and tricks done to accomplish this, they all need care and upkeep. Entropy is a force of nature that applies as much to magic as to anything. That raccoon bone beneath your bed will need some love oil rubbed into it from time to time to retain its potency. A single sip of Love Potion Number 9 may give another eyes for you, but it will wear off, just as any drug does—sometimes within an hour, sometimes within weeks, but with inevitable certainty. The question you must ask is how willing are you to constantly re-up such a spell? Every time you do so, it serves as a reminder that the person you are targeting does not love you on their own, and that knowledge can be corrosive.

Often those enacting a love spell do so because they wish to see the love they feel for an individual returned. But this gets tricky. If this emotional energy is not correctly channeled, the spellcaster can become the target of their own spell. Already smitten, their emotions intensify to an unhealthy level, so that the spell makes them obsessive and desperate, traits that push away the object of their desire, making themself a victim of their own love spell.

For Shared Residency

To get a person to move in with you, it is easiest if you keep their personal concerns at your place. An invitation for your lover to have their own drawer is an important step toward cohabitation and gives you a space you can define. A sprinkle of herbs, covered by scented paper to line the drawer, bewitches the space. When your lover is not there, you might pour honey over their toothbrush, or oil their hairbrush and ask it to whisper thoughts into your lover's head.

To move yourself into their place takes a bit more cunning, as you must find ways to dominate their space. You do not want to suggest moving your things in, as that may be too assertive for a timid partner. Forgetting the occasional sock is the best way, so long as you are tidy about it. Try to always keep at least one item there, though if they are also a Conjure worker then be suspicious of what they might do with your belongings.

To Make Them Propose

Use the following trick:

> As you eat the wing of a chicken, take the little bone that is near the end and drop it into the pocket of the fellow you are going with, without him knowing it, and he will ask you to marry him.[11]

---

11. William Carroll, ed., *Superstitions: 10,000 You Really Need*, 485.

To Make Them Accept Your Proposal

Keep in mind that the ring itself is a powerful ally. Before presenting it, bathe it in a glass of bubbly to invigorate it, telling it all the wonderful things about the person you hope will wear it on their finger.

Loyalty

Philia magic is an academic term used to describe written spells from ancient Greece that sought to secure a woman's husband. Women had little social value or means of sustaining themselves should their husband abandon them, making this type of work essential to their survival. Both men and women do similar work to keep their mates loyal.

The specifics of such loyalty vary. Some relationships are sexually exclusive to the partners involved in them, while others are open to external prospects for sexual and/or emotional commitments. Every healthy relationship has some understanding of expected behavior, and based on whatever lines have been drawn, fidelity aims to keep a partner within those bounds.

To a larger degree, loyalty means staying in the relationship, even if you occasionally find yourself with your pants down. Recognizable formulas speak to the popularity of this type of work, such as Stay at Home, Stay With Me, and I Can, You Can't.

To Keep Your Mate at Home

- It is said that burying some of your mate's hair beneath the front porch will keep them from straying.
- Plant periwinkle around your home.
- Use the power of balm of Gilead buds, such as by placing nine pieces in a glass of whiskey, then tossing them in the backyard. Unless there is an underlying issue with alcohol addiction, the whiskey may be added to the wash bucket and used to clean and bless the home.

Reconciliation

Distinct from the general type of love-drawing magic is the work of *reconciliation*, which is concerned with reuniting lovers, family members, and friends. It is a type of drawing magic, in this instance the act of drawing two distinct people closer together. Typical of reconciliation spells are practices that involve the physical movement of two objects toward each other, such as two lodestones similarly named for their targets. These stones are often dressed with general love-drawing oils such as Come Home, Kiss Me Now, Reconcile, Return to Me, and others. But beyond bringing two people together again, such spells seek to smooth things over.

Sometimes this work can bring more than a person bargained for, opening wounds even deeper, on both sides. Before going this route, I suggest finding a good psychic reader who may be able to reveal elements of the situation you are not privy to. There's no sense in going back with him only to discover the existence of his second family in Nevada that he left you for earlier.

Such warnings aside, I have seen reconciliation work defeat the odds many times. Often, after folks have been apart for some time, the chances of a reconciliation dwindle. The longer two people are apart, the harder it is to bring them together—up to a certain point at least, as after a certain amount of time the opposite can happen, whereby the wounds of the past seem less raw and concerning and there is a greater possibility for revisiting the good memories. I have worked with folks who had completely lost track of an old lover, and after doing reconciliation work suddenly found that person again in an unexpected place, one at a hospital and another at a farmers' market in a town neither lived in.

The thing about reconciliation is that you need to be able to reconcile your own feelings. Forgiving someone for having left you does not come easy, and less so sometimes when they are there in your arms again. Be aware of your true intentions. If you are the jilted party, the jab you felt at getting dumped may still be there. You may not want the person back, but you don't want to feel unwanted. I have seen folks do work to get someone back, and then when it worked they turned around and dumped that person. Some were overcome by anger they did not realize was there, while others had planned all along on making the other feel as rejected as they had.

Romance

When it comes to creating romance, action counts for everything. This is not the type of magic one can do and then sit back and wait to happen. You must take the added step of creating circumstances wherein romance can flourish. A nice dinner at home, for which candles dressed with an oil for love are set on the table, creates a great atmosphere. Here are some suggestions for bringing in the romance.

- Do magic together. Not that you want to give away all your secrets, but working together on the same magical goal of inspiring more romance should be an equally desired endeavor. Of course, if your partner is disinterested in being romantic with you, then you need to return to sweetening work. Often the issue is not unwillingness so much as uncertainty. Romance is not taught in school; if anything, most kids are taught to toughen up. Be patient with your lover, expressing your need for romance, without blaming them for not knowing how to provide it.
- Take a bath together. All the better if you can enchant the bath with blessed herbs, such as those discussed earlier in this chapter.
- Make a meal together. I suggest making something sweet, such as a dessert. Food is a wonderful way to work with some of the allies for love that we have mentioned, such as vanilla, sugar, chocolate chips, and so forth.

Of course, what you and yours find romantic may vary from this list. If you are more of a graveyard kind of person, then plan a romantic stroll among the tombstones.

Outside of committed relationships, a touch of romance livens up other loving relationships as well. Most mothers love roses, and friends enjoy knowing they are being thought of. Relationships of all stripes need to be fed, to be added to with new shared experiences.

There will always be times when a relationship needs some sweetening, though more mature relationships learn to savor the various flavors of joy, regret, playfulness, and tragedy. Just as a balanced diet relies on more than sugar, a well-rounded relationship appreciates the savory and the bitter as well.

X

The Keys to Setting Lights: Unlocking Wealth

AS YOUR EYES ADJUST to the light, you realize you have created millions of diamonds. Your altar has been set, your candle properly dressed and placed on top of a petition paper and hundred-dollar bill. The diamonds, nanoparticles, explode from your candle flame, a small but poetic confirmation of the wealth being drawn in your direction.

The desire for riches has fueled the imagination of magicians for ages. Spells abound promising the discovery of hidden treasure. The mythical Black Pullet, with its promise of golden eggs, features prominently in the Conjure ethos. It is therefore understandable that Conjure possesses a wealth of practices concerned with money. These can be broken down into three types of work: to acquire wealth, to multiply wealth, and to secure wealth. Each has its own nuanced tricks and tactics.

Aside from some miraculous exceptions, money work seldom delivers the goods that allow a person to go from pauper to aristocrat. Magic no more serves as a blank check for every expense than it does a cure-all for every illness. Yet if done right, and with appropriate real-world follow-through (such as turning in resumes and making prudent choices in spending), money magic serves to increase your potential.

The trick here is to have specific and realistic goals; otherwise your money magic is likely to be unsuccessful, each bankrupt attempt further diminishing your faith that your next working will serve you any better. Remember, many of the practices we work with were inherited by folks who did with little. Unless you believe that you are better than those powerful workers of old, you must concede that few of them were able to leave their rough lives for posh penthouses, or else much of Los Angeles would be populated by the likes of the Beverly Hillbillies. Yet if their work did not tangibly improve their lives, then their ways would have been abandoned, instead of living on as the traditions we inherited. Clearly they must have found their magic to have been successful. Likely this was because they had pragmatic notions of success. Knowing the penthouse was out of reach, they worked to mend the hole in their bucket, to get an extra penny per pound for the sale of their grain, to hide their cash savings from the tax man. The success of your money work can only be determined by the achievement of those goals you set. I am not saying to set the bar so low that any loose change found in the couch is considered a boon, but only that you should understand there are steps to be climbed before reaching the mountaintop.

Deciding what success looks like for yourself is easier than determining what it may mean for someone else. I mention this specifically because I have known more than a few professional workers who sell mojo hands promoting wealth but who themselves never make ends meet. While we all have temporary setbacks, those who persist in such conditions cannot claim to be successful at money magic (unless they have a prohibition against doing work for themselves, which is an excuse to be suspicious of). Be leery of folks promising to get you money who themselves live in squalor. On the other side of the coin, do not assume that the root doctor with the most gold teeth is the best.

It is important here to consider the culture of North America and the ideal of the American dream, with its Horatio Alger myth of rags to riches. The belief that each of us can raise ourselves up by our bootstraps leads to expectations that ignore the prejudices and lack of privileges that work to keep us down. Acknowledging all the conditions that influence your ability to amass the money you desire is essential.

It is important to realize that workers have different gifts. Always work from your strengths. You may not be strong in manifesting money. That is okay, so long as you know what your strengths are. If you have been working spells to get money but have not gotten any, then a change of tactics is in order. At my shop, the Mystic Dream, I look to see if my money magic is working to ring up the sales, and if not, then I focus instead on boosting my love magic, so that folks come in and find items to fall in love with.

Understand that money magic works best when done consistently. You want a steady income, and therefore your magic must follow suit.

Popular Formulas for Wealth

The same colorful labels typical of many Conjure products similarly appear on candles, giving a name and focus to what they are being lit for.

Better Business

This formula is ideal for self-employed people, business owners, and those working on commission.

Filthy Rich

This is the name I gave to my main money-drawing blend for my Modern Conjure brand, which uses patchouli and nutmeg and several other scents for its earthy but active scent.

Money Stay with Me

Such formulas focus on keeping you from being nickel-and-dimed to death by surprise bills. Staying within your budget, as well as steadily accumulating money to save and invest, is crucial to long-term success, and the focus of this type of work is to keep what you own from needing repair.

Pay Me Now

Maybe it's money you loaned to someone, or perhaps that job paying you under the table isn't paying you at all. Time for Pay Me Now.

Prosperity

This formula is less about drawing in new sources of money and more about expanding the opportunities around you.

Steady Work

Finding and retaining a job is important if financial security is your goal. It is much easier to achieve this than it is to pray that money will float your way on the wind.

Wealthy Way

This is another love-drawing formula, though it highlights a bit more of the high life. It may not be enough for you to feel that your needs are being met; maybe you want some bling on those fingers.

Additionally, one might rely on formulas introduced earlier in this book, such as Boss Fix in order to help secure a raise, Influence to persuade a friend to give you a loan, or Cleo May to dress the sheets so that your john leaves you a fat stack.

Curios associated with money drawing include business cards, coins and other currency, hell notes, lodestones (sometimes painted green or gold), money clips, pyrite, wallets, and similar items.

Popular botanicals for money drawing include alfalfa, alkanet, allspice, American mandrake, chamomile, cinnamon, comfrey, nutmeg, patchouli, pine, rice (dyed green is called Lucky Green Rice), rue, sarsaparilla, sassafras, and many others.

Setting Lights

Setting lights refers to the act of lighting a candle to influence a particular condition, and some use this term for lamp magic as well. This is a traditional service practiced by candle shops and independent rootworkers, whereby a candle dressed for a particular goal is burned on behalf of clients. Generally there is some follow-up from the work, especially if the way in which the candle burns suggests bad omens. While most other modalities of magic tend to be visibly static when engaged, a flame moves and is easier to recognize as a spirit that is alive and active. Candles can serve as diagnostic tools, indicating how your spell is progressing, and how it may or may not have been successful.

Figural Candles

Once you have decided which color you wish to work with based on the associations we saw in chapter 1, you have plenty of options for shapes and sizes of candles. Throughout the years the spiritual supply market has featured a variety of specialized shapes, which are collectively known as image candles or figural candles. These often are available in a small range of colors: white for cleansing, black for cursing, green for money, and red for love. The most popular figural candles include the following.

Seven-Knob Candles

Each day another section of the candle is burned, so that the spell takes a full week to complete.

Man or Woman

These candles are for working spells on people. They can be moved or manipulated to symbolically describe how you wish the spell to play out.

Adam & Eve or Lovers

These candles feature a man and a woman facing each other and embracing.

Cats

These are often burned for luck, especially when gambling.

Cross and Crucifix

These candles invoke God's power. A popular style is known as the *Master Key crucifix candle* and features a key on either arm of a cross flanking an open book, though many popular reproductions are made from molds too aged to render anything tangible, making them look like a mushed crucifix.

Divorce

Burned to break a couple up, these candles feature two figures back to back.

Genital (Phallus or Yoni)

These candles are for working on another's nature.

Marriage

These candles feature a man and a woman in wedding attire together, facing forward.

Pyramid

Like the iconic image of the eyed pyramid on US currency, these candles are used for money conditions.

Skulls

Skull candles are used to work on another's head for influencing work, or are lit in honor of ancestors.

There are a number of other figures, such as witches and devils and Indian Heads, which I will leave to you to explore.

Double Action Candles

These candles are commonly colored black on their bottom half. Each is traditionally used to reverse a condition that dictates its top color: green for money, red for love, etc. The trick to these is that the black half must be burned first. You are burning through the black, which represents negativity in this instance, in order to release the color of your ideal condition. To accomplish this, these candles are literally reversed and butted so that the black end can be lit. Once the new tip has been carved with a knife, the colored end is poked into a candle stand and the black tip lit. These are often placed atop a mirror, which reverses whatever negativity is released from the burning of the black wax back to its origin. If the candle is reversing a curse, then whoever threw the first curse gets smacked back.

Glass Vigil Candles

Dressing glass-encased devotional candles, often called seven-day candles, requires an adapted practice. When burned from beginning to end unencumbered, these candles are intended to burn for seven days; however, due to skinnier glass and cheap, bubbly wax, modern ones burn for significantly less time, and thus their colloquial name is a misnomer. These candles were introduced to North America in the 1960s and '70s, becoming popular in botanicas, followed by the more general candle shops, occult stores, and the emerging New Age and Neopagan shops across the country.

Other Candles

Tapers, household candles, chime candles, and birthday cake candles can all be utilized in various ways. First, however, folks tend to dress their candles in specific ways. Except for those candles that are encased in glass (which we will get to in a bit), there are similar ways of preparing a candle for spiritual service.

Candle Services

Working with candles in conjunction with prayer is a tradition found in Catholicism, and sometime around the 1940s this practice spread throughout the United States. This was due largely to publications such as Mikhail Strabo's *A Candle to Light Your Way*, *How to Conduct a Candle Light Service*, and *The Guiding Light to Power and Success*, which were influenced by traditions within Black Spiritualist churches. In his book *The Master Book of Candle-Burning*, Henri Gamache termed his system of candle magic the *philosophy of fire*, drawing on earlier works and influenced by Zoroastrianism. In *Legends of Incense, Herb, and Oil Magic*, author Lewis de Claremont emphasized magnetism in his instructions on how to dress a candle.

Again, we see directionality playing a part in this work. When oil is applied from the top of the candle down toward its base, this is done to invoke and draw conditions toward you. Most often this is done while holding the candle parallel to the floor with one hand, wick facing away from you, while your other hand, which has been wetted with a conjure oil appropriate to the task, moves toward you. This action is repeated, often a number of times significant to the worker. The process is reversed for work intended to send away negative conditions, to banish curses and unwanted people. A similar method involves holding the candle in the center with both oiled hands. One hand holds the candle while the other hand moves outward then grabs it again in the center, followed by the other hand doing similar. This action is thought to magnetize the candle and can be used to prepare a candle for any purpose. Some interpret such outward motions as sending energy away and use this technique solely for banishing work. To draw energy into the candle, the reverse motions can be done, from outward into the center.

Setting Vigil Lights

Again, we are talking about seven-day candles here. The outside of these can be cleansed with various products and decorated with images that adhere to it or are drawn on. Smearing oil on the glass, however, would be messy and ineffective.

Instead, holes are burrowed into the wax. Obviously, softer wax is easier to do this with than the hard, crumbly wax sometimes found. Various tools are used for this purpose. I prefer metal barbecue skewers, which are long and often flat, perfect for poking down into the candle, then winding up to remove strips of wax and leave a hole. For some folks, a Phillips screwdriver has become part of their tradition, chosen for the crossmark left from its head. I like to burrow down until I hit the bottom of the candle, but many folks go no further than an inch or so. I find that three holes are adequate. Having more than five carefully spaced holes tends to deteriorate the candle.

Into these holes is poured condition oil. Some use a dropper and are particular about how many drops go into each hole, while others just pour a bit in. Just make certain that there isn't a layer of oil just sitting at the top, or else the wick will go out. Sometimes there isn't a single formula that represents your condition fully, so a variety of oils have been chosen. It is best to focus your work on a single issue, rather than lighting something for health plus money plus revenge plus that situation with the neighbor's dog. However, issues are often complex and nuanced and require a variety of formulas to address them.

The exposed top of the candle can be sprinkled with herbs, powders, and glitter. Not only do these serve a purpose in dressing the candle, but they leave a residue that can be read as part of candle divination, which we will go over shortly. Make sure not to add too much foreign material to your candle, or it will snuff itself out or else catch fire. Small amounts are adequate.

Your magic talks back to you. Every action that takes place around your spell serves as an omen. This is evidenced most clearly with candle magic. The manner in which your candle burns indicates how your desires will manifest. It may tell you that things will take a long time or be fraught with obstacles, or it may tell you that what you wish for is not ultimately in your best interest. In lighting this candle you are creating a living spirit. Take some time to gaze at it. Acknowledge its life. See the aura of light surrounding it. Here is the soul of your spell, the spirit that will do your magical bidding. You must tell it what you need. Because it was born from you, it speaks your language, so do not fear being plain-spoken. Additionally, the spirit will speak back to you in a symbolic language that you understand.

It is best to distinguish the front of the candle from the back. This is often evident from whatever image or drawing is placed on the candle to feature its purpose.

Here are some common signs of candle magic in progress and what they might mean to the magical practitioner:

- A low flame indicates that the work will take time. Whatever you asked for may not manifest quickly.

- A high flame indicates that things are moving quickly. The universe has heard your plea and change is coming.

- A popping flame quite literally means that the candle has something to tell you. This indicates there is something needing your attention, perhaps something that has been overlooked and needs to be sorted out before success can come. If you have lit the candle for protection, then beware, as things are being said or done behind your back.

- A double flame can indicate different things depending on the purpose of the candle. Examine your feelings to make sure that you are not of two minds about what you are doing. In love magic a double flame can be a positive sign of a romantic pairing. If the candle was lit for protective work, then the double flame asserts that you do not stand alone, but have the help of other people or spiritual powers.

- A jumping flame speaks of anger. You may have resentments that must come to the surface and be dealt with before you can move. Or this could be the anger of another, someone who is holding you back. Spend some time gazing into this jumping flame and see what emotions arise in you or what your intuition has to say.

- Sparks from a candle, so long as they don't catch anything on fire, are beneficial. They are a display of power from your candle.

- Sometimes the flame will point in a specific direction, and this can also have meaning.

Since I am versed in Western magical traditions that have certain correspondences given to the various directions, I associate east with knowledge, south with lust, west with emotions, and north with respite. Therefore, if a flame reached east for a noticeable period of time, then I would have to ask myself if I had all the knowledge I needed in order to manifest this spell. Perhaps that job I am working toward has crappy benefits or a boss who'll hate me. A southward-reaching flame might tell me that things will be getting spicy, which would be good news for a romance, although for other types of work this could indicate that rivals will be worked up against me. West tells me to be aware of my emotions as well as those of whomever I may be doing work for. Finally, north tells me to slow down and that my ability to control my destiny might best be enhanced by grounding myself and letting go. Additionally a directional flame may be pointing you in a specific direction. For example, if you are doing work to enable you to move, then this flame may be telling you in which direction to go.

Reading Residue

Utilizing a candle as part of your prayer opens up a dialogue, allowing God or the spirits you have petitioned to answer you in the form of residue left on the candle. Anyone who has ever asked for something through prayer knows that prayers are not always answered, and sometimes you may be left waiting for that big win or cash settlement that never comes. If the residue left on the candle glass is read well, it can indicate the outcome of your prayer request. This allows you to reevaluate what you want, or seek alternative ways to attain it. Perhaps that lottery win is not for you to have now, but only later after you have divorced your mate who would otherwise have gotten half your earnings. An effective reading of the candle glass can help you better understand what your true needs are.

I should also point out that different people who do this work attribute different meanings to wax shapes. Here are the definitions I give to folks who come into my store looking to have their candle read:

Complete: Your candle burned to completion, successfully working toward your goal.

Incomplete: Your candle failed to complete its burn. When this occurs, it is said to have been snuffed out by either an opposing force or the will of Spirit. You may wish to get a clearer understanding through a different form of divination, or from a psychic reader.

Clean: The overall clarity of your candle glass toward the bottom signals a positive response to your petition. The path toward achieving your goal has been cleared, and you should take whatever action will lead to the fulfillment of your goals.

Cloudy: Your candle burned cloudy, which suggests a deeper need for clarity. Things are not as they seem; the fog is thick. Cleansing may be in order.

Sooty: Your candle contains soot at the top, which traditionally represents difficulty in manifesting your request. Commonly, when a candle burns black, it suggests that other forces are working against your will. You may wish to light an uncrossing candle, which helps to remove those conditions that oppose your work. Soot is a bad sign, representing a struggle; but if the candle completed its task, then it is believed to have been a success, especially the cleaner it is at the bottom. Still, some believe that the results of such a candle will be poor, and tend to favor lighting another, until the reading is cleaner.

Messy: When wax residue sticks to the glass in chaotic forms, it is called "messy" and represents a difficult situation, such as can be seen in your candle. Traditionally it would be said that the process of achieving your goal will be fraught with tension and difficulty. If you wish to help reduce this, an uncrossing candle is suggested.

Lines of Wax (Horizontal): These lines often indicate obstacles and challenges that will need to be met in the process of attaining whatever your candle was lit for.

Lines of Wax (Vertical): For me, these lines indicate being trapped. When seen on a court case candle, they can also indicate that jail time will be an issue.

Lines on Rear: Lines on the back of your candle represent past impediments, and these continue to influence your situation, especially in the form of stress and worry. Faith and confidence are called for at this time.

Lines on Front: Lines represent hurdles that must be overcome in order to achieve your goal, and those appearing on the front of your candle suggest problems in your immediate future. Often these are not large hurdles, but small ones, such as missing your ride or a phone call. Keep your eye on the situation to help ensure that things go smoothly.

If you have added glitter or herbs to your candle, they may also adhere to the lines of wax, which adds a positive connotation to their meaning. Should herbs or glitter adhere to the lines in the rear, I take it to mean that my past hurdles served as positive learning experiences. When they appear in the front, I know that my obstacles are present for a higher purpose.

Residue Halo: The circle of herbs and glitter toward the top of your candle is known as a halo, and tells us that your ancestors and spirit guides are involved in helping you achieve your goal. If you are working with any spirits known to appreciate offerings such as food, drink, or novenas, be sure to give them their due for helping you. If you do not know who your helping angels are, just know that you are blessed.

Some workers find the residue halo to imply a negative condition, which explains why one's angels might be hovering so close.

Residue on Rear: The backside of your candle represents your past, and residue adhering to the back of your candle indicates the presence of past issues. These issues continue to influence your situation. Going forward, you should identify what these issues are and work toward resolving them.

Residue on Front: The front of your candle represents your future, and residue adhering to the front of your candle represents future issues that will affect your situation.

Residue on One Side: Residue on one side of your candle represents an imbalance.

Cracked Glass: If your candle glass cracked in the process of burning, that is considered to be a negative sign. When this happens, it is time to reevaluate your situation and desired goal.

Of course, there are many shapes that the wax may take. If you see something distinctive, such as the shape of a key, then you may divine its meaning in the same manner as you would if a key were to appear in your dream. A good book on dream symbols may be helpful if you do not have an immediate understanding of what a certain symbol means for you.

Once your candle has finished burning, it is important to dispose of it properly. Your candle has done its magic, and therefore the glass is like the cocoon left behind by the butterfly. For ecological reasons, I put mine in the recycling after cleaning it.

Altars

Candles are often lit on an altar. The term *altar work* is commonly used to describe a type of focused spiritual work, setting apart the type of dedicated rites commonly done at one's altar from less formal tricks. There is no singular way to set up an altar; indeed, there are workers who never set one up, preferring to work at the kitchen table or counter. Many, however, prefer to surround their work with sacred items. These may be statues of saints, lightning-struck wood, candles, decorative incense holders, or really anything from which one might draw energy or with which one might connect with a higher power. Descriptions of altars used by American folk magicians reveal much diversity, from Helen Pitkin's 1904 depiction of a floor altar arranged with fruits, liquor, and sweets to the structured candle altars described by Mikhail Strabo and Henri Gamache.

Sometimes an altar doubles as one's work area. My working altar occupies a corner of my kitchen that has a wide, flat surface where I have room to write papers, dress candles, construct mojo hands, and so forth. Above that space are shelves, where a variety of spells are in action on behalf of clients and loved ones. I also have a candle shrine in my back yard, where I do the majority of my candle jobs. If I need additional space, I have an entire room dedicated to altars and ritual space. Unless you are doing professional work for others, then any flat surface will do. Altars need not be ostentatious, nor do they need to be dedicated solely to intense work. A vanity can serve as an altar, perhaps with simple additions such as a candle, a dish of potpourri, or pictures of loved ones. What better way to make sacred the simple act of getting your hair and face ready in the morning?

Oftentimes folks will construct altars to target a specific type of work. An altar built on a toilet tank, for instance, may be ideal for hexing work, whereas a tiny shrine occupying the top shelf of a medicine cabinet may be geared toward healing spells or success at weight loss. Windowsills, headboards, bathtub rims, dashboards, and other places can become sacred spaces and serve as altars.

Moving candle spells are another way in which directionality plays a part in Conjure. In these workings, dressing candles represent individuals or conditions, then are moved in a manner that draws them together or pushes them apart. Say you are working on behalf of two people you wish to bring closer together, such as for a love spell. You would choose a candle to represent each person, probably a figural candle related to the gender of either party. You would dress them accordingly (for instance, with a condition oil designed for love), then set them apart from each other on a surface such as an altar. You would light each candle, then progressively move them closer together. Often this work is performed over a period of time—say, seven days—with each candle being burned for a short period of time. By day seven, the two candles should meet and finish their burn together. Generally, such candles are burned on a plate, with the two plates touching on the seventh day, or else on the seventh day they are placed together on a single plate to complete their work. Moving candle spells done to separate two individuals are done in reverse, with the candles moved apart from one another each day.

Multiplying Wealth

Making money grow requires knowing which risks to take and which investments are sound ones. For example, if you are a farmer, you will want to know which chicken on the market will lay the most eggs for you. So much of this type of magic relies on being able to see opportunity as well as danger. When it comes to pursuing a business or career path, the voice of a good accountant is more important than that of any ancestor or angel. Over the years I have done many readings for folks who had been told by others to follow their dreams and do what they love, only to suffer the consequences of unrealistic goals. The You Can Do It industry of motivational speakers tries to convince everyone that whatever they wish for is possible, and when realistic concerns such as limited consumers are brought up, those concerns are written off as being a scarcity mentality. This leads dreamers to avoid relevant market signs and plow ahead with their plans, and when those plans fall through, they are left feeling as though their magic was not strong enough.

Throughout the last recession I drew cards for many a distraught person who felt they had failed some spiritual test because their home was being foreclosed on. Rather than blaming the predatory bankers who had told them a balloon mortgage was a good option, many blamed themselves instead, and suffered a crisis of faith. I am not stating any of this to dissuade anyone from pursuing their dreams or using magic to do so—

indeed, doing so is why I am in the place where I am today—but it is important to begin with realistic goals, do your research, maintain a good credit score, and expand at a reasonable pace.

For long-term goals, you might consider creating a money altar. Choose someplace high in your home or office, such as on top of a bookshelf (making certain that if you burn candles there, they do not discolor or light on fire the area above them). Statuaries of some kind are typical, such as a figure of the goddess Fortuna, or a Buddha with money bags, or a figure of Marie Laveau if you earn money from your magical talents. Flowers, incense, alcohol, and so forth are typical offerings to whichever spirit(s) stand on your money altar.

Lodestones are also great at drawing money, especially when placed upon currency. Placing such a stone on a hundred-dollar bill is said to bring similar bills toward you. You can begin with smaller bills and work your way up to a hundred; just know that this is money being given to your lodestone and cannot be taken away. Once you give it, it belongs to your lodestone. Now, you can trade bills out. Say you want to go to the casino; in that case you can trade out the bill(s) that have been sitting beneath your lodestone for others equal in value, thus giving you charmed money to work with.

Candles work well toward the goal of multiplying money, in that you can begin with a single candle, then light others directly from its flame. Take a green candle, properly dressed with a money-drawing oil, and light it. Then take three similar candles and place them in the shape of a triangle around the single one. Use the central candle to light the candle in the lower right, then use that one to light the candle in the lower left, and use that one to light the final candle up top.

Securing Your Money

You want your wallet or bank account to remain full, and any investments to remain strong. How many of us have been in the position of getting a bonus, perhaps a tax return, only to have the brakes on our car go out and have to spend it all. It's not enough to get money; you need to keep it, and you do that by securing the things that might otherwise demand your cash. One way of securing your finances is to place a railroad spike atop your bank statements. There are a number of products made for this purpose, such as Money Stay with Me.

When you do have to give your money away, there are tricks for helping it find its way back to you.

Trained Money

Keeping in mind that what you put out into the world returns to you, take a quarter and paint it with red nail polish. This is something we do at our shop, giving the coin as change to a customer. We have a little celebration whenever we receive a coin with remnants of red nail polish on it, seeing it as validation that our money is being returned to us. This is the practice of working with trained money. Others do similar work by writing on bills, which allows for all manner of creativity.

Lamps

Electric lighting all but killed the use of oil lamps; however, the tradition of using them for magical purposes remains. While there are many forms and fuels that an oil lamp may take, we will focus on the most popular variety, the kerosene lamp (aka paraffin lamp). Let us begin our discussion with the definitions for the various parts that compose such a lamp.

The part of the lamp that contains the liquid fuel is called a *fount* or *font*. The part that screws onto the font and holds the threaded wick is called a *burner*. The glass that surrounds the flaming wick is called the *chimney*.

For our font we will want something made of glass so that we may see the goodies we will be placing within it. This is perhaps why lamp magic is so popular, since we can fill the font with all sorts of curios relevant to our work, as we do with mojo bags.

There are many commercial lamps available that will suit our needs. One popular variety of burner is sized to screw onto a common mason jar, which works great, as the depth of the mason jar allows us plenty of room in which to place our curios. A trip to your local hardware store should give you some appropriate choices, and there are a variety of lamps available online as well.

Glass fonts can be found in many colors, so if you don't mind a dimmer view of the items stored within your font, you might choose a red one to serve as your lamp for love magic, or perhaps blue for happy home work. The same color correspondences used for choosing a candle can be applied to an oil lamp. Additionally, you can achieve color in other ways, such as with an oil-based candy dye like the kind Wilton sells, or through natural dyes such as alkanet, which will turn your oil red. Pre-colored fuels are available if you do a bit of searching.

When it comes to choosing an oil, I prefer liquid paraffin. It generates little smoke and burns well. While some people like to use common oils such as canola, vegetable, or olive oil, those are often thicker and not well suited to the flat wick that most burners are made for. These wicks use a capillary system to pull oil through their fibers, and thicker oils do not pull through as well. To my liquid paraffin I like to add some conjure oils, just as I do with my seven-day candles. Most commercial conjure oils contain fragrance or essential oils that have been added to a carrier oil such as almond oil or jojoba. Adding conjure oils to fuel has always worked out fine for me, although I imagine that if it made the fuel too thick overall then the wick would struggle to absorb it.

First, gather the materials needed to construct your lamp: the font, burner, and chimney.

Before threading your wick into the burner, write on it with a pen. (I find that a Sharpie whose tip is still pointed works well, which you can find in a number of colors.) You can write words, such as *This light draws wealth to the Smith family: Jane, Joe, and Jill.* The industrious and psalm-inspired worker may choose to pen the words of an appropriate verse, such as Psalm 114, which is traditionally written or recited for money petitions. Additionally you could draw symbols, such as the success sigil from chapter 4.

Place within the font whatever things you feel are appropriate to this work, keeping in mind that it must not take up too much space—a ratio of no more than ¼ curio to ¾ fuel is preferred. A picture of anyone involved in the spell works well, along with personal concerns such as fingernail clippings. This essentially serves as a type of container spell. I suggest adding a chunk of pyrite, a two-dollar bill, and a small alligator claw.

Add your fuel and assemble your lamp. You will want to add a condition oil to your fuel. Just a few drops will do. Something in the family of money drawing would be most suitable, such as Money Come to Me, Wealthy Way, or Filthy Rich.

Finally, light your lamp.

Lamps can be lit whenever you feel the need for more of whatever they have been loaded for. Sticking with money, you may light it whenever your bills are coming due and you need additional funds, or on nights when big tips are needed, or before going out gambling. The frequency and duration of the lighting depends on you.

When it is time for the lighting to be done, simply blow into the chimney. For both lamps and candles I have heard people profess a prohibition against blowing them out. If this is how you feel, then by all means snuff it out instead.

My final thoughts here relate to how many folks see the pursuit of money as being unspiritual. Given that our society requires us to earn money, this work becomes essential. What this type of work does is it allows us to engage our spirituality through our wealth work, thus creating a healthy balance between the two pursuits.

⚜ XI ⚜
The Keys to Powders:
Unlocking Justified Hexes

TO CURSE, HOODOO, HEX, bedevil, or jinx are all terms used to describe enacting harm through magic, and this is one of the more notorious aspects of Conjure work. Many examples in folklore exist regarding the nature of a curse: cords tied in knots while words of damnation are recited...dolls stuffed with herbs and hair are stabbed and buried along with prayers for the victim's demise...matchsticks are broken to encourage breakage of bone and limb...mock funerals are even performed so that the intended victim will meet a similar fate. There is no shortage of inspirational material derived from folklore when it comes to how one might do harm magically to one's enemies.

Not everyone who practices Conjure feels called to do cursing work. Typically, those who do not are called *lady-hearted*, and may prefer instead to focus their work on matters of blessing and love. The art of cursing, however, is common, and therefore a full understanding of Conjure would be incomplete without its examination.

While Christianity has served as a major religious influence on Conjure, Conjure is not a religious tradition and has adherents from a variety of religious backgrounds. In its recent history, Conjure practice has gained many practitioners from traditions within the African diaspora, such as Ifa, Palo, and Santeria, as well as Neopagan traditions such as Feri,

Traditional Witchcraft, and Wicca. While it is impossible to describe the spiritual mindset of every practitioner, there is much to be said regarding the Christian worldview that shaped the tradition. The idea that cursing work fits within a certain Christian context is unfamiliar to some people, especially those reared in denominations that focused strongly on Jesus's command in Matthew 7:1: *Judge not, that ye be not judged.* If God is all-knowing and all-powerful, then what role does the Conjure worker serve? Might it be best simply to leave justice up to God? Often the response to this is no, for the individual is seen as having a duty, one directed by biblical text, both to implore the Almighty for justice and to take physical action within the world to facilitate the work of God's hand.

The Bible is full of stories that involve cursing. Beginning in the book of Genesis, God curses Adam and Eve, and later curses Cain, then Job, and … well, you get the idea. It is easy to see how a simple reading implies that cursing is aligned with God's will, at least some of the time. Yet there is more to be found in scripture. Two laws govern how action is to be taken in matters of cursing. The first is the law of prayer, and the second is the law of action.

The law of prayer is seen throughout scripture. Though God may be omniscient and know your woes already, the devout are nevertheless directed to beseech God's aid through prayer. When an enemy must be dealt with, the onus is on the individual to pray for justice and retribution. We see this in Psalm 109, a popular psalm read for cursing. It begins with the following:

1 *Hold not thy peace, O God of my praise;*
2 *For the mouth of the wicked and the mouth of the deceitful are opened against me: they have spoken against me with a lying tongue.*
3 *They compassed me about also with words of hatred; and fought against me without a cause.*
4 *For my love they are my adversaries: but I give myself unto prayer.*
5 *And they have rewarded me evil for good, and hatred for my love.*
6 *Set thou a wicked man over him: and let Satan stand at his right hand.*

The psalm goes on to request God's aid in removing the man from his position of power, making his wife a widow, his children destitute and barren, his name forgotten, and various other unfortunate things. King David is not holding back here. He knows what he wants to see happen to his enemies, and he pleads his case accordingly. Prayer is necessary, yet if results relied on prayer alone, there would be no need to engage the world as we do through Conjure.

Let us look at another biblical story, that of Joshua and the Israelites who came to take the city of Jericho. In this passage from Joshua 6:2–5, the Lord gives Joshua very detailed instructions:

> 2 And the Lord said unto Joshua, See, I have given into thine hand Jericho, and the king thereof, and the mighty men of valour.
>
> 3 And ye shall compass the city, all ye men of war, and go round about the city once. Thus shalt thou do six days.
>
> 4 And seven priests shall bear before the ark seven trumpets of rams' horns: and the seventh day ye shall compass the city seven times, and the priests shall blow with the trumpets.
>
> 5 And it shall come to pass, that when they make a long blast with the ram's horn, and when ye hear the sound of the trumpet, all the people shall shout with a great shout; and the wall of the city shall fall down flat, and the people shall ascend up every man straight before him.

One might ask whose benefit all this marching and trumpeting is for? Why, if God is omnipotent and able to knock down the walls, must all these actions be carried out? We may not understand the exact mechanism whereby a ram's horn is instrumental in reducing a wall to rubble, but by biblical example, and through the knowledge of workers who have practiced before us, we understand the necessity of taking action. The world is ordered in such a way that certain actions are key to change. One does not simply pray that their home be free of leaks and leave it at that, not when they are capable of adding thatch to mend the roof. The practice of Conjure, although it includes prayer, focuses just as much on performing actions to change reality.

The question left to the worker therefore is not *Will God curse my enemies?* but rather *Will God find my curse to be justified?* If the answer is no, then the curse will not come to fruition. Many workers, including those who perform cursing work for payment, do not feel that cursing compromises their moral standing. If someone has done wrong and the curse is found by the Almighty to be justified, then the worker's prayer and ritual actions are seen as holy work done in service to Spirit. Many workers will not take on cursing work unless they have first employed some form of divination, confirming first that a curse is indeed justified.

I am stressing this largely due to a perception that many people have toward Conjure, which is the belief that the tradition is amoral, when in actuality a number of practitioners find their cursing work to be an ethical duty.

Of course, not all workers abide by those biblical standards. Some consider themselves mercenaries, taking on cursing work whether it is justified or not. When this is the case, God is not fundamental to the equation, and the worker may rely on other powers to get the job done. This chapter examines the power found within the formulation of certain powders.

Motivations for Hexing

Surely you, dear reader, have never been tempted to throw a curse at someone, and since you are so in the dark about what might bring someone to the point of soaking a poppet in hexing oil and setting it alight, I will tell you what my own research has revealed. There appear to be several distinct motivations for throwing a curse, including the following.

Ambition

Sometimes the easiest way to get ahead is to hold another back. Cursing a competitor to fail is not always an emotional reaction, but rather is a strategic move.

Fear

Though many folktales remind us that we may be greater monsters than those we fear, fear is nevertheless a motivation for some cursings. Better bring them down while you can, before they come for you.

Hatred

Any of the other motivations can ultimately lead to hatred, yet hatred is sometimes its own motivator. Individuals may inherit hatred through prejudiced mentors and institutions, leading them to throw spoiled eggs at the homes of people they may not even know. Therefore, hatred may or may not include a history of personal grievances.

Jealousy

What makes that jerk so special that they should get the good thing? Jealousy can be complex and personal or vague and petty.

Justice

When punishment is seen as a form of justice, it may take the form of a curse. Some people believe that karma will intercede to scold the bad guys, though a quick glance at the world does little to support this notion, as terrible people routinely grow prosperous and live long and seemingly happy lives. Though an important concept in Hinduism and some New Age theologies, karma, as it is commonly expressed in the West, is not indigenous to Conjure. When the term is used, it is often in a *God's gonna get them* manner. Some merchandisers have made use of the word, selling products said to get karma to do a job. Essentially they have taken the notion of petitioning God to enact justice in the form of a curse, and traded God for karma. When you are wanting to see someone pay for their crimes, it matters little which cosmic mind or mechanism flips the switch.

Revenge

Revenge can seem a lot like justice sometimes, especially by those who believe they were wronged. Other times we know that the wrongdoing was ours alone, but still hold resentment and seek revenge.

Metaphysics aside, hexing work can be cathartic. The notion that we should always act with love is a high goal, but is unachievable unless our less flattering desires are fully processed. Saying you do not wish to have negative motivations, though admirable, does nothing to eliminate them. The human condition, with its propensity to wish harm on others, is not so easily overcome. Denying your negative desires only makes you blind to them, so when they eventually resurface they are unrecognizable for having been so long forgotten. Better to throw a curse in the moment while the emotions are fresh. Maybe it will stick, or maybe it won't. It's often hard to judge what is justified in the moment. Either way you might feel better. That's not to say the dark arts are nothing more than a form of therapy, though I do suspect that those who throw curses, like those who swear, have found a therapeutic outlet for thoughts and feelings that might otherwise go uncommunicated and consume them.

Popular Formulas for Hexing

Banishing Formulas

When used for cursing, banishment products force someone to exit a place or situation. Depending on how it is administered, a banishing product may work by means of influence, such as causing someone to make the decision to move away; or banishment may be administered as a curse, forcing a person's life to crumble around them so that they are forced by circumstances to relocate. There is of course another way, which involves blessing them with opportunities elsewhere, but chances are whoever you are banishing has been enough of an irritant that seeing them become happy and prosperous may be another thorn in your side.

Hot Foot: This formula is said to make a person restless, as though their feet were being held to the fire, until eventually they run away.

Run Devil Run: More commonly this formula is applied to personal demons and things believed to be causing bad luck; however, some do apply it to individuals who are persecuting them.

....

RUN DEVIL RUN HERB BLEND

- Cayenne pepper
- Couch grass
- Stinging nettle

Getting rid of the people who are causing you concern is one way to deal with them; however, be careful not to harm yourself in the process. As pointed out earlier, banishing work can be cathartic; however, the opposite is true as well: bringing all your nasty feelings to the surface and stewing in them can have debilitating long-term effects. This is one issue that is brought up often to suggest that cursing work does more harm than good, as some believe that the negativity produced and amplified in the performance of a spell is just as likely to hurt the Conjurer as it is their target. It may be the case that the condition you most need to rid yourself of is your own negative emotional state. Long after you have succeeded in driving someone away, you may be left with bad feelings that need chasing away as well. To drive such devils away, Run Devil Run would be helpful.

Separation

These formulas are used in order to separate people. The motivation for those spells often has to do with someone wanting a relationship to end so that they might swoop in and make moves on one of them. An affair with someone who is married often leads to this option, especially when such a lover has made promises to leave their spouse but has not done so (as they seldom do). Other times separation work is done by a friend who has lost his bestie to some Romeo, or a mother who will not stand for having a hussy for a daughter-in-law. The purpose for separation is not always so self-serving, as there are times when folks fall into a bad relationship, such as with an addict who would have a better chance at recovery if separated from their enabling friend. Variations of separation formulas include the following.

Break Up: As this is the term more commonly used for ruined love affairs rather than friendships, its purpose is clear.

Love Breaker: This formula works as a form of separation as well, though its target need not be in a committed relationship. If you suspect your crush is crushing on someone else, this works toward squelching that emotion.

....

LOVE BREAKER CONJURE BALL

Use the directions from earlier to encase in a ball of wax the following ingredients:

- Black cat hair
- Black dog hair
- Black mustard seed

While such products get the job done, it is best to be more specific in your work. All kinds of events could lead to the object of your affection being separated from their spouse—such as running their spouse over with a car in an obvious act of murder, in which case they will likely be put on death row. Or their relationship may end after the person of your dreams suffers a disfiguring accident, and although you are not shallow, still, it is not at all what you had hoped for. This rule of specificity should be applied to all magical work. You must figure out what cracks exist in the foundation of your target's life that you can further split apart and then decide if to do so will aid your cause, or else you may encounter unexpected consequences.

Mental Distress

A strategy used in cursing formulas often entails making a person crazy, or at least making them appear to others to be crazy. This puts them at a disadvantage in many regards, likely leading to them losing their job and their relationships and being unable to defend themselves against legal challenges. It also makes it more difficult for them to get the actual help they need from a rootworker. Although a good rootworker will make diagnoses according to some form of divination, first impressions still matter, and calls from people who sound insane are not always answered with the eagerness their situation requires. Others who might be able to help, such as loved ones, doctors, and social workers, are also distanced.

Confusion: This formula causes a person to become disoriented. Behaviorally, it results in mess-ups and delays. It works especially well for attacking someone's credibility, such as a person who might say bad things abut you, the tattletale at the office, or the officer testifying against you. It can help make someone question what they think they remember.

....

CONFUSION POWDER

- Licorice root
- Poppy seeds
- Devil's shoestring

Here is an example of a formula that would be difficult to powder. In such a case, these items can be placed in a container of powder, relying on the law of contagion to imbue the powder with their essence. I suggest doing this for a period of seven days, shaking the bottle seven times each day.

Inflammatory Confusion: This is a formula for confusion, with the added element of enraged anger. Again, it is ideal for using against those who would slander you, causing them to appear not only confused but out of control. Those who succumb to this curse often lose their loved ones, employment, and housing due to their aggressive behavior.

Intranquil Spirit: Intranquil Spirit is the name given to a spirit (some say a type of spirit that numbers many). It comes into Conjure from Mexican Catholicism. It actually serves as a type of reconciliation formula, making it so that a lover who has distanced themself feels anguish, like the fires of purgatory, until they return to you. Of course, the person you get back from this is likely to be a wreck after such an ordeal.

Restless: No one likes feeling restless, certainly not over a long period of time, as the effects are harsh on the mind and body. Using this formula in tandem with Hot Foot would result in someone becoming geographically as well as mentally and emotionally unsettled.

There are multiple other ways to impact someone's mental state, though none with an extensive history of brand-name use. Similar curses might entail bad dreams, dyslexia, forgetfulness, and symptoms similarly seen in mental conditions such as obsessive-compulsive disorder and schizophrenia.

Assorted Curses

Curses, generally speaking, wreak havoc in a variety of ways. Some target individuals, or groups of individuals, and can be passed down through future generations.

Bat's Blood: These types of formulas, such as we saw for ink, contain no actual bat blood but derive power from their spooky name and the common ingredient of dragon's blood resin.

Crossing: While not everyone who is crossed has had a second-party curse placed on them, this formula is for doing just that.

Damnation: The person using this formula wants nothing less than the eternal suffering of their foe.

....

DAMNATION POWDER

- 1 part asafoetida
- 1 part sulfur

Destruction: This formula is for when you wish to burn the whole damn thing down and salt the earth it stood on. It works to destroy people, places, and institutions.

Devil: By some accounts, the Devil is the greatest tormentor, and this formula is used to direct that Devil to torment someone.

Double Cross: This formula is meant to replace or dominate more positive ones. Although many negative products smell harsh, a good Double Cross involves not getting caught, so it is subtle in scent and often light in color to conceal its true purpose.

Goofer Dust: We will discuss goofer dust later in this chapter. The classic formula is Goofer Dust, though some have been known to formulate goofer into other products such as oils and incense.

Hexing: A hex is a typically described as a curse, though the term is not commonly used to denote bad luck passed down through family lines, as is the case with a generational curse.

Jinx: Jinxes are typically less ruinous than curses, and are often used more to drive someone away than to destroy them utterly. You should ask yourself if you have been jinxed when all the little things in life go wrong, say your car won't start, or your water gets shut off, or your wallet is stolen. These are all things that irritate and slow you down, which is what they are meant to do.

Revenge: This formula's name declares its motivation and does the job of ruining its target.

War Water: This formula is used by different groups in North American folk magic. Its origin seems to be European, given that many recipes emphasize the presence of iron. At its simplest, rusty nails are added to a bottle of water. The associations with iron and the warrior god Mars make it useful for conflict and protection. War Water is often used to declare war against another, typically by throwing the bottle against an enemy's door so that it shatters and covers their porch. To make this even more unpleasant, War Water may include all manner of nasty-smelling ingredients. Some use tar water, aka *creolina*, while others include such things as snail carcasses, snake skin sheds, skunk essence, and other nasty things.

Powders

Powders are often used to dress an item, such as a candle or a person, or are thrown in a target's path. Each use has its own traditions and tricks, such as blending your powder with dirt so that it might more easily blend into the soil your target will walk across.

Most everything in the Conjure formulary can be made into a powder. This process involves taking herbs and grinding them with a mortar and pestle or coffee grinder. This is then added to cornstarch, rice powder, or arrowroot powder. (Older recipes call for talc, though recent studies suggest that talc might be connected with certain forms of cancer.[12]) All of these powders blend well with small amounts of scented oil. To keep your powder from clumping, it is important not to add too much oil, and to blend it well. Oil blends into powder best by rubbing the mixture between your hands. (Wear gloves or your skin will sponge up the oil.) Take special care when working with irritants not to get any

---

12. American Cancer Society, "Talcum Powder and Cancer," www.cancer.org/cancer/cancer -causes/talcum-powder-and-cancer.html.

in your eyes. Let us take a look at some of the more popular powders you may wish to have on hand.

Agricultural Powders

Asafoetida: This powder is used to chase away haints.

Black Pepper: This is used to drive someone away.

Cayenne Pepper: This powder heats things up.

Cornflour: This powder is often used as a carrier, to which additional ground ingredients or oils are added.

Sandalwood: This is a powdered wood that is burned as an incense for blessings and peace.

Sugar: This one is used to sweeten someone, as seen in chapter 9.

Mineral Powders

Alum: This powder is effective for stopping gossip. If you have ever put some in your mouth, as was done to me as a child to dry up canker sores, then you know how it dries and puckers your mouth—something you would want to see done to someone spreading lies about you.

Bluing Detergent: We have seen how the color blue is often used for matters requiring cleansing and protection, as is the case with this powder.

Chalk: This powder is often used to draw symbols on the ground, mostly as a form of foot-trafficking magic (which we will talk more about shortly).

Gunpowder: This mixture of saltpeter, charcoal, and sulfur is used to remove obstacles and for cursing work. Safety is a big concern when working with this powder.

Magnetic Sand: This is the name given for two different products.

In Hoodoo, magnetic sand often refers to iron shavings (a byproduct of the iron industry) that are fed to lodestones.

Another mineral called magnetic sand is *magnetite*, which can be found naturally in some places, such as parts of Santa Cruz. Magnetite sand carries its own magnetic charge and can be used to draw desired conditions to you, much like a lodestone.

Red Brick Dust: This powder is used for protection. It is important to note that bricks from different parts of the country have different qualities. Bricks often found in the southern parts of the United States tend to be softer and easier to break down into dust, whereas newer ones from the West Coast are harder and less yielding.

Salt: There are two varieties of salt commonly used in Hoodoo: white and black.

White salt, be it table salt, Kosher salt, or another, is used for protection.

Black salt is a variety that is sometimes attainable from culinary suppliers and is safe for food, though what is sold in many occult stores is table salt dyed black. There are various formulas for dyeing salt black, such as mixing it with powdered charcoal, with scrapings from a cauldron or vigil candle that has burned black, or with graveyard dirt. Black salt is used for protection to drive away evil influences, but is also used for cursing work when the evil influence is understood to be a person.

Saltpeter: Saltpeter (potassium nitrate) adds an explosive oomph to your concoction, much as does gun powder. It was once a common product to have around the homestead, used for fertilizer and removing tree stumps. Whereas gunpowder is black and has more associations with cursing work, saltpeter is white and can be used (with safety in mind) for spells needing an extra boost of power.

Sulfur: This powder is used for cursing. It is said that Hell smells of burning sulfur, which is where it draws this association.

Talc: This is often used as a carrier, especially for powders to be applied to the skin, such as a love-drawing powder. Talc has fallen into disuse in favor of other carriers such as rice or arrowroot powder.

Zoological Powders

All of the previous powders require no work to grind up, unlike the following list of zoological powders, which are ground from the following.

Bones: The bones of any creature can be ground into a powder and used to gain their qualities.

Eggshells: Known as *cascarilla* in Spanish, this is a chalklike powder made from eggshells, which you can get from most botanicas without having to grind them yourself. This powder comes from Santeria and is one of the more modern animal curios to be adopted into various styles of American folk magic. It is often used protectively, such as by marking the back of one's neck with a cross to aid against spirit attachments.

Crab Shells: These are used in reversing spells.

Snail Shells: These are used for cursing and are said to bring pestilence.

Some of the zoological curios we saw in chapter 2 may be powdered as well, such as a dirt dauber's nest.

Other Powders

Ash: Ash is often obtained from elements burned ritually, such as the ash left over from a burnt poppet, or more commonly from a name paper.

Blowing Powders

Pictured in the Standard O & B Supply Company catalogue from the mid-1940s is a woman blowing powder from her raised palm, her figure multiplied four times so she appears to have turned in all directions. Although the illustration shows her holding powder in her right hand, I've heard it said that it should be in the left hand, especially when being used for cursing work. The accompanying copy explains: "Powder Blowing is very common practice in the West Indies to purify the room and to rid it of foul, evil or unsavory 'presences,' for adverse conditions, for gaining Love affections, money, happiness."[13] If you were doing this inside your home, then you would want to stick to powders that promote peace, fidelity, protection, and so forth. Outside the home, somewhere auspicious such as a crossroads or graveyard is where you would want to do more malevolent work. Even still, something like Hot Foot

---

13. Standard O & B Catalogue (1944).

you would not want to blow at all, due to the likely possibility of getting some in your eyes.

Dressing is the term used when the powder is being applied to an item, such as a candle or document. For example, a candle is often dressed first with oil appropriate to the job, such as Filthy Rich for money drawing, then is rolled in Filthy Rich powder toward the worker. A love letter may be dusted with Fireworks of Love powder, have a heart traced in it by the rootworker's finger, then shaken clean and sent to the would-be lover. Bodies themselves may be dressed by utilizing this compound as a dusting powder.

Sprinkling involves walking backward while tossing powder on the ground, similar to the way in which seeds are scattered in a furrow. A certain number of backward steps are taken, the number of which varies. The number is often an odd amount, with nine, thirteen, and twenty-one being most common. Sprinkling powder is part of a larger practice of foot-trafficking magic, which plays a large part in Hoodoo especially.

Foot Trafficking

Be still for a moment and breathe. As your lungs gently swell, imagine that air is being swept up through your feet. Now exhale, and as you feel air leaving your lungs through your nose or mouth, imagine the air is also exiting through the soles of your feet. Repeat this until you develop the sensation of breathing through your feet. This can serve as a great way to release tension and to draw vital energy into your body. For me this serves as a trigger, switching my mindset from the mundane to the spiritual. This simple act connects me to my ancestors; I can sense them stirring in the earth below where their bones are buried, and feel them rise up into me to do work through my hands.

Feet play an important role in Conjure, an influence taken directly from African traditions. It is believed that footprints leave behind something of their bearer's identity, and that is why dirt from a person's footprint may be used in work regarding them. Furthermore, it is believed that sorcery is easily absorbed through the feet, and for that reason tricks are placed along a person's path, so that they may step upon the spell and thus be influenced by it. When this happens as a curse, it is referred to as *poisoning through the feet*. Let's look at this more tangibly through the deployment of Hot Foot powder.

....

HOT FOOT POWDER

Hot Foot, at its simplest, is a combination of peppers that is intended to make the target feel so restless that they leave. The degree to which this acts as a curse is debated. A particularly harsh Hot Foot is designed to leave them forever restless.

Which route you go likely depends on your feelings about the person. If they have caused you all manner of grief, then Hot Foot may best serve your spite. It is difficult to sincerely bless those who have done us wrong, as much as our better angels may suggest it. I find that banishing is a good solution, carrying no particular emotion but simply getting the job done and leaving you in peace. Combine the following:

- 1 part ground cayenne pepper
- 1 part black pepper
- 1 part sulfur

Optional items may include such things as these:

- Paper-wasp nest: Make sure the wasps have abandoned the nest before messing with it. This will need to be ground up.
- Tumbleweed: These are not freely available commercially, so you must live in an area where they are prevalent and chase one down. Having done this, you will want to dry it and then grind it up, which is not the easiest task.

A good coffee grinder would be helpful for transforming either of these options into powder.

....

BREAK UP POWDER

For this you will need to create two separate name papers, one for each person you wish to separate. Burn these separately, so that you are able to collect the ash of each paper.

Find a location where there is a crack at your feet, either a natural fissure in the ground or a crack in the sidewalk, and stand with one foot on either side of the crack. This work should be done at night, midnight ideally. You will need to know the cardinal directions of your location, taking note of east and west. Of the two parties, you should decide whom you wish to bless and whom you wish to curse. Beginning with the ash of the blessed party, direct your face toward the east.

Keep your feet planted on separate sides of the crack. Depending on how the crack is situated, you may need to turn to the side, or if the crack runs directly from east to west, then face east.

Place in your right palm the ash of the party you wish to bless, and blow toward the east, saying:

> *(Name of blessed person),*
> *With the rising sun*
> *You are turned from (name of cursed person).*

Keeping your feet where they are, turn west. If west is behind you, then you will be pivoting at your waist to the left and extending your arm behind you. First, however, place the ash of the party you wish to curse in your left hand. Toward the east you will throw this, as hard as you can, as though throwing a ball away from you with all the might you can muster. Say the following:

> *(Name of cursed person),*
> *Toward darkness and death*
> *You are turned from (name of blessed person).*

Understandably you will wish to do this at a time when there is no wind, lest you get a face full of ash blown back at you.

....

GOOFER DUST

Among the many cultural references to goofer dust is a song by that name recorded by Big Lucky Carter (aka Levester Carter) in 1969, which describes this infamous product. While the song does not serve as a recipe, there are all kinds of nasty things that can go into this cursing powder, such as:

- Bark from a gallows tree
- Black mustard seeds
- Dirt from a fiend's grave
- Snake sheds
- Sulfur

At the onset of the curse, it causes the target derangement (they act goofy), thus limiting their ability to get help for their condition, which appears to others as paranoia or mental illness. There are many recipes for goofer dust, although graveyard dirt (especially that taken from the grave of a fiendish spirit) is often a main ingredient, an ingredient we will examine in detail in the next chapter.

The key to a good curse is letting go of it, which serves a dual purpose. It acts as a statement of faith in the cursing work you have done, and it allows you to let go of the negative emotions that drove you to enact the curse. Let the powder sift from your fingers, and with it let your anger and hatred leave you.

∾ XII ∿
The Keys to the Graveyard:
Unlocking Spirit Conjuration

YOU SUMMONED THE COURAGE to visit the graveyard this night. Perhaps you came to bury the remnants of a spell, or to collect dirt to use for another one. Your intent is innocent enough, but the night is full of spirits, and you sense eyes upon you now. They may be friendly, helpful ancestors who have followed you to guide your magic, or a beloved saint come to heed your prayers. But in the moonlight, so much seems strange and sinister. Could it be a hellhound, or a demon even? The list of otherworldly spirits is legion. Might these be the ghosts of whatever native tribe once traveled these roads? Where are your guardian angels in this moment of fear? The tension urges you to hurriedly finish your work, as you convince yourself nothing more than an owl has spied you. The tightness in your chest at long last begins to fade, and you turn to leave, uncertain if the duplicate sounds of your footsteps are an echo or something more mysterious pursuing you.

In this chapter we will explore the powers that are to be found beyond our physical world, in the realm of spirit, where our ancestors dwell and where various ranks of otherworldly beings are called on to aid our work. Given that our labors continue here on this earth, we will study the use of materials that connect us to those spirits, giving us something tangible in the form of graveyard dirt. Spirits can aid us in all manner of work, though the primary benefit is in understanding our place in the universe and readying us for our life beyond this world. Their gift is that of wisdom, an often overlooked need, but without which we are often unable to manifest our more evident concerns. It is good to keep in mind the lesson of King Solomon, who had the choice of many riches but chose first to be rich in wisdom, a choice that thereafter led to his wealth and power.

Our ancestors are forever with us; we are their progeny, the part of them that still walks in the sunlight. It is believed that they have a vested interest in us, and that we in turn need to represent them in our lives. The history of ancestor veneration in North America is as varied as those who live between its shores. Many of the indigenous people living here, though varied in their individual cultures, venerated their ancestors through ritual and storytelling. The ancestors were known to communicate with their descendants through omens and dreams and vision quests, but were otherwise unwelcome in the land of the living. Similar prohibitions against working with the dead were prevalent among the early Europeans who settled here, especially in the English colonies. It would take a movement called Spiritualism to change that, to bring the dead out of the boneyard and into the parlor.

Spiritualism is a Christian faith rooted in a belief in the continuation of the soul after death, and in the ability of the living to communicate with those souls. Spiritualism began in the 1840s and grew in popularity in North America after the end of the Civil War in 1865. Over 600,000 Union and Confederate soldiers died in that war, making the desire to correspond with the dead a prevalent one. Spiritualist beliefs filtered into various occult societies, among them the belief in spirit guides, the evolution of the soul, and the ability for spirit to manipulate matter. Religious movements such as Theosophy, New Thought, Pentecostalism, Neopaganism, New Age spirituality, and others have much to thank Spiritualism for.

Keep in mind that Spiritualism, though unique in its genesis and popularity, harkens back to ancient ideas about how the living and the dead interact. What made Spiritualism so popular in North America, where the culture was dominated by Europeans, was that the dominant culture had largely lost its connection to ancestor veneration due to various influences, most notably Protestantism. (European immigrants who did practice ancestor reverence, such as the Irish, were disenfranchised at the time and had less impact on the dominant culture.) In other areas where Spiritualism was popular, such as South America (where it is referred to as *Spiritism* and features various doctrinal differences), the populace had not abandoned ancestor veneration and therefore the practice of mediumship seemed less radical. Among African-Americans there is a rich heritage of ancestor veneration, originating in various parts of Africa and continuing throughout the diaspora.

Those who do not work with their ancestors on a day-to-day basis often do so on meaningful holidays, such as Memorial Day (formerly Decoration Day, so named for the observance of decorating graves) and the Day of the Dead. This latter holiday originated in Mexico, and while it has long been popular in border states such as California and Arizona, it has increasingly become more of a national observance, due in part to the growing population of Mexican immigrants and their influence.

The manner in which a person works with the dead is often driven by their cultural background, and in the cultural mélange of North America there is a range of often conflicting notions of how to react toward the deceased. Before we examine such taboos, let's look at the formulas relevant to spirit work.

Popular Formulas for Working with Spirits

There are many formulas associated with the conjuration and appeasement of spirits. Since we will be exploring various categories of spiritual helpers throughout this chapter, I will not list all those formulas here. Simply be aware for now that there are formulas associated with the Seven African Powers, angels, folk heroes, Hindu deities, Native American spirit guides, kings of the Old Testament, saints, and sinners. The following belong in a more general category of formulas used to aid in working with spirits.

Conjure

This formula reminds us of the primary meaning of the word *conjure*, the ability to summon spirits. In *Golden Secrets of Mystic Oils*, Anna Riva suggests this oil may be used to empower the Fifth Pentacle of the Sun by anointing the four corners of the square that occupies the center of this talisman.

Ouija

The name *Ouija* is trademarked and currently owned by Hasbro Inc.; however, in common parlance it is used to describe a variety of similar devices more appropriately known as talking boards or spirit boards. The reputation of these boards in assisting people in contacting the dead is legendary, and Ouija formulas can be used on their own to aid in contacting the dead, or to help with the effectiveness of a talking board, such as by rubbing Ouija oil on the pointer (known by the name *planchette*).

Spirit Guide

This product is used to attract and appease personal spirit guides. How to find a spirit guide to work with is a common question. Sometimes the answer is easy, since many spells will beseech the benediction of a particular saint or devil, whereby you develop a working relationship with them. Sometimes you are simply attracted to a certain spirit, or sometimes a spirit makes its attraction to you known through various signs or through dreams. If you are lucky enough to have the direct tutelage of an experienced worker, chances are they will introduce you to those spirits who have helped in their work. The following is my suggestion for using Spirit Guide oil to aid in introducing you to a helpful guide.

To Find a Spirit Guide

Take a white skull candle and dress it with Spirit Guide oil. Place it on a white plate and set it alight, saying the following:

> *Grace me,*
> *Guide me,*

Give me sight,
To see which steps
Are wrong or right.

Repeat this nine times. Allow the candle to burn to completion, then place the wax-laden plate beneath your bed to meet your spirit guide in your dreams.

Taboos

Many cultures have taboos against interacting with the dead. In this worldview, the dead are to be avoided lest they corrupt the living, causing illness or draining life force in a vampiric manner. There may be prohibitions against using items that once belonged to the dead, and therefore their former beds are discarded and clothes disposed of. Care is given when speaking their name, perhaps followed by a petition or prayer such as *may he rest in peace*, or *may God have mercy on his soul*. Indeed, such admonishments are meant to reinforce where the dead ought to be: in another place; they should be *at rest*, or *before God*, or somewhere removed from those they have left behind. This repulsion toward the dead may have served humankind as a survival need, since corpses can spread disease and early humans likely learned that their disposal lessened illness. We can see this prohibition against human remains in various Old Testament passages, such as Numbers 19:11 and Leviticus 21:11, which imply that a person is made unclean through contact with the dead. It is my belief that this somewhat practical safeguard against disease at some point became abstract, as we can see that later Old Testament writing goes a step further to prohibit communicating with the dead, such as the famed Witch of Endor did when summoning the ghost of Samuel. The taboo against interacting with the bodies of the dead came to be applied to their spirits as well, and continues in Christianity.

Other religions and cultures believe the dead to be beneficial to the living, who are encouraged to interact with them. Often the spirits are believed to remain close to the physical plane in order to aid those still alive. Asking aid and advice from the dead is seen as natural. The living are encouraged to remember the deceased through stories. Children are encouraged to seek the guidance and protection of their namesake. Clothes and jewelry are handed down to the surviving generations. Offerings are freely given, such as flowers by the grave or a glass of whiskey beside a picture.

Many modern workers have a place somewhere in their home that serves as an ancestor altar, where candles may be lit and flowers placed, along with pictures and mementos from their beloved dead. Incense is a common offering, especially joss incense, which is used in Chinese temples for the same purpose. The extent to which a worker interacts with their ancestors varies. Among those whose practice is hereditary it is much more common, as the dead are called upon to help with whatever magical work is being done. People who had difficult relations are of course less likely to continue them, although some find it easier to work with their relations after they have passed. Generally a worker will have one or more ancestors they work with somewhat regularly. These ancestors may not be blood relations, but may be mentors from their spiritual lineage, such as deceased workers who apprenticed them. Rites of initiation are rare in Conjure, though many modern workers have undergone initiations into other traditions as part of their magical training, and in those cases identify with a spiritual lineage and include those ancestors in their work.

Graveyard Dirt

One feature of working with ancestors that is peculiar to Conjure is the use of graveyard dirt. Through the law of contagion, such dirt is seen as embodying the qualities of whoever's grave it has been gathered from. It is sometimes used as an ingredient for certain formulas, or as a means to access the spirit associated with it. The collection of such dirt is governed by traditional methods that reveal a respect for the spirit whose aid is being sought.

How a worker chooses a grave is a personal matter. However, there are some traditional guidelines and lore to help govern the process, as follows.

Researched History

Spirits possess the education and experience of their former lifetime. So if, for example, you are looking for protection, you might do well to work with the grave of a soldier, a police officer, or a gangster's heavy. Matchmakers, craftspeople, and even other Conjure workers can be approached to help with your work.

Personal Relationship

If someone treated you well while alive, then it is generally believed that they may continue their generosity from the other side. Graves chosen according to a personal relationship may include that of a relative, friend, or coworker. This category includes the grave of one's pet.

The Influential Dead

This category includes noteworthy souls—your personal heroes. If you want to petition a spirit to help you start a new business, then seek out the grave of a banker or successful CEO. If you need protection, consider the grave of a soldier. If you need healing, then surely there is a doctor or nurse somewhere in your local graveyard.

The Corrupt Dead

Not everyone is willing to bargain with the dead; some would rather manipulate what they believe are weaker souls. It is said that alcoholics can be bought with an offering of booze, with a taste given upfront and the remainder of the bottle poured only after the requested work is complete. Sexual deviants are also said to be easily manipulated and can be bought with your sexual fluids (provided they align with what the deceased fetishized); other offerings may include sweaty jock straps, bras, dildos—anything associated with the deceased's particular kink. Individuals who committed suicide are also believed to be weak-willed and easy to force into magical labor. The belief that their spirit must feel shame for their early departure leads to the practice of taunting them, such as by shaking a bottle of pills or by slicing the earth at their grave with a razor blade, mocking their unnatural choice of exit. Dead, unbaptized babies are said to be particularly vulnerable to manipulation; bought with just a bit of milk, they can be sent to an enemy to disturb their peace. This category also includes murderers, thieves, rapists, etc. Buying their dirt and favor is more straightforward. They can wreak havoc on your enemy or inspire another fiend to do the work. Working with the corrupt dead is difficult work, ethics aside, and runs the risk of corrupting you as well.

Auspicious Location

When entering a graveyard, some workers will choose a grave depending on its direction. Generally, east is for knowledge and conception; south is for sex and vengeance, west is for love and peace, and north is for wealth and healing. Except in more rural boneyards, lots are often numbered, and therefore someone buried in lot thirteen may be employed for matters of luck. A number can be determined by need (such as lucky seven for gambling luck) or chosen by lot (divination). The site is then determined based on the numbers on gravestones, or the number of steps or graves counted from a gate or monument.

Divination

All manner of divination can be used to find an appropriate site.

Spirit Lead

Follow a moving animal or insect to find a grave. Feathers, leaves, or requests written on paper or onion skin may be thrown into the air on a windy day and then followed to see where they land. If you have developed a close interaction with a spirit guide or have come to the graveyard in search of one, you may feel yourself being pulled to a certain spot or hear a voice in your head directing you where to go.

In addition to its individual inhabitants, the graveyard itself is said to have its own spirit, a caretaker who watches over the land whom many seek to appease when doing work in a graveyard. Traditionally, offerings for that spirit are left at the front gate before entering; however, it is often the case that you must first travel through the front gate in order to park. If this is the case, you can simply leave your offering at the start of any path; just be sure to make your petition prior to stepping among the graves. As is the case with an individual grave, an offering is given as payment for such dirt.

Buying graveyard dirt is a respectable transaction, whereby you offer items such as money, alcohol, flowers, and so forth in exchange for the dirt associated with a spirit's grave. There are many ways of leaving coins for payment of dirt, many of which utilize an odd number of coins left in positions above where the body is buried. The method I use is to place three coins, dimes, or silver dollars in a triangle and dig dirt from the center. You may also place them above certain areas of the body that correspond with your need, such as above the head for knowledge or strategy, the heart for love or emotional healing, the sex for vigor, the feet for success in new endeavors, and so forth. The coins are placed in a triangle pattern, and the dirt collected from the center. In most cases I will pour whiskey in the remaining hole (which should be small, as you don't want to be too greedy about the amount of dirt you extract). There are of course a variety of offerings that can be made. Those who seem not to rest in peace but are angry may be cooled down by sprinkling Florida Water over their grave. Flowers, although some spirits have their own preferences (I was once chided for offering cheap carnations), are usually a sensible choice and keep your activities at a clandestine level. I prefer to cover the coins I have left with some dirt so they are not snatched up by the living.

When offering such things as alcohol or tobacco, it is wise to know the relationship the deceased had with such substances. They may have struggled to overcome alcoholism or have quit smoking for health reasons that are no longer relevant. According to Greek mythology, the dead much prefer offerings of blood. Ritual sacrifice of animals and the offering of their blood is not unheard of; however, those who have reservations about such acts sometimes opt to use red ink in place of blood, such as the dragon's blood ink we created in chapter 4.

When most folks new to Conjure think of graveyard dirt, they think of cursing. While it can certainly be used for this purpose, there are many ways to use it positively, such as for money spells and even for love. For the former you may wish to work with the grave of a banker, and for the latter that of a successful matchmaker. Like most things, these may be placed in a mojo hand or maybe sprinkled on a candle, engaging that spirit in the work you are doing. Here is one example.

....

TO SOUND ELOQUENT

Consider this trick for when you wish to sound wise, like for a job interview or a date you wish to impress. It will make you sound wise in all that you say. You will need the following items:

- Graveyard dirt from a fair and just judge
- Solomon's seal root (powdered)
- The shoes you will be wearing for the occasion

Take 3 pinches of the judge's dirt and mix it with an equal amount of powdered Solomon's seal. The placement of this mixture is a play on words, as it is put beneath the tongue—not in your mouth, as that would be dirty, but beneath the tongue of your left shoe. As you sprinkle it there, recite Psalm 11:7. Repeat this seven times before putting on your shoes:

> *The eloquence of the Lord is pure eloquence,*
> *silver tested by fire,*
> *purged from the earth,*
> *refined seven times.*

There is a tradition of placing graveyard dirt in the shoe of someone you wish to fall in love with you, a popular enough practice that it is the theme of the 1964 song "Conjured," recorded by Wynonie Harris.

A note about leaving the graveyard: Even if your view of spirits is a positive one, you may wish to safeguard against those lost souls who are said to follow you home. For this reason, there is a tradition of returning home from the graveyard by a different route from which you came, and to not look back. There is an old saying: *The person who takes something from a cemetery will return more than he took.*[14]

---

14. Harry M. Hyatt, *Folk-Lore from Adams County, Illinois*, no. 10358.

Seven African Powers

The Seven African Powers migrated around the 1970s to North America from the Caribbean, likely Puerto Rico or Cuba, and are associated with African diasporic religious traditions. People of Yoruba descent taken from West Africa as part of the Atlantic slave trade brought with them a rich religious tradition. Their deities—the creator Olodumare and a host of spirits known as *orishas*—were purposefully conflated with Catholic saints in places where Catholicism held dominance. When the Seven African Powers became popular in North America, the merchandise associated with them commonly bore a popular image that was often copied and reprinted onto a variety of products, most notably novella candles. This image featured a central depiction of the Crucifixion, along with seven individual pictures of saints, each titled with the name of an orisha. These depictions arch over the crucifixion scene, and from left to right are as follows:

Our Lady of Mercy: Obatala

Our Lady of Regla: Yemaya

Our Lady of Charity: Oshun

Saint Barbara: Chango

Saint Joseph of Arimathea: Orula

Saint John the Baptist: Ogun

The last of these, Elegua, is depicted as a saint whose vague attributes leave us unsure of who exactly he is. This saint is variously thought to be Saint Martin of Porres, Saint Benedict of Palermo, or another.

Angels

It is a common belief that each person has their own guardian angel, one who is given charge of them at birth and helps guide their life choices and spiritual development. Guardian angels speak to us through our conscience, urging us to do good and avoid temptation. Beyond that, there are hosts of angelic races that workers might call on for a variety of needs. There are several encyclopedias to be found listing the multitude of angels and the services they provide. For this project I have focused on the most popular of them all, those being the three archangels Gabriel, Michael, and Raphael. In Catholicism, all share the same feast day of September 29.

A popular spell engaging all three angels suggests that they will grant you three wishes. Variations of it can be found online; however, I stick with the version posted to the *Lucky Mojo Esoteric Archive*,[15] originally posted by an anonymous author. All it takes are three candles (white ones work well) placed in the highest place in your home and surrounded by sugar. I suggest using tealight candles on a white plate, with white sugar. Each candle represents one of the archangels, of whom is asked three wishes: one pertaining to business, the other to love, and the third being considered an impossible wish. Three days after making your wish, you are requested to publish this spell (hence its popularity) and thank the angels, which is easy to do with access to a social media platform.

Folk Spirits

Folk heroes often differ from saints or the Mighty Dead in that they may not have lived a physical life. Nevertheless, their stories are well known, as their intercession is often on behalf of humans, making them no less real than any other spirits in this chapter.

Anima Sola

Her name translates to "the lonely soul." Catholic iconography depicts a young woman standing in the flames of purgatory, chained and barred from escape. She is beseeched by mourners to help their beloved escape the fires of the afterlife, or oppositely, to send enemies to that fire and increase their suffering.

---

15. www.luckymojo.com/esoteric/occultism/magic/spells/purple/pactspells.html

High John the Conqueror

He has been mentioned before in relation to the jalapa root that represents him as a curio. He is called upon for such things as to give strength and escape.

La Madama

In addition to recognized saints are other spirits, such as La Madama. Her name refers to a group of female spirits of African descent known in Caribbean cultures such as Cuba, the Dominican Republic, and Puerto Rico, and in the traditions of Espiritismo, Palo Monte, and Santeria. In North America she is revered among practitioners of Hoodoo and Spiritualism. Her image is often that of a mammy, with dark skin and a full figure, wearing a red dress with an apron and a headscarf. Her ideal iconography includes a broom, and she is often venerated through collectible Black memorabilia, such as cookie jars and figurines, which is a point of controversy due to their connection to an antiquated racist envisioning of African-American women.

The spirits named as *Madama* are recognized as having worked as fortune tellers, mediums, and medicine women, and they favor those engaged in similar endeavors. In addition to aiding with the skills needed to be a spiritual worker, she can also be called upon for luck in gambling, spiritual cleansing, and a peaceful home. Some workers describe their relationship as being with a particular deceased individual among the many known as *La Madama*, whereas others approach La Madama as a singular being made up of many, much as each *Our Lady of* is contained within the sainthood of the Virgin Mary. How La Madama is perceived is as varied as the backgrounds of those who work with her. More traditional practitioners of Espiritismo assert that one must have a La Madama spirit in their spiritual court to work with, while practitioners from other traditions approach her as one would a saint. My advice, if you feel called to work with her, is to call on her and see if she arrives to work for you.

To read a situation, many of us use divination cards, such as tarot decks, Lenormand, playing cards, and the many oracle decks on the market. Before working with a new deck, or after a particularly depressing reading, some folks like to cleanse their cards. While there are a variety of ways to do this that do not damage the cards, such as passing them through sage smoke, La Madama with her helpful broom brushes away any negativity such cards may possess.

LA MADAMA'S AID IN CLEANSING CARDS

To rid your cards of any negativity you will need the following:

- A glass of water given as an offering
- Other offerings may include sweet things, such as brown sugar and molasses. Cigarettes and coffee are favored, as well as flowers.
- An image of La Madama to serve as a focal point
- The deck of cards you wish for her to cleanse
- Dirt, about a tablespoon
- 9 broom straws

Present your offering to La Madama. Place your deck of cards face-down and pour the dirt on top. Next, sweep the dirt off the deck with the broom straws. When finished, burn the broom straws away from the home and blow the ash toward the west.

Hindu Deities

We have seen before how exotic influences are valued, an example being Harlem's Hindu Mysterious Store, which promoted urban Hoodoo with an Asian mystique. Many stores carry a line of products associated with the more popular members of the Hindu pantheon, such as the following:

Alakshmi: For misfortune

Durga: For protection

Ganesha: For new opportunities

Kali: For strength and spite

Krishna: For peace and renewal

Lakshmi: For wealth

Rama: For winning conflicts

Sarasvati: For creative inspiration

Shiva: For power, physical and mystical

Vishnu: For psychic powers

Native American Spirit Guides

We have seen how the knowledge of Native Americans influenced the herbal lore of North American folk magic. It is from Spiritualism and the spiritual church movement that wisdom attributed to Native American tribes came to be honored, and certain First Nations ancestors came to be recognized as spirit guides, and as powerful allies in magic. Some are well known, while others are personal contacts whom individual workers channel through mediumship, or that in other ways make themselves known to the worker. The better-known names include Blue Snake, Bright Moon, and White Hawk. Among New Age channelers in the 1980s and '90s it was popular to speak on behalf of more historical figures, such as Geronimo and Pocahontas. Perhaps the most popular of the many Native American spirit guides among modern workers is Black Hawk.

Black Hawk

Black Hawk's native Sauk name is *Ma-ka-tai-me-she-kia-kiak.* His day of celebration is December 17, and he was born in 1767 in Illinois. During the War of 1812, Black Hawk fought with the British. He is most famous for his role in the Black Hawk War of 1832, in which he led a band of Sauk and Fox warriors in an attempt to reclaim tribal lands in Wisconsin. He died on October 3, 1838. Mother Leafy Anderson, a popular Spiritualist church leader, named him as one of her spirit guides. She called Black Hawk the *Spirit of the South* (and White Hawk the *Spirit of the North*), and he has also been called the *watchman on the wall*, a reference to Isaiah 62:6, which reads: *I have set watchmen upon thy walls, O Jerusalem, which shall never hold their peace day nor night: ye that make mention of the LORD, keep not silence.* This association comes from the fact that Black Hawk is said to warn you against trouble.

The tradition of venerating Father Black Hawk requires that a bust representing him reside placed in a bucket. Oddly enough, the image of him need not be specific, and I've seen a variety of figures from a variety of Native American tribes used to represent him. The bucket, however, is specifically described to be corrugated metal. Within this bucket is placed dirt or sometimes sand, and practitioners debate the specifics of what type of dirt should be used. Certainly dirt from around Black Hawk's gravesite would be ideal; however, Black Hawk's corpse was stolen in 1839 and boiled down to the bones and was intended to be taken on tour until the governor of Iowa intervened. Despite this, the body never made it back and was destroyed in a fire.

Many modern workers fill their buckets with all types of dirt or sand, often beginning with something local and then adding to it over time with dirt gathered from places of power such as crossroads or graveyards. Other items such as stones of special significance and Indian Head coins are also often buried in the dirt. Offerings are placed in his bucket and include such items as cornmeal, tobacco, water, beans, beads, arrowheads, shells, and all manner of Native American crafts. Black Hawk is helpful in works of mediumship, aiding the medium in finding spirits sought in the afterlife. He also lends his help as a powerful warrior and is a protective spirit. When working with him for protection, practitioners often include weapons in his bucket, such as a hatchet or an arrow. An offering of incense can be made, although many workers have a preference for burning sage or sweetgrass.

Kings of the Old Testament

Moses was the greatest Hoodoo man that God ever made.
The Bible is the best Conjure book in the world.[16]

These statements are paraphrased from dialogue in Zora Neale Hurston's novel *Jonah's Gourd Vine,* which portrays Moses as a powerful magician guiding people descended from Africa. Like so many of the saints who were syncretized with African deities, this portrayal of

---

16. Zora Neale Hurston, *Jonah's Gourd Vine*, 147.

Moses evokes similarities with the folk hero John the Conqueror, while Damballa, the serpent loa of Haitian Voodoo, is seen in Moses's staff.

This patchwork of religious figures, folktales, local ancestors, and sacred iconology illustrates the syncretism of Conjure, just as North America is a mix of cultures. Saints, devils, animals, witches, angels, spirit guides, warriors, doctors, and whores all emerge as spirits that are venerated and asked for favors. Each worker has their own select group of such spirits that they work with.

Folks are always drawn to things new and exotic, including spirits. Spirits themselves seem equally driven to reach out beyond the confines of their traditions, to expand their powers and be known in new ways. There are always those people who are against immigration who will say that a certain spirit has no place in American folk magic. Additionally there are devoted initiates of traditions who apply the dogmas of their devotion to others, sometimes failing to see that this very rigidity is the reason their saints have gone on to court the attention of others.

As practitioners of Conjure continue to become more diverse, we are seeing the addition of spirits, from the ascended masters of New Age spirituality to the various gods of Neopaganism and the orishas of Ifa. As our world changes, the spirits that speak to us are changing too. This is important, as modern times present us with new challenges and new ways of seeing the world, and so new stories and heroes are needed. We need to keep the older wisdom alive while reaching for new ways to tell ourselves what it is to be human in the modern world. Spirits from other times and places often give us a perspective that is new, or else one that is old but has been lost to our culture. Issues of cultural appropriation should always be considered, as the spirit world is not ours to colonize. That said, it is important to develop a well-rounded set of relationships with spirits of different stripes. Each spirit has their own preferences pertaining to how they should be approached, addressed, and attended to. Some ask for fruits to feed them, others for faith. The depth of your belief in any given spirit is personal to you.

Some of these spirits present themselves as nonhuman, whereas others are attached to the names and legacies of alleged mortals who have passed on. These are the souls of deceased humans revered for their place in history. Sometimes we realize that their history is fabricated. Other times the evidence of their physical lives does not align with history. Of utmost concern is their effectiveness when working with you; if you ask of them a favor and they deliver, then they deserve offerings and praise.

Given all the saints and spirits that exist in the world, there is no way to list them all. There are, however, some that currently populate the altars of many modern workers, which we will now introduce ourselves to.

Saints

There are a multitude of saints, prayed to according to their patronage, and many of whom are worked with in a magical context. Though saints are not exclusively Catholic, or even *folk Catholic*, as is the term for practices not endorsed by the Church, they are often related to local traditions and remnants of previous religious influences. People who live remarkable, most often miraculous lives are recognized by many as saints. We will limit our discussion to the saints most often engaged in magical work:

Saint Agnes: For a virgin to discover her future husband

Saint Andrew: For divining the future with wax

Saint Helena: For love spells to turn another's heart to you

Saint John the Baptist: For a variety of spells including healing and love

Saint Joseph: Bury his statue upside down in your front yard to sell your house.

Saint Josephine Bakhita: For freedom from oppression

Saint Martha the Dominator: For women to dominate their men

Saint Peter: For a variety of spells including opening doors and cursing

In addition to these saints are others whom I have singled out for special note, as follows.

Saint Expedite

His feast day is April 19. Saint Expedite is depicted as a Roman centurion, most often with young features. Iconography includes a cross held aloft that bears the Latin word *hodie*, which translates to *today*. (German iconography has him holding a clock.) Beneath his right foot is a crow bearing a banner with the word *cras*, which translates to *tomorrow*. (An Armenian legend states that this crow was the Devil in disguise, trying to get the soldier to put off his conversion to Christianity until the spoils of battle were indulged in.) Saint Expedite therefore stands holding the power of today in his hand and controlling tomorrow underfoot, a champion of fate. Saint Expedite is urging folks to follow the cross today, encouraging immediate conversion to Christianity. It is also a reminder to any who may have wanted to undermine the Christian state that the Church would continue to dominate tomorrow. It is from the word *cras* that we get *procrastination*, and for that reason Saint Expedite is said to aid those of us who have problems getting done today what we can put off until tomorrow.

There is a popular, though discredited, legend concerning the delivery of Saint Expedite's statue to Our Lady of Guadalupe Catholic Church in New Orleans, in which the crate was stamped with the French word *Expédit*, causing his name to thereafter be mistaken as such. Although it is a good yarn, devotion to Saint Expedite had been well established long before then. His historical origin is unknown; however, he is a recognized saint in the Catholic Church.

Procrastinators are not his sole devotees; indeed, Saint Expedite is willing to help anyone, especially when they need help fast. Traditions vary, although there are common elements, such as in the following work to bring about a quick resolution.

....

SAINT EXPEDITE FOR A QUICK RESOLUTION
Saint Expedite delights in his pleasures, which include:

- A glass of water
- Pound cake (Some say he prefers the Sara Lee brand.)
- Red candles (Some say dressed with Fast Luck oil.)
- Red flowers (Some say he prefers carnations.)

Some give these offerings to Saint Expedite when making their request, while others wait until after he has made good on their request. You may speak frankly or in the following manner:

> *Our dear martyr and protector, Saint Expedite, you who know what is necessary and urgently needed, I beg you to intercede before the Holy Trinity on my behalf, that by your grace my request will be granted. (Express what you need.) May I receive your blessings and favors. In the name of our Lord Jesus Christ, amen.*

Thank him publicly when he fulfills your request. Though this was formerly done in newspapers, today folks thank Saint Expedite on social media. Straightforward ways work fine:

> *Thank you, Saint Expedite, for winning me that job.*

Saint Cyprian

Sometimes called *Cipriano* or *Kyprianos*, this is the name for two saints, one from Antioch, the other from Carthage, who are often conflated due to their shared name and histories, both being magicians who converted to Christianity. The fact that prayers are answered when Saint Cyprian is invoked is what most practitioners care about; they are less concerned with the exact historical identity of whomever they are speaking to. The tale told of this saint is that he burned his library following conversion, but in later years regretted this and dictated a grimoire titled *The Book of Saint Cyprian*. Various versions of this text exist, often written in Spanish or Portuguese (a reverse reading of which is alleged to summon the Devil). Because Saint Cyprian is a magician, many magic workers view him as their patron saint. Most often he is depicted wearing a purple robe, with a beard and staff.

Santisima Muerte

Though Santisima Muerte is not an orthodox saint, her cult has made substantial inroads into North American folk magic. The female personification of death, she helps with numerous concerns, which are discernible according to the color of her cloak. The traditional three colors for her are as follows:

- *Black:* Protection, revenge
- *Red:* Love
- *White:* Cleansing, healing

As Santisima Muerte's following has continued to grow, so have her colors. She is often now seen wearing a variety of other colors.

Spirits of Voodoo

Conjure workers from the New Orleans region often engage a variety of spirits associated with Voodoo. While the religion of Vodou is a structured initiatory tradition intimately tied to Haiti, Voodoo in the Big Easy is often practiced less formally, where it is sometimes mixed with practices more finely defined as Hoodoo. The spirits worked with are referred to as *loas*, and those more often called upon by conjurors include the following:

Ayida Wedo: Loa of fertility

Ayizan: Loa of commerce

Babalu-Aye: Loa of sickness and healing

Baron Samedi: Loa of the dead

Damballah-Wedo: A powerful being often represented as a snake

Dr. John (Father John): John Montanee died in New Orleans in 1885 at the age seventy, having been a Conjure doctor of such note that he is now venerated by some as a loa.

Erzulie Dantor: A passionate loa, concerned with art, love, and sexuality, and also jealousy and protection

Erzulie Freda: Loa of love and beauty

Eshu: He is the opener of doors, and nothing goes through without his will.

Maman Brigit: Loa of cemeteries and money

Mami Wata: Mermaid spirit of luck and money

Marassa Jumeaux: A pair of twins who aid in reconciliation work

Marie Laveau: The celebrated priestess of New Orleans Voodoo and a great magical ally to have on your side

Papa Ghede: A psychopomp who leads the dead to their eternal destination

My final thought for this chapter is "don't be a freeloader." If a spirit is aiding you, you should be aiding them with the proper offerings that the spirit is known to favor, be it whiskey, song, coins, or charity toward others. These relationships are traditionally ones of mutual give and take, and many spirits will simply stop working for you if you prove to be a mooch.

XIII

The Master Key

OUR FINAL CHAPTER IS not the end of the road. Rather, we find ourselves at the crossroads now, where a number of potential paths await us. What will you do with the magic you have been introduced to along our journey? How you proceed is up to you. I hope you remember fondly the adventure we have taken, though moreover I hope not only that you apply these tricks toward bettering your life but that you master them.

There is yet another key left to possess: the Master Key. This key opens the gate at the crossroads, where the brave seek the power to become masters of their craft.

Popular Formulas for Mastery

The theme of this chapter is mastery, both personal and mystical. There are a number of formulas that seek to aid folks in such endeavors.

Courage

The first step of any journey is having the courage to put your foot forward.

Confidence: You must believe in yourself, have faith in your abilities, and become comfortable in your own skin if you are going to succeed in your planned enterprises. This formula allows you to hold your head high.

....

Confidence Oil

Combine the following essential oils:

- 1 part fennel
- 2 parts thyme
- 2 parts yarrow

Crucible of Courage: In addition to giving you the courage to take action, this formula also serves to reduce anxiety that is generally caused by fears and feelings of inadequacy.

Fear Not to Walk Over Evil: This formula is especially helpful when you must go into situations against your choosing, such as court appointments or even family dinners. In addition to eliminating fear, it also serves as a protective formula, especially against foot-trafficking tricks.

Eloquence

Products for eloquence are few, and often have the word *eloquence* in their name.

....

Eloquence Bottle

Fill a small bottle with the following ingredients and carry it with you when you will be judged by your speech:

- Deer's tongue
- Honey
- Rose petals

Crown of Success: We noted this formula in chapter 2 on blessing, though it does much more, including aiding you with successful speech. It is commonly prescribed when you need your voice to be heard and to sound intelligent.

Intellect

Although nothing is going to take the facts from the book and implant them in your memory, the following formulas aid in studying.

Memory Drop Oil: This formula is found as an oil. Dabbing a bit on your forehead while studying is said to help you retain information better.

....

MEMORY DROP OIL

Combine the following essential oils:

- 3 parts clary sage
- 1 part lemon
- 1 part mint

Pass Test: This formula gives you an edge in passing tests, not necessarily by giving you the knowledge to answer the questions correctly but by providing luck in choosing the right answer to a multiple-choice question or by keeping the person grading you from noticing your mistakes.

Wisdom of Solomon: Wisdom is not the same as knowledge. I've known plenty of people who had book smarts but were nevertheless stupid when it came to many things. This formula, when applied to course work, can help you better understand how facts fit together. This is a good formula to use for essay writing.

Beyond that, Wisdom of Solomon can help when you need to make big decisions in which the appropriate action is not clearly evident.

....

WISDOM OF SOLOMON OIL

Add bits of Solomon's seal root to a bottle in which the following essential oils are mixed:

- 1 part cypress
- 3 parts frankincense
- 3 parts myrrh

Let this mixture rest for 40 days.

Magical Mastery

Abramelin: There are a number of recipes available for this oil, and much contention over which is the most correct according to translations from the *The Book of Abramelin*, from which it is derived. The following version requires only essential oils.

....

ABRAMELIN OIL

- 1 part calamus
- ½ part cassia
- ½ part cinnamon
- 1 part myrrh
- 7 parts olive oil

Black Arts: This oil can be used to enhance any magical working that involves invoking spirits. It is likewise used as a cursing formula.

The Master Key: Master Key oil was created in the 1920s by the Valmor Products Company, following the popularity of Charles F. Haanel's 1916 book *The Master Key System* (originally published as a 24-week correspondence course in 1912). Haanel's book was a popular publication on the subject of Theosophy, coining the phrase *law of attraction*, which inspired much of the New Thought literature that came later.

If you cannot get your hands on Master Key oil, such as the one I craft for my Modern Conjure brand and other spiritual merchants offer as well, then you have a couple options. The first would be to simply pour a silver-dollar-sized circle of olive oil on a white plate, then run your finger through it to make a cross three times, retracing your lines each time. This oil can then be used to anoint the keys (which we will discuss shortly). Or the following recipe will work for you to make a Master Key oil of your own.

....

MASTER KEY OIL

- Master root chips
- Frankincense resin
- Myrrh resin

The exact amount of each ingredient is up to you. The resins in the oil will break down over time and add their own scents, whereas the master root is added for its power. Next, add equal amounts of the following essential oils, at least enough for your roots and resins to be submerged:

- Sandalwood
- Bergamot
- Petitgrain

You can add a carrier oil, such as almond or jojoba, equal to three times the volume of your oil blend.

The Crossroads

The legend of the crossroads is well known, expressed in numerous folktales that share a common theme. Most popular among these is the story of blues guitarist Robert Johnson, who is said to have acquired his mastery of the guitar from the Devil at the crossroads. While this legend was originally attributed to blues musician Tommy Johnson, it became inexorably tied to Robert, whose recordings feature numerous Southern occult themes. These are evident in such songs as "Hellhound on My Trail," which references Hot Foot powder, "Little Queen of Spades," which references a gambling mojo, "Come On in My Kitchen," which mentions a nation sack, and that song most relevant to the legend being discussed, "Cross Road Blues."[17] While the lyrics of "Cross Road Blues" express a fear that many attribute to Johnson's earlier dealing with the Devil, what is likely being expressed is his fear as a black man trying to hitch a ride at night in the rural South. The final line, believed by some to indicate a literal fear of sinking into Hell, utilizes a phrase from a popular spiritual titled "Keep Me from Sinking Down," and was an idiom used to express feelings of depression and loss of stability in general. But what is of more value than Johnson's actual experience is his legendary interaction with the being described as a *large black man*, and understood to be the Devil.

---

17. "Cross Road Blues," written by Robert Johnson, produced by Don Law, and recorded in San Antonio, Texas, on November 27, 1936.

But who is this Devil who features so prominently in crossroads mythology? Some suggest that this man is a representation of Papa Legba, the loa of the crossroads in Voodoo, or one of several similar deities found throughout the African diaspora, such as Elegua, Elegbara, Eshu, Exu, and Pomba Gira, to name a few. Others suggest that he is of European origin, where we find a similar character in the Grimm's fairy tale *The Devil's Sooty Brother* and in the story of *Faust*. Just to make it more difficult, the Black Man is also known to take the form of black animals, including dogs, cocks, and bulls. The Black Man who bedevils American crossroads may well be of mixed pedigree. Whatever continent he came from, people of both African and European descent understood that his domain was the crossroads, and that he could grant folks the power to make certain desires come true.

Clearly this figure is not the same Devil as the adversary of Christianity. If you are not hip to calling him the Devil, there are numerous other names you might use: Beelzebub, Booger Man, Diablo, Funny Boy, Guy with a Pitchfork, Man with the Horns, Mr. Grim, Nick, Scratch, Splitfoot, and many more. Often such names are preceded with *Old* or *Ole*.

To deal with this Devil one must go to the crossroads, preferably at night, and bring an offering. Unlike the Faustian Devil, the cost does not include one's eternal soul. Our Devil has more practical tastes, such as for whiskey, smokes, and coins. It is customary to bring an item representing what you want to master. Some folks do this work over a series of nights, nine being common, hoping that on the last night he might physically manifest in some form or appear in the form of an animal, cloud, or tangible feeling. Once he has presented himself to you, you are to audibly ask him for what you want and present to him the item you have brought to master. With Johnson, it was the guitar. Other items might include such things as the following:

- Dice, cards, poker chips, or those things associated with gambling to learn how to win at the game
- Scissors, hair brushes, or a wig to learn how to cut and style hair

- Tarot cards, a crystal ball, or your preferred method of divination to learn how to become a seer
- Fake breasts, lipstick, or high-heeled shoes to learn how to be a drag performer

The concept here is that you are requesting his aid to master a certain something. Of the many descriptions we find regarding working with the Devil at the crossroads, mastery is the theme. The Devil of the crossroads is not invoked to bring you love (though he can teach you how to become a matchmaker) or money (though you may learn how to wisely invest the income you have) or to curse (though the art of cursing is a teachable skill). It is understood that there are various ways to achieve those things, such as we have explored throughout this book. What you are asking for at the crossroads is training.

What we wish to master for our purposes here are the various keys of Conjure that we have worked with throughout this book. So what we bring to the crossroads is a pair of keys.

I suggest a pair of skeleton keys. They need not match, but they should be similar in size. I prefer them to be about the length of my forefinger. Currently these are easy to come by, and are often found in craft stores. True antique ones are fine, though it may be good to know their history. If you do not, then give them a good cleansing first.

KEYS TO THE CROSSROADS

In addition to a pair of keys, you will need the following:

- A length of red embroidery string, 12 inches long
- Offerings (which should include a flask of whiskey) and three silver dimes
- An anointing oil, such as Master Key oil

Now we get to the heart of our working. On a night of your choosing, travel to a crossroads. Somewhere more rural is preferred, unless you want others to witness and distract you. For safety's sake, someplace without any traffic is necessary. Stand in the center of the roads and remove your keys and condition oil, anointing one key after the other. Depending on how nimble your hands are, you may need to sit or crouch down for the following task, using the ground as a surface to work on.

Figure 1

Place your keys together, laying one over the other so that they form the shape of an X, their teeth facing away from one another (figure 1).

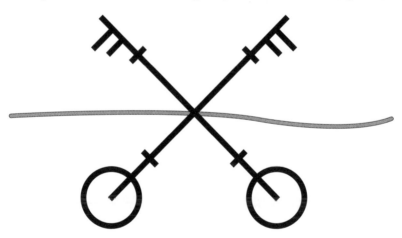

Figure 2

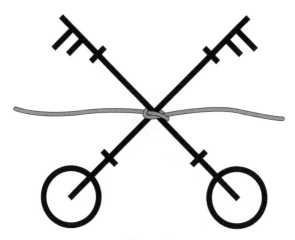

Figure 3

Position the center of your string beneath the keys where they intersect (figure 2), then bring both ends of the string together and knot them on top of the keys (figure 3).

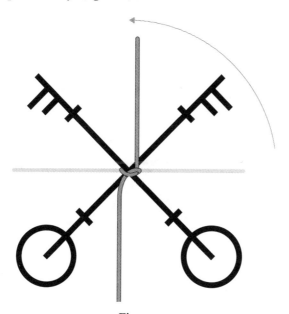

Figure 4

Adjust the string 90 degrees clockwise so that it is now lying vertically (figure 4).

Figure 5

Flip the keys over (figure 5), and knot the string again so that the knot is on the opposite side of the first knot (figure 6).

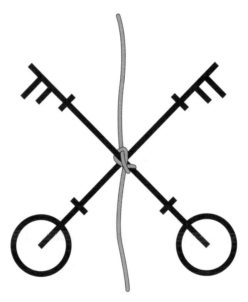

Figure 6

Continue to do this, adjusting the string 90 degrees each time, knotting the string on one side of the keys and then the other. If you were to simply tie the keys together in the center, they would end up lying side by side instead of being spaced apart to form a cross.

Keep working until you get to a place where you have just enough string to finish tying it with three overhead knots. Tie these knots with focused attention on your goal of mastering the work of Conjure, and with the tightening of each knot speak the following verse with authority:

> *Standing at the crossroads,*
> *Brought spirit as a key.*
> *Standing at the crossroads,*
> *Brought magic as a key.*
> *Knot 'em both together,*
> *Got me the secret to mastery.*

If there is extra thread, you may cut it or leave it to hang. You might also consider using a much larger length of string, such as can fit over your head, and allow the keys to serve as a necklace.

Now you wait. The Devil's physical form varies. Sometimes he shows himself as a black animal, while other times he is sensed as a presence, his form visible only through your psychic vision. Wait for clues, which can be anything from a sudden rush of wind to a chill down your spine.

Clearly you should be aware of any danger that may present itself. It is a good idea to let someone else know where you have gone, or even have them wait for you at some distance. If approached by a physical person or animal, be on guard, lest this be a vicious animal or criminal.

Once you become assured of the Devil's presence, hold the knitted keys in front of you and speak the following:

> *See these keys*
> *That unlock the secrets of magic.*
> *I will be their master.*
> *I will master magic.*

Place the trio of dimes in the center of the crossroads to form a triangle. Place your keys in the center, and pour the whiskey over them from the flask.

After this is done, remove the keys to take with you. If the Devil has accepted your petition, then the keys have been enchanted and can be used to enhance the mastery of your magic. You may wish to sleep with them beneath your pillow, and see if the Devil visits your dreams to teach you well. They may be placed on your altar, or worn as a charm when practicing magic. These keys can be placed upon a variety of items, such as petition papers, candles, mojos, and so forth, to connect them to the powerful energy of the crossroads.

As mentioned earlier, other offerings can be brought as well; however, take heed of what you leave behind in the environment, lest a deer consume a left cigar and become ill. For this reason and others, there is a secondary way to do crossroads work that does not involve travel to a sketchy physical location.

In dressing mojo hands for chapter 7, we learned that cologne or oil is often applied to a bag using a quincunx pattern, equivalent to a five spot on a pair of dice. This is a ritualized way of utilizing crossroads energy, and there is a tradition of doing similar work in order to bring the crossroads to your altar or the floor of your home. This can be achieved by drawing an X with chalk, or marking four corners with candles or stones.

This approach lacks some of the mystique and power found at an actual crossroads. There is something about the feeling of apprehension that is aroused by being alone between roads in the night. The roads themselves possess a unique energy, one that is open and encourages energy to travel. This is quite the opposite of what we find in the circles that are created for ceremonial magic and are popular in Neopagan rites, which seek to contain the energy created through ritual, as well as to keep secret the work done within them. While working within a circle or sphere has certain advantages, serving somewhat as a pressure cooker in which magic can build, the crossroads are effective in connecting the magic we make to the external world at large.

So there you have it. You may adapt this ritual if you choose, as it is not a traditional spell, not a secret initiation into Conjure. This is simply my creative way of inspiring your practice, with the hope that you will continue to pursue magic, however you find it, after the back cover of this book is closed.

Resources

Astrological

Planetary Hours

www.astrology.com.tr/planetary-hours.asp

Moon Signs and Phases

www.lunarium.co.uk
Llewellyn's Moon Sign Book
The Old Farmer's Almanac

Candle Work

The Art of Hoodoo Candle Magic in Rootwork, Conjure and Spiritual Services by catherine yronwode and Mikhail Strabo. Forestville, CA: Missionary Independent Spiritual Church, 2013.

Divination

Bone Throwing

Bones, Shells, and Curios: A Contemporary Method of Casting the Bones by Michele Jackson. Forestville, CA: Lucky Mojo Curio Company, 2014.

Throwing the Bones: How to Foretell the Future with Bones, Shells, and Nuts by catherine yronwode. Forestville, CA: Lucky Mojo Curio Company, 2012.

Herbals

Hoodoo Herb and Root Magic: A Materia Magica of African-American Conjure by catherine yronwode. Forestville, CA: Lucky Mojo Curio Company, 2002.

The Master Book of Herbalism by Paul Beyerl. Blaine, WA: Phoenix Publishing, 1984.

Oils

"Aunt Sally's Lucky Dream Oil" from Lucky Mojo Curio Company, www.luckymojo.com/oil-aunt-sallys.html.

"Divination Oil" from Otherworld Apothecary, www.otherworld -apothecary.com/oils/divination_oil.html.

"Second Sight" conjure oil from the Mystic Dream, https://themystic dream.com/products/secondsightconjureoil.

Playing Cards

A Deck of Spells: Hoodoo Playing Card Magic in Rootwork and Conjure by Charles Porterfield. Forestville, CA: Lucky Mojo Curio Company, 2015.

54 Devils: The Art & Folklore of Fortune-Telling with Playing Cards by Cory Thomas Hutcheson. Createspace Independent Publishing, 2013.

Psalms

Secrets of the Psalms: A Fragment of the Practical Kabala, with Extracts from Other Kabalistic Writings by Godfrey Selig. Dallas, TX: Dorene Publishing, 1982.

Signs and Omens

Folk-Lore from Adams County, Illinois by Harry M. Hyatt. New York: Alma Egan Hyatt Foundation, 1935.

Ozark Magic and Folklore by Vance Randolph. New York: Columbia University Press, 1947.

Signs, Omens, and Superstitions by Astra Cielo. New York: G. Sully & Company, 1918.

Bibliography

Agrippa, Heinrich Cornelius. *De Occulta Philosophia*. 1510. Reprint, Woodbury, MN: Llewelyn, 2005. Annotated by Donald Tyson.

American Cancer Society. "Talcum Powder and Cancer." www.cancer .org/cancer/cancer-causes/talcum-powder-and-cancer.html.

Anonymous. *The Black Pullet: Science of Magical Talisman*. York Beach, ME: Samuel Weiser, 2000.

Aunt Sally's Policy Players' Dream Book. New York: H. J. Wehman, 1889.

Bailey, Cornelia Walker. *God, Dr. Buzzard, and the Bolito Man: A Saltwater Geechee Talks About Life on Sapelo Island*. New York: Anchor Books, 2001.

Beyerl, Paul. *The Master Book of Herbalism*. Blaine, WA: Phoenix Publishing, 1984.

Bilardi, C. R. *The Red Church or The Art of Pennsylvania German Braucherei*. Sunland, CA: Pendraig Publishing, 2009.

Carroll, William, ed. *Superstitions: 10,000 You Really Need*. San Marcos, CA: Coda Publications, 1998.

Craddock, Ida. *Heavenly Bridegrooms: An Unintentional Contribution to the Erotogenetic Interpretation of Religion*. New York: n.p., 1918.

———. *Psychic Wedlock*. New York: n.p., 1899.

De Claremont, Lewis. *Legends of Incense, Herb, and Oil Magic: Esoteric Students' Handbook of Legendary Formulas and Facts*. New York: Dorene Publishing Co., 1938.

Egyptian Witch Dream Book. Chicago, IL: Stein Publishing House, n.d.

Fenner, Byron. *Fenner's Complete Formulary.* Westfield, NY: B. Fenner, 1888.

Frazer, Sir James George. *The Golden Bough: The Roots of Religion and Folklore.* 1890. Reprint, New York: Gramercy, 1993.

Gamache, Henri. *The Mystery of the Long Lost Eighth, Ninth, and Tenth Books of Moses.* Pomeroy, WA: Health Research, 1948.

Goona-Goona: An Authentic Melodrama of the Isle of Bali. Film directed by Andre Roosevelt and distributed by First Anglo Corp., 1932.

Grimm, Jacob, and Wilhelm Grimm. *Grimm's Household Tales.* Translated from the German and edited by Margaret Hunt. London: George Bell and Son, 1884.

Hohman, John George [Johann Georg Hohman]. *Pow-Wows, or Long Lost Friend.* 1820. Reprint, London: Forgotten Books, 2007. Translation of the German original, *Der Lange Verborgene Freund.*

Hurston, Zora Neale. *Jonah's Gourd Vine.* 1934. Reprint, New York: Perennial Library, 1990.

———. *Mules and Men.* New York: Harper Perennial Modern Classics, 2008.

Hyatt, Harry M. *Folk-Lore from Adams County, Illinois.* New York: Alma Egan Hyatt Foundation, 1935.

———. *Hoodoo, Conjuration, Witchcraft, Rootwork: Beliefs Accepted by Many Negroes and White Persons, These Being Orally Recorded among Blacks and Whites.* Hannibal, MO: Western Publishing, 1970. Distributed by American University Bookstore, Washington. Five volumes.

Jim, Papa [James E. Sickafus]. *Papa Jim's Magical Oil Spellbook.* San Antonio, TX: El Rey Botanica Inc., 1989.

Kansas City Kitty Dream Book. Eagle Book Supply, 1970.

Leland, Charles Godfrey. *Aradia, or The Gospel of the Witches.* 1899. Reprint, Newport, RI: The Witches Almanac, 2010.

Madam Fu-Fu's Lucky Number Dream Book. 1939.

Mathers, S. L. MacGregor, trans. *The Book of the Sacred Magic of Abramelin the Mage.* New York: Dover Publications, 1975. The first printed version, in German, dates to 1725.

———. *The Key of Solomon the King (Clavicula Salomonis)*. Newburyport, MA: Red Wheel/Weiser, 2016. Reprint edition.

Mickaharic, Draja. *Spiritual Cleansing: A Handbook of Psychic Protection*. 1982. Reprint, San Francisco, CA: Red Wheel/Weiser, 2012.

Peterson, Joseph, ed. *The Lesser Key of Solomon*. York Beach, ME: Weiser Books, 2001.

———. *The Sixth and Seventh Books of Moses*. New York: Ibis Press, 2008.

Randolph, Paschal Beverly. *Eulis! The History of Love*. Toledo, OH: Randolph Publishing Co., 1874.

Riva, Anna. *Golden Secrets of Mystic Oils*. Los Angeles, CA: International Imports, 1978.

Selig, Godfrey A. *Secrets of the Psalms: A Fragment of the Practical Kabala, with Extracts from Other Kabalistic Writings*. Dallas, TX: Dorene Publishing, 1982.

Skinner, Stephen, and David Rankine, eds. *The Grimoire of Saint Cyprian: Clavis Inferni*. Singapore: Golden Hoard Press, 2017.

Slater, Herman, ed. *Hoodoo Bible: Complete Compendium of Folk Magick*. New York: Magickal Childe, 1997.

———. *The Magickal Formulary*. New York: Magickal Childe, 1981.

Stockham, Alice Bunker. *Karezza*. Chicago, IL: A. B. Stockham, 1896.

———. *Tokology*. n.p., 1884.

The 2017 Lucky Red Devil Combination Dream Book and Numerology Guide. Eagle Book Supply, 2017.

Wright, Elbee. *The Book of Magical Talismans, Including All the Magical Items and Their Uses as Described in the Black Pullet*. Minneapolis, MN: Marlar Publishing Co., 1984.

yronwode, catherine. *Hoodoo Herb and Root Magic: A Materia Magica of African-American Conjure*. Forestville, CA: Lucky Mojo Curio Company, 2002.

———. *Paper in My Shoe: Name Papers, Petition Papers, and Prayer Papers in Hoodoo, Rootwork, and Conjure*. Forestville, CA: Lucky Mojo Curio Company, 2015.

Index

A. A. Vantine & Company, 44

Abramelin, 12, 86, 152, 248

African (not African American), 3, 5, 30, 31, 53, 54, 59, 98, 103, 205, 219, 225, 233, 235, 238, 250

angels, 18, 33, 35, 71–73, 86, 109, 111, 145, 153, 155, 197, 199, 220, 223, 225, 233, 234, 239

animism, 9, 63

anointing, 27, 33, 38, 95, 109, 118, 134, 152, 226, 248, 251, 252

apotropaic magic, 108, 113

Appalachian, 2, 4

astrology, 36, 37, 40, 259

Aunt Sally, 12, 22, 260

banishing, 36, 71, 169, 192, 210, 211, 220

baths, 1, 41, 91, 94–96, 98, 99

Bible, 3, 7, 13, 15, 16, 27, 42, 43, 71, 73, 79, 119, 152, 158, 166, 206, 238

Black Arts, 12, 248, 265, 271

blessings, 25–29, 35, 40–43, 45, 46, 67, 70, 71, 74, 75, 78, 90, 91, 98, 103, 106, 112, 118, 119, 135, 140, 152, 205, 210, 216, 242, 246

blowing, 10, 134, 141, 176, 203, 207, 218, 219, 221, 236

braucherei, 32, 69

broom, 9, 18, 25, 26, 91, 92, 106, 117, 121, 235, 236

candle shop, 11, 38, 76, 152, 188, 191

Catholic, 28, 44, 73, 96, 191, 213, 233, 234, 240, 241

ceremonial magic, 5, 32, 83, 256

Christian, 3, 32, 42, 69, 75, 104, 206, 224, 241

cleansing, 16, 22, 42–45, 50, 59, 70, 75, 89, 90, 92–96, 98,
    100–102, 105, 106, 113, 118, 135, 159, 189, 195, 216,
    235, 236, 243, 251

colors, 21, 119, 122, 172, 189, 202, 243

commitment, 166, 167, 179

confusion, 111, 131, 149, 158, 212, 213

conjure bag, 132

conjure ball, 130, 135–137, 212

conjure oil, 12, 41, 59, 95, 149, 151, 157, 177, 192, 202,
    260

container spells, 125, 130, 139, 203

courage, 33, 223, 245, 246

crossroads, 1, 2, 8, 14, 66, 67, 80, 81, 105, 132, 218, 238,
    245, 249–251, 255, 256

curios, 5, 12, 22, 31, 47, 50–55, 58–64, 67, 121, 122, 130,
    131, 133, 135, 137, 140, 149, 151, 169, 170, 177, 188,
    201, 202, 218, 235, 259, 260

cursing, 3, 7, 16, 17, 21, 30, 32, 35, 36, 53, 56–58, 63, 66,
    67, 74, 75, 78, 90, 96, 102, 103, 108, 109, 111, 118,
    119, 121, 129, 130, 135, 140, 158, 189, 190, 205–214,
    216–218, 220–222, 231, 240, 248, 251

Devil, 14, 30, 53, 56, 57, 81, 109, 143, 214, 226, 241, 242,
    249–251, 255, 256

divination, 9, 12, 15, 18, 70, 124, 139, 193, 195, 208, 212,
    230, 235, 251, 259, 260

Doctor Buzzard, 14, 17

doctrine of signatures, 31, 52, 58, 60

dolls, 52, 105, 122, 125, 140, 141, 172, 205

dream, 1, 12, 18–23, 33, 43, 58, 186, 187, 197, 199, 212, 213, 224, 226, 227, 256, 260

eloquence, 25, 232, 246

European, 3, 7, 30, 73, 82, 215, 225, 250

fidelity, 56, 60, 127, 168, 181, 218

folk magic, 2–4, 6–8, 18, 26, 30, 31, 37, 47, 61, 69, 82–84, 86, 140, 144, 146, 152, 179, 198, 215, 218, 237, 239, 242

folk spirits, 234

foot trafficking, 102, 216, 219, 246

formulas, 11, 12, 27, 41, 49, 50, 57, 59, 69–71, 91, 93, 94, 97, 98, 108, 109, 115, 125–128, 146–148, 151, 157, 159, 164, 166, 168, 169, 181, 187, 188, 193, 210–212, 214, 217, 225, 226, 228, 245, 247

fortune teller, 12, 15, 17, 23, 260

free will, 123, 124

gambling, 22, 40, 48–51, 53–56, 74, 91, 139, 189, 203, 230, 235, 249, 250

Geechee, 14

glamor, 40, 146, 153, 154

good luck, 47, 49, 50, 54, 65, 92, 99

Granny Magic, 2

graveyard, 57, 67, 142, 183, 218, 223, 229, 232, 238

graveyard dirt, 62, 217, 222, 224, 228, 231, 232

Great Migration, 4, 83, 152

grimoires, 32, 71, 76, 82–86, 152, 242

guardian angel, 109, 223, 233

hag ridden, 116, 117

healing, 21, 30, 36, 67, 69–71, 74, 80, 81, 85, 119, 122, 141, 164, 198, 229–231, 240, 243

herbs, 2, 30, 31, 33, 34, 40–43, 45, 50, 53, 58, 92, 94, 99,
    115, 116, 130, 131, 135–139, 142, 151, 156, 177, 180,
    183, 193, 196, 205, 215
Himmelsbrief, 73
Hindu, 6, 145, 225, 236
Hoodoo, 2, 4, 6, 11–13, 22, 31, 38, 76, 83, 119, 140, 144,
    158, 205, 216, 217, 219, 235, 236, 238, 243, 259, 260
Hoodoo drugstores, 11
Hyatt, Harry M., 13, 19, 119, 120, 151, 232, 260

intellect, 247

jack ball, 130, 137–139, 170
Jesus, 7, 32, 42, 71, 72, 102, 206, 242
jinx, 90, 93, 102, 107–109, 205, 214

Kabala, 5, 76, 79, 260
keys, 1, 2, 9, 25, 32, 47, 61, 69, 89, 107, 123, 143, 163, 166,
    185, 205, 223, 248, 251–256
King Novelty Company, 22, 58
knots, 107, 117, 119–122, 128, 138, 143, 205, 253–255

lady-hearted, 205
language, 10, 25, 26, 47, 69, 71, 73, 164, 176, 193
law of contagion, 52, 60, 64, 96, 128, 213, 228
law of similarity, 52
left-hand path, 29
live things, 107
Low Country rootwork, 2
loyalty, 60, 166, 168, 181
Lucky Mojo Curio Company, 12, 22, 149, 151, 259, 260

marriage, 54, 127, 165, 167, 179, 190
Master Key, 12, 61, 189, 245, 248, 251
mastery, 1, 12, 245, 248, 249, 251, 255, 256

medicine, 5, 15, 30, 31, 57, 108, 198, 235

mental distress, 212

mirror box, 130, 141, 142

Modern Conjure, 1, 2, 12, 70, 110, 111, 140, 149, 159,
 168, 187, 248

mojo bags, 43, 59, 108, 110, 130, 132, 201

mojo hands, 57, 132, 133, 137, 138, 159, 169, 186, 198,
 232, 256

moon phases, 36

Mystic Dream, 1, 187, 260

name paper, 76, 77, 79, 82, 137, 142, 170, 171, 174, 177,
 218, 220

Native American, 3, 44, 57, 79, 80, 225, 237, 238

nature, 5, 9, 17, 23, 25, 29, 33, 35, 54, 64, 65, 82, 118, 120,
 123, 135, 141, 143, 151, 154, 156, 176, 178, 179, 190,
 205

Neopagan, 3, 7, 73, 117, 123, 151, 158, 191, 205, 224, 239,
 256

New Age, 32, 58, 75, 123, 191, 209, 224, 237, 239

New Thought, 26, 75, 224, 248

numbers, 12, 22, 50, 59, 71, 79, 82, 86, 87, 213, 227, 230

Ozark folk magic, 2

Pennsylvania Dutch, 32, 55, 69

personal concern, 52, 120, 123, 125, 128–131, 137–140,
 142, 146, 177, 180, 202

petition paper, 73 75, 81, 84, 135, 185, 256

Pow-Wows, or Long Lost Friend, 55, 69, 71, 72, 83, 86

powders, 1, 41, 45, 57, 78, 91, 102, 136, 148, 173, 176, 193,
 205, 208, 213–222, 249

prayer paper, 30, 45, 73, 74, 76, 78, 110, 111, 130

Prohibition, 151, 152

protection, 2, 16, 20, 21, 40, 51, 55–57, 60, 61, 67, 75, 85,
    90, 92, 95, 107–111, 113, 114, 116, 118, 121, 122, 131,
    147, 157, 194, 215–218, 228, 229, 236, 238, 243
psalms, 3, 20, 74, 76, 105, 119, 121, 127, 202, 206, 232, 260
psychic, 1, 5, 9–14, 17, 23, 40, 50, 63, 64, 89, 95, 96, 109,
    116, 145, 182, 195, 237, 255
psychometry, 63, 64

quincunx, 80, 81, 134, 256

reconciliation, 21, 127, 166, 168, 181, 182, 213, 244
revenge, 192, 209, 215, 243
reversing, 56, 62, 107, 108, 111, 158, 190, 218
right-hand path, 29, 38
ritual, 10, 25, 26, 29, 30, 35, 65, 66, 70, 71, 79, 86, 103, 124,
    141, 198, 208, 224, 231, 256, 257
romance, 33, 147, 148, 166, 168, 183, 194
rootwork(er), 2, 4, 13, 17, 31, 101, 119, 212, 219, 259, 260

scent, 33, 41, 42, 45, 49, 78, 91, 95, 98, 136, 142, 143, 146,
    150, 153–157, 159–161, 166–168, 187, 214, 249
seals, 54, 82–85, 133, 147, 232, 247
seer, 13–15, 251
Seven African Powers, 225, 233
Seven Sisters of New Orleans, 13
sex, 57, 108, 125, 128, 129, 143–149, 155, 157, 165, 166,
    230, 231
sigil, 86–88, 146, 202
smoke, 30, 33, 44, 45, 116, 141, 202, 236
soaps, 91, 92, 98, 99, 103–105, 152
Southern, 4, 61, 132, 158, 166, 170, 217, 249
spirit possession, 117
spiritual cleansing, 43, 70, 75, 89, 90, 95, 98, 100, 101, 105,
    113, 118, 235
Spiritualism, Spiritualist, 5, 75, 144, 191, 224, 225, 235, 237

spoken word, 71, 144

sweetening, 163, 164, 166, 167, 169–171, 173–178, 183,
184, 216

sympathetic magic, 52, 105, 140

textile, 112, 113

Theosophy, 5, 32, 75, 224, 248

tricks, 2, 7, 15, 16, 19, 54, 56, 62, 63, 72, 84, 98, 101, 107,
110, 116, 125, 126, 139, 140, 157, 159, 171, 179, 180,
185, 186, 190, 198, 201, 215, 219, 232, 245, 246

two-headed, 10, 11, 13, 17

uncrossing, 93, 109, 118, 159, 169, 195, 196

washes, 94, 96, 102, 106

waters, 75, 96, 97, 115, 156, 160

white plate, 16, 70, 75, 105, 111, 136, 226, 234, 248

Wicca, 7, 12, 144, 158, 206

witch bottle, 130, 131, 134

witchcraft, 13, 29, 73, 82, 86, 101, 119, 148, 206

word squares, 85, 86

Index of Popular Formulas

3 Jacks and a King, 50
5 Circles, 11

Abramelin, 12, 152, 248
Adam & Eve, 166, 189, 206
Angelic Healer, 70
Anointing, 27
Aunt Sally's Lucky Dream Oil, 12, 260

Banishing, 169
Baptism, 33, 91
Bat's Blood, 78, 214
Bend Over, 123, 125
Bewitching, 147
Bible Bouquet, 27
Bingo, 50
Black Arts, 12, 248, 265
Black Cat, 9, 29, 50, 56, 212
Blessed Mary, 27
Blessing, 27, 42, 43
Blue Sonata, 168
Boss Fix, 126, 188
Break Up, 211, 220

Bridal Bouquet, 167
Broken Heart, 71

Chinese Wash, 91, 106
Chuparosa, 156, 167, 177
Cleo May, 147, 148, 161, 188
Come Home, 182
Commanding, 126, 127, 168
Compel, 117, 126
Confidence, 245, 246
Conjure, 226
Control, 126
Court Case, 127, 196
Crossing, 214
Crown of Success, 28, 246
Crucible of Courage, 246

Damnation, 214
Desire Me, 148
Destruction, 214
Devil, 214
Dixie Love, 166, 167
Do as I Say, 126
Dominate, 127
Double Cross, 214

Essence of Bend Over, 123, 125

Fast Luck, 49, 50, 157, 241
Fear Not to Walk Over Evil, 246
Fire of Love, 168
Fireworks of Love, 168, 219
Florida Water, 95, 98, 103, 105, 116, 135, 151, 231
Follow Me Boy, 127
Follow Me Girl, 127

Fortune Teller, 12
Four Thieves Vinegar, 92, 96
Free from Evil, 109

Get Well Soon, 71
Goofer Dust, 214, 221
Good Luck, 49
Goona Goona, 148, 149

Happy Home, 28, 165, 202
Healing, 71
Hearts cologne, 151
Hexing, 214
High John the Conqueror, 33, 53, 57, 133, 151, 235
Hold Me, 169
Holy Trinity, 27, 73, 80, 242
Holy Type, 27
Hot Foot, 210, 213, 218, 220, 249
Hot Fucker, 149
House Blessing, 28
Hoyt's cologne, 134, 151, 161

I Dominate My Man, 127
I Dominate My Woman, 127
Intranquil Spirit, 213

Japanese Lucky, 50
Jinx, 214

Kiss Me Now, 147, 182

Lady Luck, 50
Lavender Love, 149
Life Everlasting, 41, 71
Look Me Over, 147

Lottery, 50
Love Breaker, 211, 212
Lucky Buddha, 50
Lucky Clover Vulva Oil, 151
Lucky Dice, 50
Lucky Dream, 12, 260
Lucky Mojo, 49
Lucky 7, 50
Lucky Swastika Penis Oil, 151

Marriage, 167
Master Key, 248, 251
Memory Drop Oil, 247
Mighty Magnet, 59

Nature, 151

Ouija, 226

Pass Test, 247
Passion, 169
Peace in the Home, 165
Protection from Envy, 111

Q, 149, 158

Reconcile, 182
Red Fast Luck, 49
Restless, 213
Return to Me, 168, 182
Revenge, 209, 215
Reversing, 111
Road Opener, 93
Romance, 166

Rose of Crucifixion, 111
Run Devil Run, 128, 169, 210, 211

Safe Travel, 62, 111
Satyr, 150
Second Sight, 12, 260
Seventh Heaven, 150, 151
Speak No Evil, 127
Spirit Guide, 226
Stay with Me, 109, 168, 181, 187, 201
Stop Gossip, 109, 127, 142

Uncrossing, 109

Van Van, 47, 91, 152, 157–159

War Water, 6, 155, 215
Watchful Eye of Protection, 111
Wheel of Fortune, 50
Wisdom of Solomon, 247

Yellow Fast Luck, 49, 50

To Write to the Author

If you wish to contact the author or would like more information about this book, please write to the author in care of Llewellyn Worldwide Ltd. and we will forward your request. Both the author and the publisher appreciate hearing from you and learning of your enjoyment of this book and how it has helped you. Llewellyn Worldwide Ltd. cannot guarantee that every letter written to the author can be answered, but all will be forwarded. Please write to:

Chas Bogan
℅ Llewellyn Worldwide
2143 Wooddale Drive
Woodbury, MN 55125-2989

Please enclose a self-addressed stamped envelope for reply,
or $1.00 to cover costs. If outside the U.S.A., enclose
an international postal reply coupon.

Many of Llewellyn's authors have websites with additional information and resources. For more information, please visit our website at www.llewellyn.com.

GET MORE AT LLEWELLYN.COM

Visit us online to browse hundreds of our books and decks, plus sign up to receive our e-newsletters and exclusive online offers.

- • Free tarot readings • Spell-a-Day • Moon phases
- • Recipes, spells, and tips • Blogs • Encyclopedia
- • Author interviews, articles, and upcoming events

GET SOCIAL WITH LLEWELLYN

Find us on     @LlewellynBooks

www.Facebook.com/LlewellynBooks

GET BOOKS AT LLEWELLYN

LLEWELLYN ORDERING INFORMATION

 Order online: Visit our website at www.llewellyn.com to select your books and place an order on our secure server.

 Order by phone:
- • Call toll free within the US at 1-877-NEW-WRLD (1-877-639-9753)
- • We accept VISA, MasterCard, American Express, and Discover.
- • Canadian customers must use credit cards.

 Order by mail:
Send the full price of your order (MN residents add 6.875% sales tax) in US funds plus postage and handling to: Llewellyn Worldwide, 2143 Wooddale Drive, Woodbury, MN 55125-2989

POSTAGE AND HANDLING

STANDARD (US):
(Please allow 12 business days)
$30.00 and under, add $6.00.
$30.01 and over, FREE SHIPPING.

INTERNATIONAL ORDERS,
INCLUDING CANADA:
$16.00 for one book, plus $3.00 for each additional book.

Visit us online for more shipping options. Prices subject to change.

FREE CATALOG!

To order, call
1-877-
NEW-WRLD
ext. 8236
or visit our
website

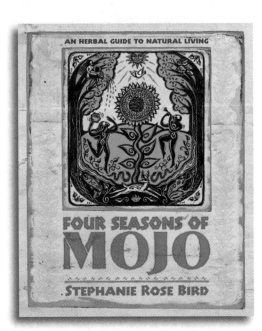

AN HERBAL GUIDE TO NATURAL LIVING

FOUR SEASONS OF
MOJO

STEPHANIE ROSE BIRD

Four Seasons of Mojo
An Herbal Guide to Natural Living
STEPHANIE ROSE BIRD

The changing of the seasons can feel magical-greens changing to browns and golds, snow melting to show fresh buds. We all recognize these tell-tale signs, but few are aware of the powerful impact each season has on our spiritual lives. *Four Seasons of Mojo* infuses ancient techniques, rituals, and methods from around the world to use each season's inherent energies to supplement body, mind, and soul.

Designed to further spiritual practices by learning from neighboring cultures, this book provides readers with useful ideas unrestricted by geographic borders, ethnicity, religion, or magical path. Included are recipes and concepts from the Caribbean, African American soul food, Buddhist Meditation practices, sacred Hindu rites, Old European traditions, Australian Aboriginal dreaming lessons, and Native American wisdom.

978-0-7387-0628-3, 240 pp., 7½ x 9⅛   **$16.95**

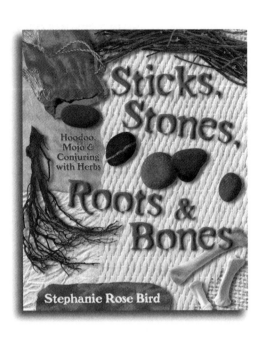

Sticks, Stones, Roots & Bones

Hoodoo, Mojo & Conjuring with Herbs

Stephanie Rose Bird

Sticks, Stones, Roots & Bones
Hoodoo, Mojo & Conjuring with Herbs
Stephanie Rose Bird

Hoodoo is an eclectic blend of African traditions, Native American herbalism, Judeo-Christian ritual, and magical healing. Tracing Hoodoo's magical roots back to West Africa, Stephanie Rose Bird provides a fascinating history of this nature-based healing tradition and gives practical advice for applying Hoodoo magic to everyday life. Learn how sticks, stones, roots, and bones—the basic ingredients in a Hoodoo mojo bag—can be used to bless the home, find a mate, invoke wealth, offer protection, and improve your health and happiness.

978-0-7387-0275-9, 288 pp., 7½ x 9⅛   **$19.99**

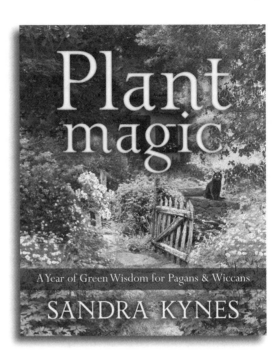

Plant magic

A Year of Green Wisdom for Pagans & Wiccans

SANDRA KYNES

Plant Magic
A Year of Green Wisdom for Pagans & Wiccans
SANDRA KYNES

Connect to the natural world in ways you never expected with the many magical uses of ordinary and classically witchy plants. *Plant Magic* presents a unique approach to working with plants in concert with the cycles of nature. Learn which ones best align with the sabbats on the Wheel of the Year and which are most useful for the time between them.

Sandra Kynes guides you through a year of plant magic, providing significant dates and detailed information on garden, wild, and household plants associated with each month. Discover activities to grow your connection with nature, such as plant-based rituals to celebrate the seasons and incense burning to attract love and prosperity. Explore ways to develop your self-expression in the craft, from placing flowers on your altar to using herbs in your divinatory practices. Featuring lore, recipes, spells, and more, *Plant Magic* helps you better understand and be inspired by the green world.

978-0-7387-5017-0, 264 pp., 7½ x 9¼   **$19.99**

UNEARTHING *the* MAGIC & MYSTICISM *of* DEATH

TOMÁS PROWER

La Santa Muerte
Unearthing the Magic & Mysticism of Death
TOMÁS PROWER

This is the first book written by a practitioner that presents the history, culture, and practical magic of La Santa Muerte to the English-speaking world. As the patron saint of lost causes, the LGBT community, addicts, and anyone who has been marginalized by society, La Santa Muerte has a following of millions—and she's only becoming more popular. Join author Tomás Prower as he gives step-by-step instructions for spells, magic, and prayers for practical results and long-term goals, including money, love, sex, healing, legal issues, protection, and more. *La Santa Muerte* also includes detailed information on:

Her Names • Tools • Altars • Offerings • Spells • Prayers • Rituals • History • Myths • Symbols • Meditations • Ethics • Colors • Correspondences

978-0-7387-4551-0, 264 pp., 6 x 9 $17.99

Llewellyn's Practical Magick Series

CHARMS
SPELLS &
FORMULAS

for the Making
and Use of Gris-Gris, Herb
Candles, Doll Magick, Incenses,
Oils, and Powders...

to gain Love,
Protection,
Prosperity,
Luck, and
Prophetic
Dreams

Ray T. Malbrough

Charms, Spells, and Formulas
For the Making and Use of Gris Gris Bags, Herb Candles, Doll Magic, Incenses, Oils, and Powders
Rev Ray T. Malbrough

Hoodoo magick is a blend of European techniques and the magick brought to the New World by slaves from Africa. Now you can learn the methods which have been used successfully by Hoodoo practitioners for nearly 200 years.

By using the simple materials available in nature, you can bring about the necessary changes to greatly benefit your life and that of your friends. You are given detailed instructions for making and using the "gris-gris"(charm) bags only casually or mysteriously mentioned by other writers. Malbrough not only shows how to make gris-gris bags for health, money, luck, love and protection from evil and harm, but he also explains how these charms work. He also takes you into the world of doll magick to gain love, success, or prosperity. Complete instructions are given for making the dolls and setting up the ritual.

978-0-8754-2501-6, 192 pp., 5¼ x 8   **$12.99**